THE WINTERING

Stephen Bowkett was born and brought up in a mining valley in South Wales. He taught English at secondary school in Leicestershire for many years before becoming a full-time writer, and a qualified hypnotherapist. He has published twenty-five books, mainly science fiction and fantasy, for both adults and children. He also writes poetry, plays and educational non-fiction.

Ice is the first part of The Wintering, a major trilogy.

THE WINTERING

ICE

STEPHEN
BOWKETT

TED SMART

First published in Great Britain in 2001
as a Dolphin Paperback
by Orion Children's Books
a division of the Orion Publishing Group Ltd
Orion House
5 Upper St Martin's Lane
London WC2H 9EA

This edition produced for
The Book People Ltd
Hall Wood Avenue,
Haydock,
St Helens WA11 9UL

Reprinted 2001

A catalogue record for this book is available
from the British Library

Typeset by Deltatype Ltd, Birkenhead, Merseyside

Printed in Great Britain by
Clays Ltd, St Ives plc

ISBN 1 85881 873 7

Now is the globe shrunk tight
Around the mouse's dulled wintering heart.

from 'Snowdrop' by Ted Hughes

To Wendy – who warmed me
through the wintering.

Contents

Note: a few terms used by the culture of the Shahini Tarazad derive from old Anglo-Saxon. These are:

hlaf-weard – the provider of bread, the protector, ultimately the lord.
weorthan – to be, to become or to happen.
wierd – fate, destiny, one's personal journey. It is spelt thus by Michael Alexander in *The Earliest English Poems* (Penguin Classics, 1970) to distinguish it from the modern 'weird' and all its connotations.

Learn more of the world of The Wintering and check Steve's other books by visiting his website:

www.sbowkett.freeserve.co.uk

1

A Wraith on the Road

It was a kind of peace for the thin fair-haired boy as he sat against the cushiontree staring into the distance. His body was relaxed, his long legs stretched out in front of him, hands folded behind his head. But in these past few minutes a frown had crinkled his forehead and his eyes looked troubled . . .

He was thinking of the previous afternoon when curiosity – and something much deeper which was growing in him day by day – had drawn him away from his work. He had left a furrow half-ploughed, left his mox alone to idle away another sunny hour, and climbed from his terrace on the midslopes to the place where the land joined the sky.

This was a thing that Kell had attempted several times before. At first the wonderment of childhood impelled him; for old Gifu had spoken of the High Places at the top of the world. More recently, aware of a rebellious streak, he had deliberately done what his tutors forbade him to do. But now, this last time and the time before that, Kell's imperative was not only to test the rumour that the sky was solid and curved like eggshell: no, Kell wanted more, to go beyond the boundaries of Perth and to see for himself whether past that point lay Nothingness, as the Mythologies asserted – just the endless dark and cold of everlasting Ice . . .

He thought back to yesterday with mixed feelings of pride and frustration and more than a little fear. He had climbed for three hours, struggling on past the highest terraces towards the chaos of rocks that gathered up and up against gravity until somehow they blended into a sky that was sheer-smooth and utterly unclimbable. And there he had lost both his nerve and the trail and was forced to return tired and defeated.

But just for a minute, as he accepted his failure, he had turned and looked back across the entire world and knew, deep inside him, that one day he would succeed . . .

A faint brief smile touched Kell's face – wiped away instantly as a fat spherical amber bee came buzzing and blundering into him. It bumped against his forehead, his cheek. Kell startled and swatted it away. The bee, covered in a powder of coloured pollens, swung confusedly to and fro for a moment before flying off in a zigzag path that took it back towards the grove of nightberry flowers, where it disappeared among its kind.

Kell watched it go, and shook himself out of his daydream. Like the bee, he could not stay away from the ideas blossoming in his head. They came as questions that so far had brought no answers, for the Knowledge only dealt with the enclave of Perth and what happened there. The All Mother in her wisdom denied that there was anything else.

Kell found his mouth dry and uncomfortable. He gathered saliva and spat, watching the plug of spittle soak quickly into the dust. The sun, fully gathered now and at its hottest for the season, shone down directly into his face. But at least, working here on the midslopes, there was the relief of the wind that streamed endlessly upward from the plain as the great lungs of the world did their work.

Kell eased back into reverie and soaked up the warmth – until a voice came bellowing up from the lower terraces and snapped his mind back to the present. How long had Gifu been watching his ploughlad doing nothing, just musing the day away? If the fieldsman was in a temper, Kell knew he would get a cuffing for sure.

He stood up in a flurry of indecisions. His animal – having pulled free of the share how long ago? – had grazed a wide swathe through the honeygrass and was feeding contentedly among a stand of lantern-apples two furrowlengths distant. Luckily they were still several handfuls of suns away from overripening, so the beast would not get drunk on fermenting fruit. Even so, its belly might be full and its motivation lacking. So Gifu would beat them both!

Kell pursed his lips and gave the signal whistle, a trill of ascending notes. The mox, as big as a wain and the most powerful animal in the enclave, swung up its huge horned head and let out a flat, nasal answering call: a honking drone that might be heard right down on the flats. Kell signalled again. The beast snorted and with a hiss and pump of pistons shifted its bulk and lumbered over.

Kell grinned and shook his head. The mox stank of fruit and its mouth was sticky with molasses-like juice. Gifu was bound to spot Kell's lax management. But the brute was so happy-eyed and content that the boy couldn't find it in him to be severe. It was his fault after all. Instead, he kissed the mox's wet black nose and patted the bony ridge between its eyes, lifting a small cloud of dust. Then, more deliberately, he searched for the hard nodules in the animal's heavy wool close to the base of its horn: they formed a cluster fashioned just right for a human hand. Kell pressed out a sequence of instructions and the mox responded immediately: small driver devices whined inside and there came a sharp hissing as hydraulic pressures balanced. The beast's internal fires gathered up and it stirred, sweeping round so that Kell could chain it to the share.

The mox was moving almost before the boy could leap aboard. He snatched at the grab handles and plugged in the feed cable that connected the mox to its master; and was happily folding stubble back into the soil when Gifu appeared

3

over the lip of the terrace. He was big, square, solid; florid-faced and bulked with muscle from a lifetime of work on the land. His shaggy grey hair and beard gave him a wild and windblown look. A leather tunic strained across his huge chest, and his great boots lifted billows of dust as he strode towards the boy.

'Kell – Kell! Why has the mox been standing idly by? Why have you been wasting your time? I saw you from the ridge.' The fieldsman was in a hot temper. He hated lazy workers.

Kell looked innocent. He whoaed his beast and sank the plough's anchor-spike deep into the ground so the mox wouldn't wander again. Then he jumped lightly down and dusted himself off as he walked over grinning to his workmaster.

'And you can wipe that expression off in case I take it for smugness!' Gifu thundered. In an instant he had looked at the neat furrows to calculate Kell's labour, and was surprised and almost irritated to note that the boy had done a decent day's work. Apart from the dredge of crushed honeygrass and the lantern-apple trees looking a little ravaged, the terrace was in good order and the ploughing well advanced.

'If I have annoyed you, Gifu, I'm sorry,' Kell said, and he meant it. His face was so open and filled with fondness for the old man that Gifu's tetchiness vanished.

'You worry me more than you annoy me, Kell,' Gifu replied with equal honesty. He sighed and ruffled the boy's mass of curly blond hair and then dropped his hand on Kell's shoulder. 'What am I to do with you? What kind of life will you make for yourself?'

'A grand life.' Kell's smile did not falter. 'A life of adventure and wonder. A life of danger, perhaps. I will see new things, go to new places . . .'

He shrugged and became self-conscious. They both knew

that what he was saying was, according to the strictures, forbidden.

'We are wheat, Kell.' Gifu had said this on many occasions. 'There is nothing beyond the planting, the growing, the reaping and the ploughing under. That is all we know and all we need to know.'

And Kell had nodded as though at the wisdom of the teaching, while inside, his heart clenched with the beauty of that single magical word – Beyond.

Now, as friends, they sat on the very viewpoint stone where the boy had been dreaming the afternoon away. The fieldsman took out a flask, poured a deep tumbler of water for Kell and added two zest crystals, half his daily allowance. They watched the liquid foam and fizz and take on a bluish hue sprinkled with tiny scintillating particles. Gifu passed over this gift of energy, and Kell lifted the tumbler high.

'With thanks to the All Mother, for the warmth of her heart and her brooding wings.' It was the right thing to say.

'The All Mother,' Gifu echoed, and Kell felt unaccountably disturbed by the tears of reverence in the other man's eyes.

They sat quietly a while in a companionable silence. Down below and far away the plain spread into the golden haze of distance, scattered with small villages fringed by trees and fields, separated by tracts of shadowy woodland. Halfway to the far rim, the city of Odal glittered in the heat like an intricate lattice of metals and glass. Its farthest reaches bordered the Central Lake – and even at this range Kell could see tiny bright dots of watercraft as goodfolk went about their leisure or the more arduous business of fishing. Then there were more villages like flat smudges on the map of the land; the threads of roads, shadows of trees; the far rim masked in pearly vagueness. Kell had never taken the trouble to visit there, but he knew what he'd find – other lowslopes where the breadroot crops were grown, the mid terraces for wheat, the high pastures given over mainly to fruits and grazing for the moxen ... And ploughlads coming up to their man-years, smiling into the sun, caught on the hook of the moment, never bothering to rage against the emptiness inside their own heads!

Perhaps Gifu felt the boy tensing beside him. He put out a brown weatherworn hand and rested it heavily on Kell's taut shoulder.

'It's a paradise, lad, for all you disdain it. Instead of carrying the stone of your anger much further, think how it might have been if the All Mother had not touched this place with her presence.'

'I think of little else,' Kell answered truthfully, 'except ploughing to your standards, Gifu,' he added with a sidelong look that the elderman caught and appreciated.

'Yes, no doubt. I don't know, you younglings have more wit than's good for you! Which reminds me that the minutes I'm wasting here I could be using to chase some other sitabout whose head's filled with dreams and smart quips.'

They laughed together. Then Gifu stood up with a weary groan. Kell watched him clump his way back heavily to the terrace edge, and then move out of sight as he climbed down the steps he had walked thousands of times before.

Kell laboured on with a will through the remaining hours of daylight. Shortly before the sun's ungathering, he unchained his mox from the plough and retrieved a disc of dark glass from the metal-edged slot built into the bone behind the beast's ear. He replaced the disc with another, which gave the animal the sense of its own way home to the common byre in the high pastures where all of the moxen herded overnight.

Kell had brought food for his vigil. He had also told Enjeck and Munin, his current kin, that he would not be oversleeping at the village. It was common enough practice, when there was much work to do on the terraces.

So, Kell regained his spot against the soft bark of the cushiontree. He calmed his thoughts and set himself down to outwait the sun and watch the darkness come on.

It was a marvel that had never lost its fascination for him. All of the people Kell knew took the undoing of the sun completely for granted. Shamra, his heartbond, had mentioned on occasions how pretty it was: she was perhaps the most intelligent and most sensitive person Kell knew, yet even she didn't wonder beyond the phenomenon itself: she never wanted to know the magic behind the mystery.

Now it began again, as though for the first time, since every ungathering was different. One moment the great diffuse yellow ball was too bright to look upon – then there came a fading, a sudden blink of dwindling brilliance, and the sun-sphere was larger and a little fainter and tinged with orange now and streaks of red. This was always a feature, and Kell suspected it was a signal to let the animals know of the onset of dark. Come to that, it alerted the fieldsmen to make an end to their work and return home, or else find a sleepingplace on the slopes, which many of them did during busy times; harvesting and ploughing-under.

This phase lasted for many minutes, and Kell watched patiently but with a tense anticipation for what would come next.

The sun guttered like a ball of flame wreathed in smoke. It began to expand, its interior filled with a scribble of purples and reds. Lights sparkled deep within, flaring and then dying down again quickly. At this point the spectacle was nearly over. The edges of the globe were now almost too faint to be seen, a dimly glowing rim of subtle violet that tantalised the eye. Like mist on a fall-season morning the swelling, cooling gas was vanishing away into the air. A tight cluster of glowing brands burned briefly where the globe had been, but they too darkened swiftly and were gone. It was over, and presently the sky gleams appeared; little dots and points and discs, some near, some far off, most motionless, but a few even now drifting slowly across . . .

Far away a cliff-owl called its long mellow note. Kell loved that sound of the night – which a part of him regarded as his own domain. Not unreasonably, for virtually all of the inhabitants of Perth got themselves under cover when the darkness came. The Mythologies were rooted deep in their minds, and in those stories connections were made between the brief dark of the enclave and the total terrifying blackness of the wilderness Outside. It was an irrational superstition of course, for the All Mother saw to it that her children were safe, safe and warm under her bright and brooding wings.

Kell wondered what part the sky gleams played in the picture. Perhaps they were her eyes, mysterious elemental beings. Or maybe the teachers were right, and the streaks and points were the All Mother's thoughts, dreaming the existence of Perth moment by moment . . .

Kell smiled at the way the old lessons came back to him unchanged. He was an able pupil, he had been told, but unconventional in his thinking. Instead of simply accepting the Knowledge as his fellows did, he challenged it – as though his Initiate's tiny intellect could shake the foundations of the world's long-held wisdoms! Still, his assertions and pointed questions made for a certain entertainment which the other students enjoyed.

Kell put these thoughts behind him. There would be enough of it tomorrow, which was his next learning day. Instead, he cleared his mind and simply let the night soak into him; the sweetness of the cooling air, the cries of the

8

enclave's noctural creatures, the wonderful sight of the sky gleams drifting and streaking across the heavens. Sometimes they made a sound, maybe a sizzling or a low buzzing: occasionally they came close, and at such times Kell felt the childlike thrill of imminent discovery, as though the All Mother had spotted him awake as she trod the paths and pastures normally reserved for men.

In fact, one gleam now swung down from the left and came spinning in Kell's direction. As it drew closer he heard the rapid fluttering it made, and its glow was so strong it cast shifting shadows around him. He held his breath, his body tight as a wire with excitement.

The sky gleam seemed to reach a point directly in front of him, high above the midslopes, then it slipped sideways and dropped away very rapidly. It moved out of sight so quickly that Kell was forced to scramble up and run to the terrace edge to see what became of it.

His eyes swept across broad puzzles of shadow below. For a second he thought he'd found the gleam and that something was wrong with it; for down there among a tumble of rocks there was not one light but several. And then Kell realised with a shock that *the sky gleam was elsewhere, hovering above*. A second later the group of lights he'd first spotted went out and left the gleam hanging alone, watching like a scrubcat for the treemice to reappear . . .

They never did. There was only the solitary jewel in the night, which held its position for many minutes before slowly moving away. Kell waited longer hoping to glimpse some other clue, but remained disappointed. Eventually he felt sleep coming on, and resigned himself to the fact that this was yet another mystery to add to the many that tantalised his mind.

Enjeck and Munin had grown used to Kell's unconventional

9

ways. He had shared their home since the last ploughing season, and the upbringing ritual required that soon he must move on. None of them would be very saddened by this. To Kell the elders were simple, honest, undemanding folk who tolerated him but seemed rather embarrassed by his presence. They fed and sheltered him but took little interest in his education and were even frightened sometimes by the things that he said. Though to be fair, that had been a common pattern among the kin Kell had stayed with since leaving the communal nursery in Odal.

Such was the way in Perth. The All Mother insisted that the population was a single family; no man or woman having any special right or influence over the offspring they authored; and that all heartbond couples should welcome any children who entered their houses for as long as they wanted to stay. This would ensure the broadest and most balanced nurturing, and would prevent a stagnation of thought in adults and children alike.

This regime had brought Kell only frustration. Often he longed to know just who his original father and mother had been. Yet at the same time he dreaded finding someone like Enjeck and Munin, dull and old before their time, locked into a routine that found no room for a son.

Kell ate his breakfast in silence. Munin never asked him where he had been, or why, and Kell felt no impulse to tell her – even though the story of the sky gleam and the group of lights was almost bursting to be out of him. Enjeck had not even bothered to stay for first-meal: the sounds of his wood lathe came busily through the wall from his workshop. He had laboured since earliest light.

'I have a learning day today,' Kell told Munin conversationally, determined to make some effort of friendliness. She was standing over the washplace by the window, cleaning vegetables for the main after-work meal.

'There is food in your pack, and I've bottled some nightberry juice in case you get thirsty on the way . . .'

To Kell's surprise he found himself suddenly and desperately disappointed not to have come up to Munin and Enjeck's expectations. They were well into their middle years, and soon would no longer be required to house youngsters. But they would not grow lonelier as they grew older, for the village-family was even closer-knit than the world-family of Perth. Yet Kell, being one of their last children, was not the source of pleasure and pride that they would have wished for.

At that moment Kell wanted nothing more than to leave his food and go over to Munin, hug her close, and tell her he loved her. But even that small lie was beyond him, and probably she would not believe him anyway. Instead he finished his fruit, muttered that he'd be back before last light, and went quickly into the fresher and more honest air outside.

The village of Othila stood an hour's brisk walk from the midslopes and ten minutes' stride from the main road that led to the city. There were a number of students making their way to the Tutorium, some already sporting their bright Initiate's gowns; yellows, blues or greens according to their level of achievement. Kell, who had the right to wear the blue gown of excellence, with two gold shoulderstripes, avoided doing so whenever possible. He hated showiness. Shamra, a stripe ahead of him, was coming round to his way of thinking and likewise kept the uniform tucked in the pouch at her hip.

He met her soon after, waiting beneath the peacock palm at the first crossroads as they'd arranged. She, like many girls of Perth, was trained to inner sight and may have followed the progress of his mind from its waking – though he hoped not, since he wouldn't have wanted her to know what he'd thought about Munin and Enjeck, or their opinion of him.

He greeted her formally with a small bow, which she returned according to custom.

'How are you today?'

'I am well,' she said. Kell used the moment to look at her. She was as tall as he, but dark where he was fair, and much finer featured. People would think of her as thin, yet soon the appearance of womanhood would make her voluptuous. Kell had already noticed some of the older male students gazing at her with longing, and at him with an envy that they could do nothing about. Shamra was unselfconsciously beautiful and Kell was glad of that, since it would have been so easy, if she felt superior, for her to have treated him with disdain.

'I have been studying the Elemental Precepts,' she told Kell, and then went on to explain some of the ideas she'd learned. Her green eyes glittered with excitement, but they were distant now and Kell came to feel that she was talking to herself. She usually excelled at her work – which Kell truly admired – yet it pained him to see her so absorbed with teachings that no longer compelled his faith. The Precepts, the Mythologies, all ended where Perth ended and anything else could only be delusion and lies.

'. . . so as Pennek says in the ninth codicil of the Fourteenth Precept . . .'

And then Shamra stopped, for it was Kell's turn to look distant and preoccupied. She laughed at his dreamy expression and touched his face. He startled and smiled. Then, because she was his special companion, he kissed her briefly on the cheek. As a heartbond couple, made so by the All Mother on their first birthday, they were allowed to show such intimacy in public. He loved her, but if he was true to himself, he wasn't sure if he loved Shamra enough for them to be together all through their lives. She was his first, fast,

12

last friend, with him together in spirit for life. He had decided long ago that he would die for her, the only one. Yet was that the same as being a good husband to his wife? Somehow he doubted it – but put the issue aside now as an irritation.

He watched her closely for signs that she'd been *reading* him, but her eyes were clear and her face was open. She was simply glad to see him.

'So, tell me everything that's been happening since I last saw you,' Shamra said brightly. That had been two days ago, when they'd both had a rest day from their work. Kell ploughed under Gifu's instruction, and Shamra was an artisan of ideas. Her function in the Community was to be an Academic, so all her tutors said, and there was no doubt of it. Others, craftfolk like Enjeck, would be left to realise her imaginations.

Kell shrugged and made a story of how one of the other ploughlads had got into trouble for misdirecting his mox, sending it blundering into a field of feathercane instead of along its intended path. He also added his own misdemeanour, before making light of it and speaking of Gifu with a special warmth . . . But Shamra's expression was darkening, almost in parallel with the darkening sky that Kell had fixed in his mind, and the memory of the sky gleam and that strange exciting cluster of lights below.

'You should have been asleep!' Shock broke Shamra's silence. She shivered with the dread of the night, and her breath came faster as she caught the deeper and even more terrifying thoughts beneath Kell's immediate vision.

'What are you doing?' Kell said, pretending to be offended by her intrusion but secretly glad that she was coming to discover what he held to be so important.

'The night – the night!' Her whole body was shuddering now, and passers-by turned to glance curiously at the tall trembling girl, before looking away again politely.

Kell understood that Shamra's abilities were not refined or strong enough yet to control the force of his own emotions. He helped her, turning his mind to other things – to the village, to Munin peeling vegetables, to a caricature of the tutor he most detested, to a memory of the last time he and Shamra swam together in the sphere-pool at Odal . . .

Gradually she calmed, soothed by his thoughts. She was dark-haired, with deep black hair almost down to her waist, and this contrasted strikingly with her paleness now.

'I'm sorry,' Kell said, sincerely. 'I have wanted to tell you about these things, these feelings I have and these notions I can't get out of my head. And it's better if you do it by inlooking, rather than listening to my clumsy words . . .'

They were walking on, an arm's length apart, and impulsively Shamra waved to halt one of the big air cars that came their way along the road. It was going to Odal, and now it slowed and stopped with a gush of hot air and a deep drumming of hidden blades. Kell and Shamra climbed aboard, and she looked away from him as she spoke.

'I know these things about you are different, Kell.' She sounded serious, her voice quiet and on one level. Gifu sounded the same, sometimes, when matters were bad and there was no laughter inside him.

'Maybe I've always known. Heartbonding is more than just bearing children and dwelling together.' She entered his mind for the merest moment and left a knowingness behind that made him ashamed.

'We don't even need to think about that yet,' Kell protested with a weak impulse to defend himself. 'We are four or five ploughings away from children, let alone settling in a home—'

'So we just blunder into trouble when we're older, is that it? When our responsibilities are greater? How will you be then – idling your nights away, wandering the slopes, gazing at sky gleams, searching the rocks – searching the rocks – for – a – way . . .'

She could not bring herself to say it, and gave a little splintered laugh and shook her head as if there was nothing to be done.

'Searching the rocks for a way Outside,' Kell said, and felt an amazing lightness come over him; a clarity, a revelation. 'There. It's said.'

Shamra turned to him and seemed years older. Kell wondered cynically who else was directing this conversation through her eyes and words.

'There is nothing Outside, nothing that we would want to see. You know that. You learned that the first time the All Mother gave you the Knowledge.'

'Here, in Perth, we are safe,' Kell said carefully. 'The world beats with the rhythm of an unworried heart. It has been like this for many generations.' He was quoting his lessons almost to the word. 'And Outside there is just the terrible cold, the endless ice, the infinite darkness of an everlasting winter, and the Ice Demon forever prowling.'

'Just horrors . . . monstrous things.' Shamra's imagination reached for them and failed. She glimpsed only shadows underpinned by a deep sense of dread without any shape.

'But what if that isn't true?' Kell felt powerful in the asking. Powerful but frightened. Shamra's jaws clenched tight, and some of the other passengers shuffled uncomfortably, concerned that this young couple were having a serious argument.

'I said—' Kell began.

'I heard what you said. And it's meaningless. How could things be otherwise? How could the All Mother be anything but perfect in her understanding, and in her caring for us? What is the point of asking what is beyond Perth – your blood knows there is nothing.'

'But just to *see*,' Kell said. 'Just to go there and to find out for myself!'

'How can you see nothing? How can you go to a place where you couldn't survive for a second?'

Kell hated the cool calm relentlessness of Shamra's logic. It made nonsense of his most cherished ideas, which she trampled with the heavy boots of her reason.

'It can't be that bad,' he said limply, knowing they both knew he had already lost the day.

They were coming to the outskirts of Odal. The Tutorium, a delicate architectural arrangement of marble and glass, followed the contours of a low cluster of hills a short walk away from the main road into the city. Kell, Shamra and perhaps twenty other passengers disembarked from the air car which then drifted on its way like featherdown once the last traveller had left. There was no driver, but the machine, like Kell's mox, had enough intelligence to know where it was going. Which was more than could be said for some people, Kell thought bitterly.

The two paused briefly to don their academic gowns, woven from a weightless black sylk. To Kell's intense annoyance Shamra made a point of attaching her shoulder-stripes, as if to reinforce her success. He tutted audibly and she pretended to take no notice.

They walked on and soon crested the rise of the first lens-shaped hill and looked across at the beautiful jewellery that was the Tutorium complex.

'One day,' Kell said with a quiet determination, 'I *will* go beyond the world of Perth. And I'll either die Out There, or I'll return to admit you were right. Or . . .' He shrugged and made out that his imagination had failed, though in fact a wonderful prospect was blowing through him like a gale.

'But for now, Shamra, will you keep that secret to

yourself? I wouldn't want the Praeceptor to find out, or the All Mother—'

'Oh,' Shamra answered lightly, and not in any way to frighten him, 'I'm sure she already knows.'

There were teachings, and there was the Teaching; knowledge, and the Knowledge. There were no thoughts beyond those in the mind of the All Mother, and the job of the tutors was merely to see that the ordinary students and the more advanced Initiates had correctly understood what were unquestionably the ultimate lessons.

'With thanks to the All Mother, for the warmth of her heart and her brooding wings.'

The students chorused the supplication in the Great Hall of assembly and in unison made the symbolic gesture of folding their arms across their chests, until the hands rested on their opposite shoulders. The one-voice-that-was-many rose in a soft thunder to the faceted vaults of the roof and echoed back in a cascade of coloured sunlight. Kell gazed at the rainbow panes and the smooth pale marble columns and walls, and marvelled that faith needed to be supported by such an immense volume of stone.

The prayer ended, and each student checked his glass for the day's instructions. These most precious items, lovely oysters of smooth silver, were given to all children upon their birth as a gift from the one Goddess. Although every glass looked identical, there must have been a subtle uniqueness built into each, for everyone in the Community knew his own by instinct, and would never be parted from it for a second.

Kell let his glass lie in his left palm and felt its warmth and weight and the utterly natural way his hand moulded its contours. Then, once he felt settled, he opened his fingers and looked down at his own distorted reflection. He saw a boy of thirteen ploughings with wry-dark eyes, a curly tangle of straw-coloured hair and a rather thin face; these had given him an innocent look as a toddler, but now made him seem scruffy and slightly gaunt. He was growing beyond the cuteness Shamra had used to tease him about.

The other students were going about their business and the Hall was emptying. Kell let out a gentle breath and his mind was washed with reassurances and the spirit of the All Mother. He was embraced by the Goddess, enfolded by her, drenched in the love of her . . .

And out of it came the clear command for him to accompany Shamra to the park, where more of the Knowledge would be imparted.

'I am concerned for you Kell,' Shamra said a few minutes later. They were walking down through the grove of windchime trees beyond the Hall, following the moss-fringed steps sunk in deep greenery towards the park and its central crystal lake. The air was filled with tinkling music, meaningless as the breeze but incredibly soothing.

'Don't be. If the All Mother knows what I have been thinking about then my punishment is already set. Besides, what is the worst she could do – banish me to the Outside?' His grin looked fractured, so that Shamra came to wonder how this damage had been caused in him, and why the Goddess in her wisdom let it go on.

'I just hope it passes,' she told him, presenting a different aspect now: her superior know-it-all self had faded away.

They reached the bottom of steps and came to the little park among the trees and the stands of filigree bushes that confused and delighted the eye. And although they had walked hand in hand, something suddenly changed for Kell and he found himself alone. There was an enormous power here in this hidden and intimate place. Shamra had gone . . .

And where was his bravado now and all of his rebellious ideals?

Kell went down to the water. He felt dizzy and sick, and his glass, safe in the small pouch on his belt, burned like hot iron in his brain.

It isn't good that you should be alone.

He didn't know if he was listening to his own mind, or to the voice of the Goddess, or to the faraway jingling of the windchime trees. His head spun and he dropped to his hands and knees by the edge of the turquoise lake. Kell's eyes throbbed and the world seemed to writhe and rearrange itself strangely.

And out of the voice or the red marrow of his bones came a piercing sense of loneliness. It was so acute and so intense that he cried aloud and his stomach heaved and he vomited into the water.

You are never alone under my wings.

'No,' he choked out. 'No.' He desperately wanted Shamra's reassurance, or at least to know that she was nearby. But the All Mother's illusion was as cruel as it was complete, and look as he might Kell could not find a trace of the girl.

Here you are safe. Here is warmth and shelter, food and companionship forever.

Kell could not prop up his own weight now, his arms were weakening.

Elsewhere is nowhere.

He slumped sideways and flopped on to his back, his mouth open and gasping.

Elsehere is nowhere.

Above him hung a huge web attached to the corners of the sky. And at its centre a vast cool eye looked down upon him. And terror burst into the ocean of loneliness and carried him to a brink and forced him to gaze into the dreadful abyss.

Elsewhere – Elsewhere – Elsewhere . . .

'Is nowhere!' he screamed. 'Elsewhere is nowhere! Elsewhere is nowhere!'

It was a terrible lie, he knew that; a transgression. But the only way to be rid of the pain.

Kell did not see Shamra again that day. He knew the Goddess had deliberately arranged for that to be so, and that was a minor punishment. Until last ploughing he had only heard about such isolations from the mouths of other students, hearsay and gossip in the main; but then Kell experienced it for himself after the notion of going past the high slopes first came to his mind. He recalled vivid dreams over a period of several nights and how his eyes had troubled him; they were itchy and watery as though infected. Shamra had seemed distant to him (which had frightened her as much as it had done Kell). And then, on the fourth day after the forbidden thoughts, he had forgotten his kin and his home and even where he was going. He remembered wandering without reason across the slopes with only the moxen and scrubcats for company. Going towards villages brought the sickness upon him more strongly: he was compelled to be alone, to experience as exquisitely as possible what loneliness meant. It was a solitude that had struck at him deeply.

Now, as Kell made his way up to the midslopes where he felt safer, he understood that this time the withdrawal was more subtle, and designed to appeal also to his reason. Simple separation from Perth and its people had little power over him, given his personality. But to be torn from Shamra, to have their bond cut, was an altogether more profound kind of torture.

Kell tested the idea and put out his thoughts towards her. Like the abalone doves that always flocked back to the nest, he knew that their minds were connected. But even as he turned his attention in Shamra's direction, the nausea that had gripped him in the park returned – one, two, three times the awful cramps doubled him over and dropped him to his knees, and his eyes burned and watered, and his head spun.

After that Kell resigned himself to the fact that he would need to forage around the fields for as long as his chastisement lasted – reduced like the mox to feasting on lantern apples and sugarnuts until the All Mother's will had been satisfied.

But he was not troubled too much. The threat of his own company was not the worst that could happen. And it wasn't as if he had been detached from Shamra forever. He would see her soon, once his penance was paid.

It was late in the day and there was a certain tinge to the light that told Kell the ungathering would soon begin. He was already high on the slopes far above Odal, walking along a terrace that was being left fallow for a season. His sylken Initiate's gowns swished through the flitch grass and, noticing this, he removed them and packed them away. Kell felt weary now, but the mysterious excitement at the onset of night was growing in him again. Nearby an old cushiontree had been ravaged by moxen; they had stripped off its bark to get at the milky phloem beneath, and large mats of bark lay scattered around.

Kell collected a bed of the spongy material, arranged it so he was sitting propped against the tree, and then waited.

Soon the spectacle began, that wonderful sight which perhaps he alone, among all the people of Perth, relished and loved. This evening the sun's globe seemed to expand like a bubble, darkening to the colour of old brass threaded through with red vein-like lightnings. A green flash ripped across the surface, while at its heart the pattern of lights brightened to a bluish brilliance . . .

Then there was a wing, a slow shadow cast somewhere across. Not by the sun – the display was continuing – but in Kell's head. He realised he was no longer alone.

Now a different fear touched him: Kell, who marvelled at unknown things, grew tense as the apparition approached. He knew it was a wraith of the road, not part of the human population of Perth. Such spectres were rare, and there were many mysteries attached to them. Most people believed they were the essences of the dead, somehow continuing like mist through endless, meaningless years. If that were so, then Kell could see how his meeting with one now need not be a coincidence. The Praeceptor's teaching (his opinion, really, Kell thought cynically) was that road wraiths were elemental beings: they had minimal identity of their own, but rather were aspects of the All Mother, facets of her greater personality.

Whatever the true explanation, the wraith came closer and Kell trembled. It had taken the form of a small girl, no more than seven ploughings old. She was dressed in her sleeping gown, a long white garment of simply woven cottoncloth. Her hair was the colour of Shamra's – and in fact there was a passing resemblance in their features, as though the Goddess was emphasising the point of Kell's foolishness. And the wraith's eyes were dark beyond imagining. Behind her innocence Kell sensed something more. She had a sweet smile, but he suddenly fancied that smile could split and grow and become dangerous and evil. He felt no shame in realising his fear. This road wraith could kill him with a glance.

The wraith was the first to make the small bow of greeting. Kell, slightly surprised by this ordinary formality, responded awkwardly from his seated position. Then like a lick of fog folding in on an autumn morning, the shade sat beside him and sighed. It reminded Kell of the wind streaming upwards over stones.

'Why have you come here, little sister?' He asked this without trying to betray his fear.

You have a heart, Kell, while I have none. You have friends here, whereas I am alone. You are all that I am not, warm flesh to my cold emptiness.

'Have you come to possess me then?'

The little girl smiled and Kell watched apprehensively to notice how far her pale lips would stretch.

My concern is that you will come to possess me, ploughboy — or at least come to possess what I am.

'Ah, then you're here to warn me!'

Beyond Perth the whole world is like me. Cold. Empty. Friendless. Dead. Is that what you would give up your life to find?

'I just want to know.'

You have the Knowledge, and I am part of it. Think of me, if you like, as a soul that once strayed too far, too far beyond what was right and true. You are being punished for a few days, Kell. My punishment is endless.

Kell wasn't sure if these words were spoken aloud to him or were shaped in his head, as Shamra sometimes did. Was he dreaming the whole thing?

The wraith reached out its hand and touched his bare arm, and Kell was left with a memory of cold weight and fingers as unfeeling as the ice.

'Thank you, little sister, for troubling to appear to me tonight.'

Nothing is beyond you, Kell. Remember you are a man in the making. You are defined by your choices, as I was once . . .

Again the creature beside him sighed and was drawn down into that whisper and vanished.

It was full night. Already the sky gleams streaked and whirled and glittered in the heavens.

Kell stirred stiffly. The chill had gone from the air and he felt safe again. Way down along the track, almost as if this were a part of the night's deliberate weaving, a dancing cluster of lights came into view and drew closer.

23

Excitedly Kell scrambled up and hid behind the cushion-tree, ready to follow them once they had passed.

2

The Way Through the Rocks

Behind the lights were shadows, vague figures of women or men. It was difficult to tell, for each of them wore dark cauled cloaks over what seemed to be work clothes, the heavy tunics and breeches and boots favoured by the cityzens in the industrial quarter of Odal. Sensible clothes and good protection against factory hazards, or the barbs of thornweed on the high slopes – or cold.

The figures passed by, five of them. Kell saw that one was a man of colossal proportions who brought up the rear. He swung round several times to cast his beam downtrail as the party made their way onwards and upwards. Swiftly their lights dwindled to sparks, and Kell knew that soon he'd lose sight of them. The warning of the road wraith came back to him: he had been punished once this day for disregarding the laws of Perth. Whatever followed would be worse . . . And yet the actions of these strangers were no less questionable. What were they up to, unless it was to find a way beyond the world, putting into practice Kell's most audacious dreams?

The conflict inside him was an agony. If he followed these people then the All Mother's retribution was likely to be severe. Yet if he turned back then his shame and disappointment would be a weight he'd carry forever, because he would have betrayed himself completely.

Kell rose from behind the cushiontree – and like a passenger on an air car ride allowed his legs to take him where they would; along the track until it passed beyond the line of cultivated ground, through the zone of thornweed and wirebroom that even the moxen would not eat, past the end of the trail itself to the chaos of rocks that continued up and up until it met the mysterious and eternal substance of the sky. He had never been so high, and the prospect was dizzying. Kell paused to look back and was stunned by the sheer sense of volume and space. Far away the lights of Odal and its surrounding villages twinkled with distance: the whole beautiful map of the world resembled a spiderweb laced with dawn dew. And perhaps even more amazing was the fact that a number of distant sky gleams seemed to be moving *below* Kell's present position. He had climbed even higher than they. And that, he felt, was a fine achievement indeed.

Smiling drunkenly with self-satisfaction, Kell turned to continue his journey – and was struck with a sudden freezing horror to realise that the lights of the strangers had vanished.

Panic tore through him like the stomach cramps had done earlier, wave after wave as the danger of his situation came home to him. Even though his eyes had grown familiar with the night, there was too little light for him to see his way forward, or back for that matter. He might proceed by touch, but in which direction? Ahead lay the jumbled rocks of the highslopes, and increasing danger. Behind him sure enough was safety, but defeat. An alternative might simply be to wait to be found by the strangers on their return; or, if they didn't come back before dawn, then Kell's problem would be solved by the gathering light.

With these choices open to him, Kell became calmer. His heartbeat slowed and he felt his fear-grip on the rock face beside him lessening. And as he quietened he made an interesting rediscovery.

It was a mundane item of the Knowledge that although Perth remained self-sufficient, air was continually drawn in from beyond the world and breathed out again once used.

The tutors were at pains to explain that such air was filtered and tested and made absolutely pure. It was the last and only gift from the Wilderness. Kell had sensed the air-flow previously during his explorations of the highslopes; a steady streaming breeze continually awash around the scoured rocks. At lower levels its effect was undetectable, and Kell doubted that anyone he knew had ever experienced it directly.

Now, as his nerves steadied, he felt that soft constant breath at his back. Since the sky — as far as anyone knew — was sealed, then the night wind must lead to a cleft in the rocks. Perhaps the very cleft that the strangers had entered, or at least one where Kell could hide until he was safe.

He moved on with a purpose, his hands and feet sensitive to the contours of the uneven ground. Several times his clambering dislodged loose stones, which went tumbling with a clatter. And once a misplaced step caused a larger fall: Kell felt a slab of stone sliding away. He jumped ahead and waited with a pounding heart as the block dropped and spun and shattered into a rattling cascade of smaller fragments lower down.

He dared a glance into the darkness. There was nothing to see below, but what Kell did notice was a stirring amongst a number of the nearer sky gleams. Four or five of them slipped across the heavens as though alerted by the rockfall. After a few moments they repositioned themselves and hung hovering, perhaps waiting for signs of further slippage. As Kell carried on he kept a wary eye on the gleams, but all through the rest of his journey they showed no further indications of activity.

Presently, despite the coolness of the night, Kell found himself sweating. And his muscles now were trembling with exertion. He became aware of slick wetness on his hands, touched his fingers to his lips, and tasted blood. He knew he couldn't continue much further; sheer tiredness would beat

27

him. For a while he had been bypassing cracks and openings in the rock wall: some were impossibly narrow, others seemed to end after a few paces. Kell reflected that at least if he failed in his mission he'd have somewhere secluded to sleep.

But then those thoughts were swept away. His probing hands suddenly found nothing beneath them. He took a stumbling step to correct his balance, tripped over and landed hard on a downslope of sliding sand.

It might have meant nothing. He might easily have scrambled up and cursed and carried on. But the message of the breeze held him spellbound, for its direction had changed – it was streaming outwards now into his face, *and the air was so cold it made him shiver.*

Kell gasped. It felt like being plunged under water. He nearly cried out, though a natural caution restrained him. For long minutes he lay there drinking in the freezing draught, until it became too painful to bear. He laughed, his teeth chattering, laughed stupidly with cold and then crawled on until he came to a boulder big enough to shelter behind. There he rubbed warmth into his arms and his numbed and stinging cheeks. His eyes watered tears of frost and elation. He let them out, along with all the huge feelings he could not fully understand or control; love and fear and hate and a pride so intense it pierced his heart. After that, after many minutes when he was wrung out like a wet washcloth, Kell came back to himself. He sat slumped against hard rough stone, he was desperately tired; and in that tiredness came the slow understanding that he had done enough for tonight. Maybe the strangers had passed this way, but even if so they might not return for many days, if at all. Kell had to consider himself alone. There would be other times. But for now his flesh and his imagination both failed him and he closed his eyes, and slept soundly at the top of the world.

Voices woke him. Immediately afterwards a drenching brilliance shocked his eyes open. Momentarily he thought the strangers had found him with their lights. Then he realised it was sunlight striking into the cleft. The sun had regathered. Daylight had come.

Hurriedly Kell scurried under cover of nearby boulders, groaning softly at the stiffness in his limbs and the cuts and scrapes on his hands. As the voices came closer, the temptation to peek was almost overwhelming. But he understood his danger and stayed silent and hidden.

One of the men's voices, high and neurotic, was explaining something technical at great speed. Kell caught certain snippets, and was intrigued by mention of 'the Traveller' and 'the shiftings of the ice'. Another voice, deeper and slower and altogether more commanding, responded after a second's consideration.

'You know well enough, Skjebne, that our time here is limited. Once the fire has been lighted, it will spread by itself—'

'Yes, but Kano, we must make adequate provision for the journey. This is such a huge responsibility—'

'The dispossessed are responsible for their own freedom, once they are given the choice. The stores are there for the taking.'

'But not the knowledge. And, if we aren't careful, nor the opportunity either!'

The one called Skjebne seemed frightened and unsure. Kano, apparently their leader, was much more assured. But he was also relentless, Kell felt. There was a hardness to him. Kano the dangerous one would not be a man to cross.

The strangers passed by Kell's boulder and their silhouettes filled the entrance to the cleft, misty black shadows surrounded by a haze of amber dawnlight. Their words began to fade. A third voice, a woman's, spoke briefly, and the group laughed before moving beyond the threshold and out of sight and hearing.

After a few minutes Kell dared to crawl until he could peer along the trail. The strangers were no more than dots bobbing in the distance. Then, once again, the triumph of what he had done, and the scale of the panorama before him, melted into Kell's mind. The whole of Perth was laid out before him in a vast round arena. The Central Lake was a blue agate slice bedded in the green-and-gold of the fields. Odal, a day's determined walk away, was no more than a grey and silvery smear. People were impossibly small. Above him the dome of the sky covered all, and even higher than Kell could hope to go, a cluster of red garnet birds dropped a thousand armspans and shattered apart and went streaking away like splinters.

With the chill wind of the future blowing over him, and with the world of the enclave flooding his eyes, Kell thought hard about what he would probably do next. And, after many minutes of careful contemplation, he stood up – having made no decisions at all.

The journey back was easier, but Kell was still aching and weary and the morning was gone by the time he arrived at the lowslopes. On a whim he continued, making for Othila and home.

Surprisingly, he found he was able to approach the village and then enter it. The All Mother's spell was broken and his punishment presumably had ended.

He enjoyed a certain wry amusement at the glances he got from the villagefolk. His shirt was torn, his breeches dirty, and his boots were badly scuffed. In addition Kell realised his face was covered in dust, while his nails were broken and his fingerends crusted with blood. He smiled benignly to all he met and waved cheerily to a few. Then he entered his kinhouse, smelt Munin's excellent cooking and was instantly ravenously hungry.

To give her due credit, Munin was seriously concerned about Kell's absence. As she fussed around the table, setting him a bowl and spoon and three slabs of brown nutbread, she explained that the evening before Shamra had come to tell what had happened.

'She was distraught, poor girl.' Munin's eyes filled with the memory. 'Like a little lost child.'

'Don't know why,' Kell muttered, hiding his deep guilt in a shallow petulance.

'It's not been the first time—'

'That doesn't excuse it boy!' This *was* the first time, however, that Munin had shown any temper at Kell's wayward behaviour. And he almost admired her for it. She brought the brothpot over from the stove and slopped out three large ladlefuls, not troubling that some of the piping hot stew splashed on the table and, a few spots, on Kell's hand. He snatched it smartly away. The broth, like Munin herself, was substantial and wholesome and smelt warmly of onions.

'I did not mean to alarm her,' Kell said more reasonably. 'I simply don't understand why the thoughts I think are forbidden.'

'Ah but it's not just thoughts, is it Kell?' Her sudden perspicacity surprised him.

'Old Gifu has seen you wandering the high trails . . .'

Kell imagined the fieldsmen down at the tap-house, smoking their hava leaf, swilling their juggons of beer, chewing over morsels of gossip as though they were starving for news.

'The world is safe,' Kell said defiantly, quoting the Knowledge. 'There's nothing up there to harm me.'

'Except yourself.'

'I am almost into my man-years. It's my responsibility.'

'You also have a responsibility to Shamra. If you were to die, her heart would break and she would soon follow you.'

'Why should I die?'

'Because you refuse to live the life the All Mother gave you,' Munin said, and without thinking crossed her arms over her breast in thanksgiving to the Goddess.

And she would say no more. She took Enjeck's broth through to him in his workshop, and that more than anything else told Kell of the burden he was placing on these good people's shoulders.

The guilt that Munin had caused in him made him pick at his food and leave it unfinished. Then he washed and went outside to study his glass in peace, beneath the shade of a lime tree whose leaves here and there were touched with gold, first sign that the summer was ending.

The glass, the warm, dear, marvellous glass bedded perfectly in his hands. It could be read directly – words and images flowed readily through its substance – or by impression. Kell closed his eyes and visioned the lens in his head, where it expanded and filled his mind exactly. Then, by settling back, he could enjoy a rich panorama of all that was known throughout Perth. He might visit any person he'd met, study again any lesson he'd learned or any he'd failed to remember: he might swim into his moxen's dulled consciousness and plant instructions for the next day's ploughing: he could dance with Shamra or challenge an acquaintance to a fierce game of battleboard . . .

Kell smiled. He would dance with Shamra. Though first, perhaps, he should apologise.

He put out his attention to find her – and gasped when she was with him immediately, vivid and insistent.

Oh Kell, what have you done!

'I – well – what?' His eyes snapped open, and although Shamra's image wavered it stayed with him.

Your tutor is coming to see you – he's on his way now – I want to be there Kell – I only hope I reach you before him . . . Even the Praeceptor has heard of this. This is very serious!

She sounded stern and hugely disapproving so that Kell felt thoroughly scolded. He felt worried also, for a visit by one's tutor was no minor matter. He began to bluster out some explanations, but Shamra broke contact and left him alone.

Aquizi and two clerics arrived minutes later; the tutor in his royal blue sylken gown and professorial regalia, the priests in their more modest fawn vestments. They came in an official Tutorium air car, sweeping into the village above skirts of red dust and setting down just within the borders of Enjeck's property. Aquizi, like all of the tutors, was a strict methodologist and did everything according to the Knowledge.

Kell had worked hard to compose himself, and although he still felt cowed and nervous to be paid such formal attention, some part of him relished the encounter – for if his ideas were being taken so seriously, then there must be some truth behind them.

Kell rose and exchanged bows of greeting with the delegation. He brought some wicker seats and set them out facing his own beside the lime, including a fifth seat for Shamra, who was hurrying along the street to join them. Munin had been watching almost horrified from the kitchen window, and at Kell's glance busied herself with refreshments, wheatbeer, t'cha, and fruit juices of various flavours.

The men waited on their feet until Shamra reached them. She was breathing heavily and her cheeks were reddened from rushing. She made the bows, but beneath the surface of the etiquette sent a wave of love and reassurance to Kell that filled him with warmth to his bones. Like all of the heartbonded, their deepest feelings went beyond words.

'So.' Aquizi seated himself with a swish of gowns. The

33

others followed. 'There has been a grave violation here, Kell. You have not taken account of your warnings; you have paid no heed to the feelings of those who care for you; and, most crucially, you have continued to doubt the teachings of the All Mother herself. Is that right?' the tutor said, in a tone which indicated there was no possibility of it being in any way wrong.

Aquizi's eyes were small and blue and penetratingly accusing. They held all of the life within him, since his skin was dry and wrinkled, his lips pale and dead. He had been mummified by the Knowledge, Kell thought (smothering that thought swiftly). The Answers had been delivered to him long ago, and he had believed them and never questioned them since.

'From your point of view, that is right.'

Munin bustled out and set the drinks. She poured t'cha politely for her guests and Aquizi, just as politely, took a sip and then pushed the cup away.

'And from your point of view?' Aquizi said. Kell forced himself to look away from the cold fire of his inquisitor's gaze: the man was here only to condemn him, not to understand him.

He looked back.

'If the All Mother gave me the ability to ask questions, why shouldn't I then be allowed to ask them?'

'All of the important questions you ever asked have been answered.'

'I have been told,' Kell agreed. 'But not shown. And now I am being punished for wanting to see for myself.'

Aquizi was leaning forward hawklike in his desire to rip the heart out of the boy's contentions. Kell felt sure the tutor would like nothing more than to beat surrender out of him. One of the clerics, the younger one with the supercilious smile, made a note on a small paper pad he had for the purpose. He used a gold-nibbed pen which was pure affectation. Kell made a point of ignoring him.

'Perth,' said Aquizi, 'is an egg. A fragile living thing. If the shell is fractured or breached in any way, infection sets in. There is ferment and rot. Do you understand?'

'I understand that an egg must hatch or die, and that the only purpose of the creature inside the egg is to break out of it.'

Aquizi sat up slowly, drew himself away from the boy and looked at each of his attendants in turn, and then at Shamra most meaningfully. He folded his hands neatly in his lap and offered a thin insincere smile.

'The egg must bide its time. It knows when to hatch.'

'When is that time?' Kell wondered, feigning an expression of open innocence that he knew Aquizi would love to slap down.

Instead, the harsh censorial light in the tutor's eyes moderated. He gazed at his hands as though in earnest consideration. They were rather fleshless hands, thin fingered, the nails long and well kept. Those hands now came up out of their resting place and fluttered like skeletal birds and touched Kell and Shamra briefly between the eyes.

Immediately there followed a sense of great tranquillity. Aquizi's mood seemed to mellow, and even the clerics' air of superiority faded away, so that they smiled and nodded easily at all that transpired. Munin reappeared with hot food and more drink. Astonishingly all three of the delegates poured frothing wheatbeer into big pottery juggons and quaffed the ale, Munin laughing heartily at the foamy moustache left on Aquizi's lip when he had supped his fill. And even Enjeck, shy and respectful, came out of his workshop to thank the tutor for his concern, and to congratulate Kell on his patience and ultimate common sense. The afternoon unfolded brightly and naturally, like a flower; the air sweetened, and a slow-

35

drifting flock of whisp came sailing across the village on their leisurely, endless migrations round Perth. They resembled little parachutes, each carrying an opalescent seed. Kell had never known if they were animals or plants, but they were delightful and beautiful, and seemed now to represent the freedom that could be achieved even within the enclave itself.

'With thanks to the All Mother,' Aquizi said devoutly, 'for her warm heart and brooding wings.'

'With thanks,' the others chorused, 'with thanks.'

Kell looked about himself at the trees and the sky, and was awed: it was the ultimate art of the Goddess, like the most perfect picture, never finished, ever changing, always complete; nothing less than exquisite. And how wonderful it was now to consider that he, like a fleeting brush-stroke within this greater panorama, should be so much an essential part of the whole.

The conversation and good cheer seemed to continue for a long time, lapping like quiet waters around the edge of a tranquil pond.

Then presently it was time for Aquizi and the clerics to leave, and there was a small sadness of parting. Kell found himself looking forward to his next lesson at the Tutorium, for Aquizi was so wise and understanding, so tolerant of Kell's raw stubbornness and his over-eager desire to seek the heart of a dream that was only ever a dream.

But it was over now. Kell realised how precious was this benign and gentle world where he was nurtured and protected, given all that anyone could reasonably ask for.

He stretched out his hand to touch the miracle of the lime tree . . .

. . . And came upon hard stone and the whisper of sand under his feet. Shadows folded behind him like the swirling of an immense cloak. He jolted and turned, confusion sweeping through him like an illness.

'We're in the cleft . . .'

Shamra, nearby, was wearing a thin blue shift, ideal for late summer but thoroughly impractical here. She too looked startled and then afraid.

'I don't understand what is going on—'

'The Ice! Something's happening to the Ice!'

The words and the fear beneath them came tearing out of Kell's throat. He did not comprehend his dread, but neither did he doubt it. Ahead of them the walls and contours of the cavern were oddly vague, little more than slabs of varying shadow. The needling wind that Kell had experienced before whined keenly into their faces, a cutting wind whisking scraps of white dust and harsh fragments of sound spiralling out of the gloom.

Shamra touched her forehead and stared at the ice particles slowly melting on her fingertips.

'It's coming in . . . Kell, the Ice is coming into the enclave!'

Her words were caught in a rising note of alarm.

'We must do something!'

And before he could stop her, Shamra was running forward stupidly, holding out her hands as though to deny entry to the wilderness.

Instantly Kell bolted after her, but the headwind was powerful and filled with stinging crystals, so that after only a dozen paces he was exhausted and making no progress as he battled against the gale.

'Shamra!' The call was futile, snatched out of his mouth and flung away behind him. 'Shamra!'

Kell forced himself on into the storm, into the curtains and veils of snow borne on the howling gusts. Intitial discomfort had become a complex pain; sharp and lancing through the flesh of his hands and face, a dull throbbing numbness in his bones. He bent his body forward and trudged on, pausing at the high ragged sound of a scream up ahead. He lifted his eyes, almost closed, to peer into the dimness.

Something red spat out of the dark at him and landed wetly on his cheek. Another shred struck his hand and stuck there in ghastly contrast to his own frozen white skin. The oncoming snow flurries were laced with spinning red flecks and spittlings of fresh bright blood.

Kell stumbled on a few steps, too horrified to think. When he saw the glistening mass crumpled on the floor of the tunnel he knew without doubt it was Shamra. She had been flayed by the tiny flying blades of the ice particles, which were now coating her completely in a white crystalline crust of rock-hard frost.

And yet *I'm* still alive—

Kell had time for a foretaste of puzzlement. Then there was more red in the air nearby, a cavernous tooth-filled redness. It became a mouth, jaws gaping hugely above the height of his head.

The creature was like nothing Kell had ever seen, a monstrous thing. It walked heavily on two legs, its pelt of shaggy white fur swinging to its pace. Pendulous forelimbs hung down level with the knees, each massive paw armed with a row of curved black claws, as deadly as fish hooks. And the eyes, the demon's little black eyes, held a knowing evil.

Kell realised that, defenceless, he was doomed. Pointlessly he stood over Shamra's pitiful tattered body in a protective stance.

The beast loomed forward, then struck out. One paw swung round in an effortless arc and swept Kell easily off his feet. He screamed with the agony of the claws in his chest.

Then he was being hauled along, hung like dead meat, his

feet dragging, his hands clutching and scrabbling at the frost animal's terrible grasp.

By now the sound was almost unendurable, an endless wailing shriek of wind over measureless wastes of ice; for they were close to the far end of the tunnel. With what remained of his senses Kell concentrated on the blurred slash of the cleft as they approached it. The ice beast was forced to turn itself side-on to pass through, lifting Kell easily up and out into a total chaos of storm.

Then the creature gathered its voice in a rumbling roar that rose and rose to a high keen howl as it called its kin to feed.

They came quickly, five, six of them, loping eagerly into sight. Weeping in his hopelessness, Kell spent his last seconds searching for any glimpse of the world he had so often imagined . . . But there was nothing.

And swiftly and savagely that nothingness was replaced by another.

His senses gathered slowly, as though he was reluctant to leave the restfulness of death. Only when his eyes opened fractionally and he saw Shamra lying beside him did Kell stir himself to move.

He became aware of someone crying. With all of his meagre strength he hauled himself over, on to his side, on to his back. He was lying on the ground close by the lime tree. Sunlight came speckling down, gold and green, through the swaying canopy of its leaves. It was late in the afternoon.

Munin moved into view, her face blotched with weeping. She knelt heavily beside Kell and one salty tear dropped from her reddened eyes into the corner of his mouth.

'Oh I thought we'd lost you – I thought they had killed you both!'

They. Aquizi and the false-faced clerics who had accompanied him.

Kell opened his lips but all that came out was a dry croak. Munin wailed anew, collected him up and squeezed him to her bosom. Her faint warm oniony smell was the most soothing thing in the world.

'They – hurt – Sham – ra –' As he spoke Kell struggled feebly, pulled himself away from Munin and flopped round to face the girl. He moved aside her wing of black hair and was shocked to see blood on the grass.

'She has bitten her own tongue,' Munin reassured. 'Nothing more. But I cannot wake her – just as I couldn't wake you, Kell. You went into a madness soon after your tutor had left. I didn't know what to do – I – All he did was touch you—'

A coldness came over Kell that had nothing to do with the late afternoon chill; it grew from deep inside him and left him feeling frightened and exposed. Aquizi – bumbling old Aquizi whom the other students made an object of ridicule and fun: Aquizi whose life was only a mirror reflecting the Knowledge . . . Who would ever suspect the power of those thin little fingers, the power of the All Mother to scold her children to the very point of their death?

'She's waking,' Munin said. Kell let his thoughts go and bent to Shamra's care.

'Make t'cha would you Munin, please. Give me time with her now.'

The woman didn't argue. She hurried away and as Shamra's consciousness returned, Kell eased her over on to her side. She looked pale, and one side of her face was crusted with dirt and with blood. But most startling was the expression of gathering anger that lit in Shamra's eyes; a fierce and defiant light warning of a towering temper.

Kell nervously searched for scraps of argument in his

defence. Shamra gripped his hand so hard her nails dug painfully into his skin.

'He did this!' She struggled to sit up, wincing with pain and discovering the soreness of her tongue. There was confusion and some fear and disbelief, clearing like clouds from her eyes. 'Aquizi did this!'

'He touched us,' Kell said. 'He put insanity inside us . . . Trying to warn us away from the Outside.'

'I felt myself die.' Tears came hotly and suddenly, but Shamra refused to weep. 'And then somehow I saw you die too, Kell. That terrible animal – do you think things like that really exist outside Perth?'

'Who knows? Which is why *I* want to know!'

To Kell's alarm Shamra began shaking in the aftermath of her ordeal, clenching her fists and clamping her jaws together while the trembling grew and reached a peak and then gradually subsided. He held her through it and then, when the fever was done, he helped her back to the wicker chairs where they had earlier been sitting.

'I need to know,' Shamra said, when Munin had brought the hot drinks, and been reassured and gone away again. 'If I am to be with you, I need to know it all, Kell; what you've seen, the ideas you've had in your head . . .'

Kell understood what that meant. Such a complete surrendering of one's thoughts to another was a profound and intimate thing, an act of total trust. Once the gates were opened freely in this way, Shamra would have access to all of Kell's mind. Nothing would be secret, should she choose to look.

She smiled, guessing his unease.

'I only want to know about your explorations, Kell. Of course you could tell me about it, but that would take time.'

'I am afraid that what you know, the All Mother will know . . .'

She nodded, understanding his fear. 'With the gift of seeing comes the equal gift of hiding. Or, at least, of confusing one's thoughts for others. If the Goddess is inside our hearts so completely, she will already be aware of your intentions. Your experience disproves this. And so, if you will trust me – more than you have ever done before – then I will keep your secret safe.'

They both glanced at the sun, which was misty round the edges now and close to its ungathering. And in that moment Kell acquiesced and straight away had a sense of Shamra sweeping gently and elegantly through his head like a ghost, a poignant and welcome presence, a gentle haunting filled with respect.

It was over with quickly. Kell felt her leave like a sigh, and then she was staring at him in a new way, as though she had learned more of herself through this process.

'Such passion, Kell. You have kept so much inside.'

'And even that has got me into trouble,' he said wryly.

'I think,' she went on, 'they will not stop – the tutors, the All Mother. If we ignore Aquizi's warning, there will be another punishment. And then another. In the end – I don't know – maybe they can take away our thoughts completely, so that we have no remembrance of things past.'

'You said "we",' Kell reminded her. Shamra shrugged as though her decision had not been a big one.

'We are heartbonded. Our lives are twined.' She looked up at him openly. 'But just as importantly, what has happened here is wrong.'

Kell's voice was quiet, his thinking simple and weary. 'So what should we do?'

'Stay together,' Shamra said. 'And at first light, go to the city to find this man you call Kano.'

3

A Very Deliberate Eye

It was the first time that Shamra had ever watched the ungathering through to its end, waiting on for the sky gleams to appear. The Knowledge had nothing to say about the nature of the sun or its mysterious behaviour; nor about the equally engimatic lights that sometimes streaked and flew, sometimes swarmed in dense swirling clouds, but which usually hung motionless in the air above the silent land of Perth.

'It's beautiful,' she whispered once, her head resting on Kell's shoulder as they sat in the little garden against the lime. There was no actual taboo against being out in the night, though most people felt uneasy about the dark and chose to be in their beds by the time the sunlight dissolved. Kell knew that Shamra would not be here now but for his company and her deep and simmering rage.

Neither Munin nor Enjeck had attempted to coax the youngsters inside. Shamra sensed their agitation, blended with a sense that they were losing Kell as their kin, and with a fainter thread of guilt that they had failed in their responsibilities towards him. They had watched from the kitchen window briefly, until the shadows pooled outside and engulfed the two figures. Then they turned away, Munin weeping quietly, and went to their sleep, their minds open and heedless of the All Mother's vast and brooding wings.

Even Kell and Shamra slept eventually, though hers was a different slumber. So it was with all of her kind, with the inward-looking. Some part of her was always aware, the way a cat sleeps, even in unconsciousness; like a faint but steady light shining on the landscape inside, so that Shamra knew when the morning was coming, woke with a will and stirred Kell out of his dreams.

'I'm cold,' he complained, and began rubbing life back into his arms. 'The sun will warm us . . .'

Kell was reminded of the nightmare, of the endless cold Outside. Shamra felt it too and shivered.

'If we are to search for Kano today we'd better get going,' she said in a strong and strident voice, before she could talk herself out of it.

They walked from Othila while the sun was still weak. There was a jewelled dew on the grass and for a short while their breath made faint feathers in the air. No one else was about, although Kell knew that on the midslopes the fieldsmen and ploughlads would already be at work. He thought about his mox standing like a monolith in the byre, waiting for the instruction that wouldn't come today. At some point perhaps one of the other fieldsmen, Gifu most likely, would notice Kell's absence, shackle up the beast and do at least a proportion of his work.

'The crop is mainly gathered and there's only the stubble to plough under . . . Though I'm in enough trouble already . . .'

Kell wondered if he'd spoken or just thought of these concerns. Either way, he grinned sheepishly as Shamra shrugged.

'Our way is set, Kell. Always remember we did this by choice.'

He nodded resolutely, but even then wondered how those words might come back to haunt him.

They took an air car most of the way to Odal. Nearer the city there were more passengers, some of whom looked on

44

the two children curiously; at this rather scruffy farm boy who avoided their eyes or replied with a nervously hostile glance; and the taller, darker, deeper-minded girl – one of the seers most probably, whose destiny would be as an acolyte of the All Mother, or maybe as an academic at the Tutorium, or both. She smiled more readily and was pretty when she smiled, though like all inlookers she would be adept with masks and deceptions: the honest clarity of her face was unnerving, and most people turned away after only a moment or two.

'Do you suppose we will be caught?' Kell said. He was thinking of the horror that was Aquizi's emotionless face and the ready cruelty beneath.

They had disembarked from the air car and were moving through an area of busy galleried plazas that formed the shopping and commercial area of the city. Fewer people stared at them now, because this was a place where a great variety of cityzens visited; people from all over Perth going about their diverse business.

'We will only just have been missed at home,' Shamra said. Her eyes held the bright and distracted look which told Kell her mind was sensitive and searching. 'I can't feel any suspicion, at least nothing that points our way. I think we are safe for the present.' Kell took her word, as he always did.

Although everyone in Perth probably visited Odal at some point in their lives – and many people regularly – there were few who knew the city intimately, or would go to certain of its quarters unless the need was great. The industrial sector was one such place. It sprawled on the far fringes, a grey, drear, unwelcoming labyrinth of manufactories and ware-houses built between the Jara Hills and the shore of the Central Lake. And while the All Mother surely saw to it that the waste products of the zone's industry were cleansed from the enclave, even so a pall of pale mist hung above this part, suspended like veils in the sky.

'There is something very strange here,' Shamra declared. Kell squinted harder along the hazy streets, which at this point sloped gently down towards the water. 'I mean,' she added, 'the people.'

Kell's eyes scanned among the crowds. Folks here seemed rougher and less welcoming perhaps than those in the outlying villages, and the diversity of their appearance was greater. But apart from that . . .

'Look at that man—' Shamra half pointed for fear of him noticing. He was a big square-boned freightworker leading a train of moxen on a firechain. The beasts were loaded up with bags of cargo, carrying them easily as one would expect, but with a sluggish and lumbering gait, their heads hung low. It was obvious to Kell that these animals were badly cared for: metal showed through the bedraggled fur in places, and the left forelimb of one of the poor creatures sparked and sizzled due to the poor contact of bared wires. Their instruction discs were probably dirty or damaged, which was why they needed the leash to keep to their track. The freightworker seemed oblivious.

'You're right,' Kell said, 'he deserves to be punished for the way he maintains his beasts!'

'No.' Shamra's reply carried a stinging impatience. 'I don't mean that—'

She reached with her mind and Kell saw a little of what she saw, and suddenly realised.

'There is some of him missing!'

Shamra chuckled at his expression. 'Well that's not quite what I intended . . .'

They watched the worker threading his way through the bustle of people, a fading mental echo, like off-key music poorly played.

'He is . . . disconnected,' she added, arriving at this startling idea intuitively. 'Somehow that man has lost his link with the All Mother . . . He does not know – he cannot receive The Knowledge – He . . . he is entirely on his own . . .'

A sense of what that loneliness must be like swept through them both. Shamra was shocked and rather frightened by it, but Kell's blood tingled with excitement. To be detached from the Goddess was another kind of Beyond; like being cast out even while you lived in Perth. Did that make it a prison or a paradise? The notion was too strange to contemplate. Whatever, thought Kell, that didn't excuse the shabby treatment of the moxen!

They watched the man disappear in the distance, then walked on as the middle of the day came and went and the afternoon stretched out ahead of them. Now and then Shamra noticed others like the freightworker, cityzens cut loose from the All Mother's influence, outsiders within the populace. They looked no different from any other stranger passing by, though to Shamra they carried a terrible emptiness inside them; or perhaps a barrier of independence she found it impossible to penetrate.

'I don't like it here,' she decided at last, after some hours of searching and tentative enquiry after Kano. They had reached a straggling market-place that followed the line of the street. Stalls laden with every kind of produce stood under many-coloured canopies that kept off the heat of the sun and the droppings of the mergus flocks as they circled above the city. The lake, not more than five furrowlengths away, glittered green and coppery orange under a tainted light.

'It is simply unfamiliar,' Kell said, although his own discomfort was obvious and Shamra would surely be picking it up from him now. On an impulse – and it was an impulse, for Shamra would never have advised it – Kell walked over to the nearest market stall and asked the trader outright about

Kano, the rebel. Shamra watched the eyes of the stallholder, a jewellery seller gaudily decorated with her own wares, and for a moment brushed by her mind to check its honesty.

'She doesn't know,' Kell reported seconds later. 'The work clothes Kano and the others were wearing are common.'

'Clever Kano.' Shamra's sarcasm was very gentle. When Kell opened his mind to her she had gleaned an impression of Kano and his followers. It was a glamorised vision, and that amused her; containing little fact and much imagination. Kell had never seen the man's face, but in his thoughts pictured someone vaguely like himself and more strongly like Gifu, though more daring and free-thinking.

'If he is deliberately hiding,' she added, 'we might not find him for days.'

'But how can he hide from the All Mother?'

'By breaking the link, as the freightworker did, and those others . . .'

They had noticed many whose souls were detached, people seemingly sketched on the fabric of reality rather than embedded within it. Shamra called them the dispossessed, and her heart went out to them whenever she became aware of their strangely lost and haunting presence.

'I think we should go on for a little longer today—'

And then leave before dark was the part she did not say, but which her expression conveyed clearly enough.

They made their way through the market, pausing to buy food and drink and make more enquiries as casually as they could. No one had heard of Kano, although a pot seller did know of a huge man similar to the one Kell mentioned. His name was Hora and his work was to fish the waters of the Central Lake. At this time of the day Hora would be out on his boat, but shortly before the ungathering he would most likely be found in one of the taverns close by the waterfront.

'At least that's a start.' Kell was grinning as though their search was already over. His head was full of boyish dreams and excitement which made Shamra smile with a deep fondness for her friend. But she was worried about him too, and for herself: a fishers' tavern in this part of the city would not be as comfortable or as safe as a grassy spot beneath a lime tree in Othila!

And so it proved to be. They found a number of drinking houses ranged along the street that fronted the water. Many floating piers stretched out into the lake, and crews were busy tying up their boats to these as harbourmen unloaded the day's catch and stacked the fishboxes on low slung mox-drawn waggons. There was a great bustling and energy about the place: men wanted their work done and to have some ale inside them before the darkness came.

'Kano could be anywhere,' Kell said at the sight of these crowds. His disappointment was obvious.

'Hora will be easier to spot.' Shamra tried to sound buoyant, but she was uneasy. The dispossessed were every-where, as though this was their territory; and once a severe looking man walked right up to them and told them to go home, that this was no place for children.

'I think he gives us good advice, Kell . . .' Shamra pulled him away from an open tavern door as he peered inside. She did this absently, because something was shifting in her mind: there was a kind of tension, elusive, powerful, huge. It felt as if she was hanging in the deepest waters of the Central Lake, and just at the edge of her seeing some vast and monstrous thing moved.

'Come on Kell, we've done enough for today.'

'Maybe he's in the next one—'

'I don't feel so well,' Shamra mumbled. 'Come on!'

He looked at her then, and was immediately concerned. He touched her face, and the shadow of his hand was fringed with red. High above the lake the globe of the sun was

49

changing; expanding like a ball of gas torn through with rags and banners of crimson.

'All right. I'm sorry. I have left it late.' Kell held Shamra's hand and led her purposefully back the way they had come. 'When we are outside the city we can keep to the road. We'll be safe enough in the dark.'

His reassurances came from far away. Shamra seemed to be drifting, drunken; her eyes were swimming and she was not able to look at him with any focus. Kell quickened his step but needed to pull her as Shamra's pace slowed and her feet started dragging. Around them now the crowds were thinning as people took to their houses, but a number of strangers looked oddly at the children as they passed – and Kell became convinced that a group of three or four were following them at a distance.

Behind the lakeside frontage of taverns and stores lay a web of narrower streets of dwellings, warehouses, mills, forges and factories. Above them the sun was dissolving and the shadows were flowing like ink.

Kell pulled Shamra through a press of people as they hurried from a drinking house, and out of sight of the followers took one of the sidestreets, then turned again sharply into an alley. On one side a high wall of red bricks glowed like hot iron in the last of the sunlight: to their left was a yard where moxen were being hosed down after a day's hard haulage. The man who sluiced away their dirt wore rubber boots and waxed trousers and a thin grubby vest. He yelled something after the youths as they passed by, his words twisted with the hard flat nasal accent of the city.

'I think we should hide,' Kell said, even as he thought of this sudden imperfect plan. 'At least until we know whether the strangers are after us or not . . .'

Shamra wasn't listening. She seemed distracted and far away. Suddenly she laughed and gabbled out a rush of meaningless words, spilled links from a broken chain. She stopped and her expression grew wide and wondrous.

'She is in my eyes and in my seeing . . .'

'Shamra?' Kell's alarm was turning to panic. She started to sway.

'She is in my heart, and in my understanding—'

Then she fell forwards, her legs collapsing under her. Kell took her weight and eased her down to the ground. Her breath was fluttery and the skin of her face was taut and white. Kell was now dreadfully afraid. He wondered if the man in the yard could help him – glanced up into the gloom, and saw the group of shadowy figures walking decisively towards him.

Far above the sun was a cooling mist laced with fading blue filaments. Streetlights were flickering on across the city; but sparsely here, just a few faint globes fixed by brackets to the wall. Their illumination offered only glimpses of vague shadows coming closer, and then of one particular figure that broke from the rest and strode forwards and loomed above him.

'Don't worry. She is only stunned. She'll come out of it soon.'

It was a woman's voice, hard and clipped, the words reluctantly spoken. She was tall and looked strong and fit. Her boots were made of glossed leather and her leggings and tunic of mox hide. Her hair, longer and blacker than Shamra's, was brushed severely back and woven into a single tight plait that hung down to her beltline.

'My name is Feoh. I am not going to hurt you, Kell.'

His brief surprise that she knew his name became a jolting shock as she knelt and turned more into the light. Half her face was a mask of polished black material that might have been metal or some kind of ceramic. Around its fringes

Feoh's flesh was ruttled and scarred. She would have been beautiful but for this great damage.

Kell swallowed back his immediate horror. Feoh's one dark eye glittered at him coldly.

'What . . . What has happened to Shamra?'

'She will tell you herself in a moment. She is recovering consciousness now—' Then Feoh surprised Kell with a beaming smile. 'I think she will not be well pleased.'

Even as Feoh spoke Shamra's eyes opened and she hissed like an angry scrubcat and her hands struck out. Kell fumbled to restrain her, but Feoh simply reached and touched the girl's forehead with a fingertip. She calmed instantly, though her tears of outrage and frustration came freely.

'You – you went into my mind. I did not invite you, but you went in and you saw everything!'

So much was drawn together in Shamra's voice; intense anger, disbelief, perhaps a touch of embarrassment and shame. The woman shrugged it off easily.

'It was necessary to know your motivations, and what you intend. Kell we already knew about—'

Before he could ask how, Kell's mind filled with his memory of the cleft and the group of figures he'd seen; Kano, Hora, the others, and Feoh among them.

'You are an inlooker like Shamra!'

'But much more powerful.' Shamra sounded awed. 'Much, much more . . .'

'I thought that since you enjoy breaking rules, you wouldn't mind if I did it too.' Feoh's voice had gentled. There was even a touch of humour. She looked briefly over her shoulder so that her strong human profile stood out starkly in the streetlight.

'We should get you inside now, before the opticus finds us.' Feoh beckoned the ones that had hung back, four powerful angular labouring men, one of whom helped

Shamra to her feet and carried her until she declared she was strong enough to walk by herself.

'Where are we going?' Kell felt lost among the alleys, and although he trusted Feoh without knowing why, he sensed clearly enough that there was danger here.

'Where you have wanted to go,' Foeh said. She pointed ahead. They had reached an area of vast low buildings. The air was richly laced with the stinks of manufacture, while the walls and roadways around were grimed with a crust of industrial dirt. Deep inside the sheds machinery pounded automatically, and once Kell glimpsed a driverless air car pulling a train of freight waggons. It moved along steadily at twice head height, moving at an angle away from them, its heavy-duty engines throbbing resonantly.

Beyond the manufactory rose a complex of towers whose lights stood out against the contoured shadows of the Jara Hills.

'That's it,' Feoh said. 'Not far now.'

Kell noticed above the towers and the faint cityglow a small cluster of sky gleams following a zigzag path.

'The opticus,' Feoh told him, as though Kell had asked the question aloud. 'The eyes and ears of the All Mother.'

'You mean, they watch us? The sky gleams watch us?'

Feoh's tone was tolerant. 'Of course, you would never have suspected it . . . The Goddess has many ways of keeping the community in check. It has been like this for generations, probably for thousands of years, from the time that Perth was first made. What you have called the sky gleams form part of a much larger organisation, so that the All Mother knows where you are and what you say, and how you think. And while her means are powerful, they are imperfect. She cannot know everything—' Foeh gave a tight, hard, bitter smile. 'Else we would be dead long ago.'

They reached an empty yard bounded by high fences. One of the small side gates was unlocked. Feoh turned and dismissed the four men who had accompanied them. They bowed respectfully and made their way home by different routes, each keeping carefully to the shadows.

'They are all dispossessed,' Shamra said, knowing that Feoh understood her meaning.

'Instead of possessed,' the woman answered wryly. 'We will tell you what you need to learn presently. Now let's get out of the night.'

Whatever purpose the towers had once served, they seemed to be deserted and silent now. Foeh took Kell and Shamra up several flights of stone stairs, through bare corridors and past many empty rooms, towards the topmost level high above.

'I never thought there were parts of Perth that lay unused,' Kell said, and he felt a sense of sadness he was unable to explain. Feoh's voice was gentle and close and perhaps entirely inside his head.

Perth is an old culture. It was not made to last forever, though my feeling is that the All Mother would have it otherwise. All eras end. We are living through interesting times, younglings. Let me prove it to you now.

They came to a door of layered steel with many devious locks. Shamra felt a shove of thought, a forceful pulse that was the mental equivalent of a dazzling light or a deafening sound. The door opened, and the giant named Hora stood aside to let them in.

The room, like the door, was clad in metal. It was sparsely furnished – a table, some chairs – and there were racks of shelves piled with papers and mysterious devices. Kano, whom Kell somehow recognised immediately, was sitting at the table examining charts. When he stood up he made a striking figure; tall and thin, honed like a blade to his purpose. His hair, swept back, was thinning, and his beard was peppered with grey.

'So. These are the young bloods of the future. Kell the dreamer and Shamra his heartbonded, his shadowlove. The Beholder has worked on you well, but I wonder how much you are pained by the splinter in your eye!'

He sounded angry and cynical, though Kell did not exactly know why.

'Treat them courteously, Kano,' Feoh advised. 'They are simply children and they are true and sincere in their hearts. They did not ask for any of this. And she—' The woman glanced at Shamra. 'She has great potential, if the will is strong enough.'

'You are a complication,' Kano told them abruptly. 'Events are finely balanced and even the smallest circumstance could tip the scales towards disaster.'

He came round the table suddenly, dropped to his haunches, took Kell's head in his large powerful hands and stared penetratingly into his eyes. Kell could smell liquor on Kano's cool breath and felt the force of the man's personality bursting into his head.

'She has given you nightmares, hasn't she?'

Kell nodded fractionally between the pressure of the hands.

'And they were frightening, and they hurt, and they made you realise the love and the peace and the safety you find here in the enclave. Didn't they?' His grip tightened. 'Though they are not the worst ones. Could you survive horrors ten times worse, little dreamer? Could you endure the cold and razor claws of the Ice Demon, the Wilderness Lord? Could you deal with your heartbonded being torn away from your life and her memory wiped from your mind? Would you betray us if you were threatened with those, eh boy?'

'I – I –' Thoughts and resolutions scattered like shattered

glass in Kell's head, and tears forced themselves into his eyes. He tugged and struggled but Kano held him tightly. Finally the fight went out of him and Kell sagged weakly, defeated.

'I don't know.'

'Good,' Feoh said, before Kano had his say. 'We wouldn't expect you to know. Total certainty now would be simply a delusion.'

Kell found himself released. He stumbled a step as Kano let go and bumped against the table.

'He was like it with all of us,' Hora said, his voice as broad and huge as the man himself. The others in the room, a thin-faced and intense figure, and a stockier dark-haired man, were introduced as Skjebne and Birca.

So these are the five, Kell thought, small and secret and touched with doubt; these are the ones who challenge the Goddess and seek a way beyond Perth . . .

Kano walked over to the window and opened the shuttered steel and looked out. Somewhere far away, in the cool whispering darkness of the countryside, lay all that Kell knew and found familiar; the people and the places and the simple ways of his life were out there and waiting. Perhaps Kano would understand if he and Shamra chose to return to them now. Or maybe the man in the heat of his rage would kill them both and be done. However it was to be, Kell knew that the time for their decision had arrived. He had come so far, and the path ahead of him was open.

'We are numerous,' Kano said, offering small answer to Kell's huge questions. 'The ones you have seen in the city – the dispossessed – have made an act of sacrifice to prepare themselves to leave. We have daring plans nearing comple-tion. And soon, when the time comes, hundreds of us will go into the great Outside, into the world beyond the world. It is an exodus that needs to be made, for we foresee a time when the people of Perth will perish like neglected plants in sterile soil. Then the Goddess will rule over stillness and silence and fading memories of human voices. It must be the same in many places.'

'You think there are other enclaves?' Kell's excitement was tentative. The Knowledge spoke of regions other than Perth, equally vast territories shielded and safe from the Ice. But the Mythology also made it clear that the outer cold was an ancient and fearsome enemy, and that its weaponry of storms and frozen slow-moving rivers might crack the fragile eggs of Man's future despite the All Mother's protection. In other words, the Knowledge was vague on this matter. Kell wondered how Kano could be so sure.

'Other enclaves?' Kano gazed beyond Kell into his own imaginings. Then he nodded slowly. 'There will be others, and maybe many of them. Some, like Perth, will have reached a critical point. Others will have been devastated and long ago laid waste by blizzards, or by other kinds of chaos,' he added darkly. 'But some will have released their cargo of life into the greater world. So that when we go, we will not be the first. Others will have made the journey before us.'

'But how do you know?' Kell demanded, weary of this high rhetoric as he was weary of the low threats and promises and half-truths he found at the Tutorium.

'Because we have seen them.'

'Feoh has seen them in her mind,' the one called Skjebne joined in. 'And we have caught glimpses with our own eyes.'

'You have already been Outside?' Kell could hardly believe what he was hearing. Skjebne nodded eagerly and smiled.

'Just briefly. It is still the dark season out there and we cannot spend much time in such conditions. Beyond the cleft there is a valley, and at the end of the valley a line of low hills. Not long since – fifty suns at most – we looked out on a clear day and saw a group of riders. They were perhaps two hundred furrowlengths away. Their beasts were not so large as moxen, but much more agile and lower to the ground. From what Feoh could gather they were traders . . .'

'What is a "clear day"?'

'Fortune preserve us,' Kano said, 'He would be worse than useless out there!'

Skjebne answered patiently. 'The sky and land outside is full of changes. The sun comes and goes as it does in Perth, but by some vastly different mechanism. Its position, and other factors as well no doubt, affect the quality of the air. Sometimes the distances are crisp as crystal, sometimes hazy with mist. When the air is clear and the sun is high, you can see much farther than two hundred furrowlengths, actually . . .'

Kell knew that Skjebne must be lying, or else was badly self-deceived, and his anticipation snapped like a stitch breaking and ruining the weave.

'Two hundred furrowlengths is a great distance,' Kell pointed out gently. He was thinking of the times he had gazed over the panorama of Perth and seen tiny particles of detail without knowing quite what they were.

'Your skepticism is healthy,' Skjebne said. He had a look of wild enthusiasm in his eyes, as though he had met a kindred spirit in Kell; some other who shared his own urge to know, but whose energy was balanced with doubt.

'Shall I show him the farscope, Kano?'

'It can't do any harm.' Kano came over to Shamra and Kell as Skjebne hurried into another room. 'You are reaching the point where you have to decide,' he told them both, his voice level and calm. 'We are telling you of our plans, but it would be so very easy for the All Mother to withdraw them from your mind.'

'But we wouldn't—' Kell began. Shamra stopped him with a gentle touch.

'He knows our intention,' she said wisely. 'The Goddess would take our thoughts anyway.'

Kano acknowledged Shamra with a nod. 'While we've talked, I have been thinking. Taking you with us would be a risk. You are young, you have not yet gained the strength and resilence of your adult years. You may be impulsive and disobedient and reckless . . .' Kano grinned severely at Kell's look of outrage. 'And yet, you have the necessary strength of purpose; you have courage and vision and other gifts in the making. You may be more of an asset than a hindrance. As for the All Mother discovering your part in our plans – well, Feoh can oversee Shamra at least . . .'

'So can we come with you?' Kell's heart was pounding fast, fed by dreams and fears and the imminence of the moment.

'That's my offer,' Kano said. 'And if we survive the escape, you will see what we have seen, and know the depth of our truth.'

There was more. Kell sensed that as keenly as Shamra, but just then there came a clatter and bustle at the doorway, and Skjebne reappeared carrying a most remarkable instrument; a long silver tube mounted on tall tripod legs. Kell noticed the glint of worked glass inside, and the glitter of lights along the tube's length.

'There is more to Perth than meets the unaided eye,' Skjebne smirked. Feoh accompanied the man's words with a soft wash of thoughts: the children gained the impression of vast hidden places and secret ways, and storehouses filled with such wonderful devices.

'The farscope can see into space!' Shamra deduced this with a silent bloom of understanding, helped perhaps by Feoh's elegant guidance.

59

Skjebne was nodding furiously. 'This is how we saw the riders Outside, at the end of the valley. Look now – look at this now!'

He went over to the window and planted the tripod solidly, then angled the instrument with the tube pointing out into the dark. Above the city the sky gleams were still swarming and wheeling, breaking off into scattered patterns over the length and breadth of Odal. Then Hora extinguished the dimly burning lights in the room, and they were ready.

Skjebne spoke a few words. Kell heard the soft whine of a motor; the farscope swung fractionally and held steady.

'Behold the eyes of the night.'

Kell peered into the tube's near end. For a few seconds he saw only a soft bluish glow. Skjebne explained that the farscope was working out the focus of Kell's eyes, and adjusting itself to compensate. As the glow faded, Kell was amazed and startled to see the sky gleams much closer, and looming behind them the shadowy shapes of the hills.

'I could touch them!' His astonishment bubbled out and made the adults smile.

'What do you see?' Kano wanted to know.

'Well . . . Well, the lights. The sky gleams – but bigger, Kano – globes, spheres with colours in them . . .'

'He is still being influenced,' Feoh confirmed. 'Even now he has not broken free.'

'Lights,' Kell said more quietly. 'Only lights . . .' He stood away from the farscope. 'That's not right, is it?'

'It's not everything,' Kano told him. 'The All Mother rules us in many devious ways. You know some of them. Shamra knows more, deep down. But the Knowledge is silent on this matter. You have only ever seen sky gleams, rather than the truth.'

'So – what must I do?'

Kell's heart was still racing, but for different reasons now. He had noticed the tension in the air, appearing suddenly like a threat. He noticed how Feoh and Skjebne and Birca had fallen silent, and how Hora had moved closer to the door.

Shamra, leaping ahead with Kano's thoughts, felt a drenching cold and opened her mouth in horror.

'Please – Don't do it!'

'Feoh can cleanse your minds of all you've seen here and you can go back to your life in the fields—'

'No, no!' Kell was adamant on that.

'Or come with us and see the truth. But know this, Kell – that if thine eyes offend thee, pluck them out!'

4

Behind the Shadow

Before Kell could react, Hora moved forward and grabbed him, each huge hand entirely circling the boy's upper arms. Feoh similarly lunged and held Shamra fast.

'It's all right, it's all right,' she told the girl. 'It's just a passing pain.' She accompanied the thought with waves of reassurance, but even so it was a torture for Shamra to stand and watch as Kano pushed Kell's head back so that he was staring straight up at the ceiling. And then, with long black cracked fingernails, he picked at the surface of his eyes.

Kell let out a choking, gargled scream. Kano's grip on his forehead was solid, immovable; while the fingers of his other hand probed and snatched. He knew with a blood-red certainty the man was going to kill him, or at least blind him for the secrets he had seen. All of it – all of it – had been a terrible trick, part of an evil, hidden side of Perth that crawled with rot underneath the placid surface.

'Hold still ya damn' brat!' Kano snapped. He grunted, tore – and more screams burst from Kell's mouth in a spray of spittle. The pain was intense, and increasing. Before the agony turned him dizzy, he had time to regret his foolishness in allowing himself to be led to this end. And, more poignantly still, he grieved for the hurt he'd caused Shamra; for she would surely be next to suffer at the hands of these brutal savages.

'Here it comes!' Kano sounded triumphant. Kell experienced a final climax of pain, then an awful, wonderful, bottomless relief before the man was at his other eye and the torment started once more.

Foeh was impressed with the speed of Shamra's understanding. She released the girl and knelt to pick up the scrap of stuff that Kano had removed.

'The All Mother cares so deeply for our souls that she even directs what we see . . .'

She dropped the pellicle into Shamra's hand. The membrane was as thin as the most delicate skin of frost, though slightly thickened at the centre. Tiny, almost invisible, wires radiated out around the edge: these would have anchored the film to the eyeball; or perhaps their purpose was far more subtle than that.

'When—'

'Soon after birth,' Feoh said, 'when the baby is weaned and first goes to the Tutorium. And then, as the youngling grows, the integuments are changed to fit the enlarging eye. Kano discovered the existence of the lenses by chance, when he was injured at the manufactory where he worked. That was the first step of the journey that has brought us all here today—'

She broke off as Shamra went over to Kell. Kano's work was done, and Kell had dropped to his knees. His eyes were badly inflamed, and there was water and some blood on his face. Blue eyes, Shamra saw with a shock, bright clear blue eyes rather than the dulled pastel she had always been used to.

'Shamra . . .'

He waved his hands feebly towards her. The world was sinking in deep water, shapes and surfaces and colours rippling madly as Kell tried to make sense of what he saw.

'He – he didn't blind me. Kano didn't blind me. I can see . . .'

'Now you can see for *yourself*, instead of the world that the

All Mother and the Praeceptor and the tutors have chosen for you.'

Kano helped Kell to his feet, his gentleness in total contrast to the violence of moments before. Hora passed Kell a dampened cloth, then Skjebne showed the boy one of the lenses, a delicate smear of transparent material, almost not there at all.

'It is beautifully crafted.' Skjebne's admiration was obvious. He waved a hand about himself. 'Nowhere in Odal do the workshops exist that could have produced such an artefact – and yet there must be millions of them, many pairs for each child until he is grown and his seeing is set.'

'Then where . . . do they come . . . from?' Kell was only half listening despite his best intentions. His face throbbed deep to the bone, and the soreness in his eyes was acute. But these things hardly bothered him, for as his vision was clearing, so was his mind. Suddenly the people around him had depth and solidity: suddenly they were somehow more real. There was a sheen of sweat on Skjebne's forehead, and his nervousness showed too in the smell of his sweat. Foeh's hardness, Kell knew now, covered a dark tragedy: so strong and capable outside, inside she cried with despair. And Kano, whose hatred went to the core, was driven by the fearsome engine of his passion and out of control of himself . . .

'There must be hidden places.' Skjebne's voice was high and fast and excited. 'Manufactories unknown to the ordinary populace. And yet, which cityzens make these lenses and the other apparatus of the Goddess – the sky gleams, as you call them, and perhaps more devices we haven't even suspected?'

Kell had no answer of course, nor was he troubled to search for one. His attention was drawn again and again to Feoh, and to Shamra, and to the tide of knowing that flowed between them.

'It will be more difficult for her,' Foeh said, picking up

Kell's concern as though he had spoken it aloud. 'Those of us who have the insight are more closely leashed to the All Mother.' She gave a ghastly smile. 'Her influence goes deeper. For now, I can protect Shamra and guide her. The time is not right yet for her to sever the link – Not for one still growing; not for one so pretty.'

Almost without realising, Feoh's hand reached up trembling to the smooth black mask on her face. She made a strange and moving sound, a little sob stitched with regret and self-pity and a deep and abiding resentment. Then her expression cleared. She reached into a leather pouch on her belt and drew out what Kell at first took to be a large and exquisitely wrought piece of jewellery; a webwork of silver wires linking tiny silvery beads. Shamra gasped and put her hand to her mouth.

'With thanks,' Feoh said with quiet intensity, 'with thanks to the All Mother for her warm heart and brooding wings . . .'

Kano came and put his arms around Feoh as her bitterness collapsed and she started to cry. The other men stood with their heads hung, Hora for all his vast power looking helpless and clumsy and lost.

'Hers has been the greatest sacrifice.' Kano hugged the woman to him and then stepped away. 'And I cannot even promise her revenge. When we go, it will be once and for all. There is no intention of returning.'

'When will it be?' Kell asked.

'Soon. But we haven't finished here yet. Each of you has a treasured thing, the reflector that has guided your growth—'

'No, not that!' Shamra's hand went instinctively to the beltpocket where she kept the glass.

'It is made of the same substance as the lenses, and is one with them. Remember that a window allows vision both ways.'

Kell had no hesitation. Something inside him had changed and he was caught in a deeper and more complex mixture of feelings. He took the beautiful translucent oyster, cradled it in his palm for the last time, then hurled the thing forcefully into the corner. It shattered in a shower of sparkling fragments that rattled and skidded across the floor. Hora let out a deep barrel–chested laugh and Birca nodded his savage approval.

'And now you are dispossessed,' Shamra said simply, 'like these others.'

'And you,' Feoh told her, 'are caught in a terrible dilemma, which you must realise clearly. If you come with us the Goddess will still know you. She will journey with us inside your head, and defying her will be a constant battle. Should you choose to stay, then you must break from Kell your heartbonded, for he will surely travel with us when we go.'

Kell's face reflected the decision he'd already made; fierce and proud and frightened, old and young and sure and filled with doubt. *How could I leave him? I love him.* Shamra's thought bubbled up into Feoh's mind and was filled with warmth and compassion. She withdrew her glass, held it for a while, then gave it over for Kano to destroy. That was something she could never have done for herself.

'Now,' said Skjebne, 'before we leave here there are one or two more things you should see . . .'

He beckoned Kell back over to the farscope, made some rapidly spoken readjustments, and invited the boy to observe.

The sky gleams had increased in number rapidly, as though like moths they had been attracted to the lights of the city.

'The All Mother is thwarted, because you have vanished from her sight. And Shamra is being shielded by Foeh's mental protections. And so she is searching for you by clumsier means. Take a look.'

Kell did so, and now the lights were not quite so mysterious. One or two that hovered closer to the towers

66

were not the sprites and elementals of Kell's imagination, but seemed now more like mechanical contrivances of spinning metal and glass.

'If they find us then the tutors and the clerics will come.' Kano's voice was close beside Kell's ear. 'And we will be taken forcibly and reintroduced to the Knowledge, and our punishment will be severe.'

'Then let's go immediately—'

'Not before we have shown the All Mother our teeth. Hora!'

The big man was behind them and had anticipated Kano's order. He carried a device of sleek blue metal, a kind of tube, though far thinner than the shaft of the farscope. The mechanism incorporated various attachments, including a strap so its weight could be borne on the shoulder, and a stock of contoured wood that nestled against Hora's chest as he hefted the apparatus, positioned it, aimed and . . .

There was a sudden great boom and explosion of fire and smoke. The force of it clapped at Kell's ears like punishing hands. Then, a momentary numbness, a silence . . .

Far away in the sky one of the gleams erupted into a flower of red flame and a cascade of sparks that trailed down through the dark. Its neighbours whirled and swarmed in agitation.

Hora fired again, and once more a gleam was destroyed by the weapon's marvellous wrath.

'They will have the measure of us in a few seconds,' Skjebne said.

'Time then for one more!' Hora was enjoying himself greatly. He rebalanced himself on his vast muscular legs, eased the fire-rod up to his eye and touched a stud underslung on the belly of the thing.

The thunder of the weapon was matched by a harsh sizzling spitting sound that seemed to hit the room and fill it all at once. The air was instantly charged with a prickling energy: it ran in blue trickling threads along the walls and the outlines of the furniture and shelves; it sparked between the teeth and crackled along fingerends and jabbed at the eyes with tiny fiery needles.

Hora howled as the lights on his weapon all blinked to red and the metal grew too hot to hold. Skjebne's farscope glowed for a moment like a wand; then all the lights failed and everywhere was shadows and faint blue afterglow.

'The Goddess has defences of her own,' Feoh pointed out wryly.

'We leave now.' Kano's voice was urgent but without panic. Efficiently all of the adults packed up a small number of essential items, slung the carryalls over their backs and ushered the children to the door.

Kell, taking one fast last glance back, was satisfied to see Hora's third target spiralling down in flames like a winged bird.

They slammed steel doors clang shut behind them and clattered down steps away from the hiding place. Kano knew that the gleams would have found it by now, but even he was surprised by the thunderous crashings that echoed down the stairwell from above, and by the high whining shrieks and rendings of metal that followed them for many minutes afterwards.

'The streets will be dangerous—' Shamra was thinking fearfully ahead.

'We won't go there,' Feoh reassured. 'We know other places, cellars, caverns deep under.' And even as she told them, Kano came to a doorway in the wall and tricked its sly locks and pushed it open.

'Quickly. We mustn't be seen going through.'

Hora shouldered his way forward first with Skjebne close behind. Fire flared and steadied into the uncomfortable light of a firetar torch. Feoh guided Shamra and Kell, then Kano

68

clapped Birca on the shoulder to usher him in, Kano himself finding safety last of all. The door closed, and Kell knew he had turned his back on everything he had ever known.

This was the world behind the shadow; an immense place of tunnels and caverns, towering chambers and uncountable rooms. Many were locked and sealed shut and could never be opened. Others, breached by ancient explorers or Kano's craft, yielded a variety of surprises. As they made their way, Kano and the others explained to Shamra and Kell how things had been.

'Like you Kell, I was troubled by questions and dreams from my infancy. Looking back now, I am not sure if such a need to know came out of my own head, or was fed to me by the All Mother's artistry—'

'But why would she seek to undermine her own authority in Perth? And why haven't others before you made their escape?'

'These are philosophical puzzles that we have not been able to solve. Perhaps men and women left Perth in the past. If so, the Knowledge does not speak of them. It is as though we are the first. But it's certainly true that people have come this way before us. When we look upon these treasure hoards, we find much that is missing or disturbed . . .'

'I think the Goddess knows her own weaknesses,' Feoh added. 'Perth is not eternal. There must be an ending of it. Maybe in the complex cycles of her mind there lurks the death wish, which in its granting will give life to the enclave's future generations.'

Kano nodded with understanding, if not with agreement. 'However it may be, provision was made long ago for people to move Beyond, into the outer darkness. During one of our explorations, Skjebne found the farscope and fathomed its workings. On another, we came upon the fire-rod which only Hora can wield.'

69

'Luckily for us.' Skjebne grinned. 'I'd break my back trying to carry it!'

'Everything we need for the journey is available to us – although we must supply the strength of our hearts for ourselves. We will show you these things,' Kano went on. 'Whoever laid up these stores envisioned an exodus of thousands.'

'Yet there are only hundreds like us,' Feoh said. 'These are the ones we've found who are sympathetic to our cause, the ones who dream beyond their confines. But the power of the Knowledge runs deep, and the terror evoked by the Mythologies controls the lives of most of the cityzens of Perth.'

Kano thought about Enjeck and Munin, and about Gifu's simple honest ways, and he had to agree.

'And even those who are with us in spirit may not accompany us in the flesh when the final great doors to the Outside are opened.' Kano's expression was reflective, perhaps anticipating disappointment. 'But we will see. For now, come and look at some of the things we have discovered.'

They walked many furrowlengths through the metal tunnels, pausing here and there to rest. Sometimes their route was illuminated by the dull unwavering glow of the lamps such as those to be found in the streets: othertimes they made their way more slowly by the smoky stink of firetar flames. Kell's excitement was intense, though he could see that the others were wary. And once Hora called them to stop.

'I thought I heard a sound – back there.' The big man turned to face the solid blackness of the tunnels, and pointed his weapon and waited. Feoh sent a ghostly wash of thoughts behind and around and ahead, but found absence and emptiness in equal measure.

'There are no people coming after us . . .'

'The sky gleams then,' Skjebne suggested. 'Since they are mindless, you cannot detect them.'

'Quiet and listen,' Kano cautioned. A minute went by and then came a faint metallic clink and a whisper far away, followed by a silence that went on until it became a distant rushing in the ears.

'Ditchrats,' Hora decided. 'That's all. They have found a way down from the sewers. We are frightening ourselves.'

'Maybe so, big friend. But would you mind walking backwards with your eyes honed, just to be sure of your guess?' Birca wasn't smiling as he spoke, though Kell felt he was not being serious, and Shamra knew this for sure. He was intense in his beliefs, a quiet man whose strengths were restrained and held back; but not one without humour.

'Certainly, little friend, if you walk beside me with a firebrand to help my aim.' The two men smiled at each other, but the smiles quickly faded, for they both knew the danger of the business they were about.

Shortly afterwards the group came to a chamber whose great double doors had been forced open ages ago. Kano indicated the way, but in stepping through Kell felt a pang of betrayal: the dark was aswarm with sky gleams, hundreds of them in varying colours, all motionless but for a slight dimming and flaring in a few.

Feoh picked up Kell's impulse of panic and sent it back changed to a reassurance. She laughed at his brief fluttering confusion.

'A place of stories?' He wasn't sure what she meant.

'There is knowledge recorded here,' Skjebne said. 'Images and sounds from past times and places – and Feoh suspects sensations too, locked in the glass.'

'So far we haven't the wit to open most of it, though what we have found out has thrown light on other discoveries we've made.' Kano moved through into the room and touched the walls, and pale ambient light appeared. Kell and Shamra found themselves moved and amazed by its beauty.

'Is it like the glass we have given up to you?' Shamra wondered nervously.

'I have found no trace of the Goddess in the crystal.' Feoh went over to a glittering repository and removed some mirror-like discs of glass framed by smooth silver metal. 'Here.' She passed a coin each to Shamra and Kell, who immediately felt the delicate crafting of the discs' outer rim. 'By handling the metal edge suavely it is possible to govern the messages in the glass—'

Kell discovered this for himself an instant later when the crystal brightened and a burst of song and a whirl of coloured costumes swept below the surface. He was so surprised he almost let go of the coin.

'An ancient celebratory dance . . .' Kano took the disc from Kell's shaking fingers and manipulated the tiny dints and studs of its perimeter. The scene reappeared, and the faces of the dancers were flushed with happiness and pride.

'These people have been dust for thousands of years. Look at the structure of their bones – different from ours. And listen – do you understand even a single word of what they are singing?'

They listened, and found the melodies entirely strange, but stirring nevertheless. After the first shock and wonderment, Kell and Shamra noticed finer details of the dancers' world. There were architectures of wicker and wood, clean and bright and yellow with sillion shine; trees of graceful and remarkable arrangement; animals of unusual appearance; and people, dancing people of all ages in their coloured robes with skin as glossy and dark as ravenfruit.

'And – look – here –' Shamra's lean finger came trembling and touched a portion of the glass. Beyond the village a reddish globe was hanging in the sky, its light soaking the folds of nearby clouds. She giggled a little with fear and astonishment.

'It's the sun—'

'But not the sun of Perth,' Feoh said. 'It's a sun that we have never seen. A sun that shone before the Ice invaded the world.'

Caught in the little reflector was a marvel almost too large for the mind to contemplate. Kell watched the tiny fleeting images and believed them but could not somehow absorb them. He felt the beginnings of a powerful anger.

'Why doesn't the Knowledge tell of all this!' He gazed around the room and was dazed. 'These thousands of coins, all filled with learning – and we have not been allowed to see them. We have not been allowed to choose!'

'Who knows the mind of the Goddess or her innermost heart?' Feoh sounded calm, as though she had thought this way, but now her fury had passed. 'Perhaps these are her dreams as much as they are ours . . . But think of the horror, children, if when we pass through the portals we find the world ravaged and know that the Mythologies are true, and that all of this glory has gone.'

It was something none of them wanted to contemplate. Feoh explained that during their explorations they had hoarded coins in a place close to where they would make their escape from Perth . . .

'In the cleft where I first saw you?'

'No, not there. That was the first site we found with an opening to the Outside, but it lies far above the valley and is impassable. There is another way – an intended way.'

'Which you will see,' Kano said, 'when we are ready. But to end our day's adventure, we will satisfy the thirst of your eyes.'

They spent some brief time gathering up a few more of the coins. It was impossible to know how much information each one contained, although Skjebne told of how he had spent a whole day wandering like a wonderstruck traveller through the imagery of a single disc.

'And I discovered a most amazing thing . . . As you come to know the glass, so it comes to know you. And at the end I was able to talk with some of the people contained there: I could ask of their world and their ways, and they were always ready to answer.' He patted a pouch on his tunic. 'Here I have a treasury of doctrines, the secrets of many artful devices known to men before the enclave was made.'

'Secrets lost until now,' Kano said, 'or held back by the All Mother for reasons of her own.'

They left the great room to its own darkness and went on. Kell wondered if they would pass this way again, and felt a powerful regret that he had not had and might never have the time to search through its infinite riches.

Kano led the party through the seemingly endless tunnels. Once they paused in a small chamber with many passages leading off.

'We have ventured along three of them.' Skjebne indicated three portals daubed with a splash of firetar. 'Where these others lead, we have no idea. But down this one . . .'

He guided Kell and Shamra to the entrance and from there ten paces along. Then Shamra stopped and would go no farther, for from a great distance, deep down in the fathomless black, came a low and steady pounding; a drum-drum-drum that resonated through the body so that it was felt in the flesh as much as heard with the ear.

'What is it?'

'The beating of the All Mother's heart, perhaps?' Skjebne was being mischievous, but Shamra's eyes were wide and dark and as frightened as a night-squirrel's, and then he felt guilty and was forced to apologise. 'We don't know. It must be part of the mechanism that keeps the enclave alive. It is nothing that need trouble us now.'

They went on. Soon after, their track tilted upwards and they climbed. Skjebne stopped them several times to make notes on a paper chart that he had been compiling.

'We've mapped some of these tunnels, and we know in a few instances what lies above. Actually, we are not far away from Othila here . . .'

It both amused and annoyed Kell to think that he had ploughed his simple way through life and never realised the grandeur that lay beneath his feet. How Munin would shriek if he dug his way upwards and came out in the middle of her kitchen floor!

'Have you met other cityzens down here?' Kell wanted to know. Kano shook his head, but Hora shrugged a little self-consciously.

'I saw a wraith once. We had come to an immense place filled with pipes and conduits. A cavern. We separated to explore, and moments later I noticed the ghostly one watching me. It did not speak, and its expression never changed, and it vanished when I took a step closer—'

'Too much ale,' Feoh quipped, then chuckled at Hora's indignant grunt.

'That's why I never mention it!'

Kell smiled, but not at Hora's expense. He felt a fondness for the big man, and decided that at some time, when the moment was right, he'd tell of his own experience of meeting the wraith on the road. But not now, not with such spectacles to see.

Soon the slope steepened and they needed to labour along. There were flights of steps, metal ladders; a cooling of the air, and moisture condensed out on the steel walls. Then, quite unexpectedly, the sand was damp under their feet and rock had replaced the metal.

'I smell the fields,' Kell said.

'We are high above the levels, higher even than the slopes you work.' Kano pointed ahead. 'Not far now. Come on.'

The breeze became keener and steadier. Kell suddenly knew where he was, and in a dizzying flash he understood Kano's intention.

Moments later they stepped out from the cleft in the rocks and gazed over the broad lands of Perth. The night was old and there were only a very few sky gleams visible. Things seemed quiet, though both Feoh and Shamra detected a certain tension which they felt must be linked with what happened in the city.

'This is what you'll be giving up Kell, Shamra,' Kano said. And Kell respected him for allowing them this final opportunity to return.

'It feels warm in here.' Kell made a pretence of wiping sweat from his brow. 'I need some fresh air.'

And so they made their way back through the rocks until they came to a deep niche where some overclothes of moxen fur had been cached. They struggled into these and then forged on, their faces growing numb with the cold.

Presently the wind's keenness became painful to bear, as it whined around the rough, frost-shattered surfaces of the stones. Hora showed Kell how to fold out the caul of his hood, then repeated the courtesy with Shamra. Up ahead, Kano yelled something to the others but his words blew away downwind and were lost.

Hora grabbed the children's hands. Tiny white powdery flecks came whirling past, and for a brief moment the great horror of Kell's punishment nightmare engulfed him.

But then the crags seemed to fall behind and they emerged between tumbled boulders and stood on an icy brink.

The land below was plunged in darkness, while across the sky clouds flowed and streamed, laced with a pale marbled light in one quarter. There was so much detail, so much to take in. For a time Kell was too confused to make anything of it, but by degrees as his eyes and his mind adjusted he understood something of the nature and size of the scene. There — those immense looming shadows — were the towering summits of ice-streaked mountains around which the snowclouds swirled. And above them, among them, lost in the sky, a gentle silver light shaped like a crescent of ice . . .

Kell shouted. He shouted defiance and fear and wonderment into the night. And as though in answer there came a lull in the wind and a patch of ragged cloud thinned and vanished. And for the first time in all his life, Kell saw the stars.

5

Traces

After the storm came the calm. Kell felt himself being taken back into the shelter of the rocks, to a cold, still, stony room where Hora lit firebrands and a kindling pile. Skjebne opened a hotflask and poured steaming t'cha into a cup and pushed the cup into Kell's trembling hands. In his head he was still out there, his senses stripped to the bare bone by the everlasting wind. It had melted him away and laid a coat of tiny crystals on his skeleton. There was frost in his eyes and his brain and his future.

'It isn't possible to live there – so huge – so empty—' Kell looked up at Kano and his eyes wept from more than the sting of the cold. 'We couldn't survive Outside. There is too much dark and ice and desolation.'

'It was only a night gale,' Kano said matter-of-factly. 'When the sun goes down the temperature drops and sets the air astir. It blows up from the valleys and becomes channelled by the slopes and contours of the surrounding mountains. Skjebne can tell you in much more detail,' he added with a momentary grin. 'Besides, we are coming to the end of the season of short days. There will soon be longer light and better travelling weather.'

Kell didn't understand all that Kano was saying, but still he felt himself troubled by doubt. 'How do you know this?'

'From what the discs have told us,' Skjebne said. 'And from what we've seen. You don't think we would knowingly walk to our deaths, do you?'

'But there seemed to be nothing.'

'Would you prefer the seeming the All Mother feeds you through false eyes?'

Kano came and sat by the fire, beside Shamra and Kell. 'How long do you suppose Perth can go on, deceived by its own dream? The preparations to leave were made centuries ago. Perhaps the knowledge has been lost until now, but even so we are simply completing the plan.'

'You have made us distrust the Goddess,' Shamra spoke up, her quiet voice drawing the attention of all. 'Perhaps her wisdom and goodness are greater than you think. Perhaps she knows that the outer world has become a dead place, and removed thoughts of discovery from our minds. What you call a curse may be a kindness.'

'What I call a curse is that the All Mother has not let me choose for myself. Whatever I might find Beyond, I cannot forgive her motives in stopping me from trying.'

'Then we must disagree.' Shamra gazed steadfastly at Kano, whose face was a mask of shadows that danced and flared by the fire's inconstant light. It was a hard face, and Shamra thought that that maybe all of Kano's life was filled with such bleak unforgiving.

'We are not walking blind,' Skjebne said. 'That is the point. Our decisions make us what we are – and we are not choosing ignorantly.' He scrambled up off the cool sand and beckoned the others. 'Come and see this.'

They followed him through a gap in the rock to another small chamber. Stacks of packages stood against one wall, and against another was a table laden with many curious objects.

'I told you that through the farscope we had once seen a caravan of huge beasts. Well look here . . .'

He lifted a big heavy lump of yellow material and passed it over for Kell to handle. It was made of bone, with deep

79

grooves and channels worn or carved into one flattened surface; an ugly thing, gross and barbaric.

'It's a tooth,' Skjebne said with a certain delight. Kell tipped and tilted it until the grooved surface was uppermost. Shamra gave a little gasp at the beast that Kell just then imagined.

'As you see, it's a grinding tooth, not a meat-tearing tooth. And where there are teeth like these, there must be plant material to graze, and plenty of it.'

'No mox has a jaw big enough to fit this!'

'Quite so.' Skjebne hefted the tooth from Kell's hands and placed it gently back.

'And see these other things here . . .'

There was a skull, small and streamlined, with the look of a weapon about it. Two long stabbing teeth curved down from near the front of the upper jaw. Smaller teeth, equally dangerous, hooked upwards. When Skjebne brought the jaws together the trap of blades was completed and any prey would be locked in place. Kell noted that the skull was no ancient relic: the bone was recent, whitened by snow-scour.

'And here—'

Skjebne showed them hard nutty seedpods, a silvery feather, a delicate, lethal catlike claw of black horn, a cluster of flies preserved in a jar of dry vapour; their backs shone a glossy metallic green and their tiny eyes were a wonderful brassy gold.

'These are things we found on our short trips Outside,' Skjebne said with a boyish delight. 'And the flies we actually caught live with a strip of brock meat as bait.'

He shook the jar and the flies' hard carapaces rattled like beads inside. 'If these small creatures have survived, so can we.'

'And don't forget the riders we saw on the pack beasts,' Kano added.

' "Riders", "pack beasts".' Shamra shook her head. 'Did you really see them, or are you building your own dreams now?'

'Whatever. But we have the means to find out.'

He walked from the room and the others followed, taking Kano's lead to another much bigger cell which was part of an even larger complex. Through an arched way lay a road of black meltstone that ended in a portal sealed by huge steel doors. Neither of the children needed to be told what lay beyond them.

No firetar was necessary here. Skjebne called some swift commands and cold blue-white light bloomed throughout the chamber. Kell jolted with shock, but Shamra had caught Feoh's anticipation of the trick an instant before and was prepared for it.

'Like moxen, and like my farscope, this room listens to human voices and understands their meanings.' Skjebne shrugged as though it was nothing, but inside he was filled with glee at these marvels.

'Now come and see why we are so optimistic.'

Nearby stood a huge shape draped with grey waxed canvas and secured to the ground by guyropes. Hora and Birca strained to draw the ropes' anchor-spikes, then Hora hauled the canvas away with a show of pure brute strength.

Underneath squatted a big hunch-shouldered machine; built low against whipping winds, with streamlined flanks to cleave aside the drifting snow. Grapplechains were sunk in niches along the sides: at the back was a lowered ramp leading within, and below hung an array of vents and inways which Kell took to be part of the driving mechanism. The whole weight sat on an assembly of six stout axles whose wheels were linked with studded metal chain. Kell could imagine this brutish device crunching and crushing its way over rocks and ice with a tireless determination.

'There is room enough inside for the seven of us – if Hora doesn't move about much,' Skjebne said. 'Elsewhere in the cavern complex you'll find other chambers with more machines such as these. Ancient technology, but artfully built by people who understood the Ice and the need to face it again one day.'

'We are not fools,' Feoh added, looking at Shamra more than at Kell. 'Nor are the ones who would join us.'

'But what about the cityzens you leave behind? What kind of chaos will they be forced to suffer when their beliefs are uprooted by your going?'

'The Goddess will soothe their minds, as she has done all down the generations. They will forget we were here. And I suppose that is the great difference between us. Life is easy in Perth, easy and unknowing. Let them stay who wouldn't dare otherwise. We go, Kell – we go, not because it is easy, but because it is hard.'

Kano smiled, but struggled to keep his tears to himself at the faces of the two children. He had been helped by his own adult experience and resiliency in making his choices. Despite this fine and plentiful equipment, the way over the Ice would involve many extreme and unexpected dangers. And even if by wit and good fortune they survived beyond the time of the long nights, there was no guarantee that they would find another place in all of the whole wide wilderness to call home.

This boy, Kell, reminded Kano so much of himself when he was young. Except that Kell's thoughts had a wonderful freedom about them. And he possessed a noble determination too. Now his jaw was set and his eyes were fierce; and Kano felt a surge of admiration, because Kell had already suffered some awful trials and was still prepared to face the Cold. There was, Kano admitted in a secret corner of his mind hidden even from Feoh's insight, something special about this boy. Something significant. It was not readily apparent yet, and Kano's own sense of it was purely instinctive. But among all of the souls that Kano would lead through the gates of Perth, Kell would surely prove to be the most valuable.

Yet this other, the girl Shamra; she had neither the strength of the oak nor the pliancy of the reed. A delicate jewel, she was the weak point in the armour. If she had not been heartbonded to Kell, Kano knew he would have rejected her immediately. More worryingly, whereas Kell had tasted the venom of the Goddess, Shamra still had all of her ordeals to come, and without the healthy cleansing of her eyes. Feoh knew, and only Feoh could protect her.

'There may not be time for goodbyes,' Kano warned as he noticed the resolution in the youngsters' expressions. 'The time is late and there are still some preparations to make . . .'

He explained that the people who were leaving Perth had been organised into cells of five or six, each cell having its own co-ordinator. Over the course of many weeks individual cells had gathered up their own provisions from the subterranean store rooms that Kano and his friends had discovered; and each too had staked claim on one of the robust travel machines that would take them out over the Ice.

'Once beyond the enclave, the separate groups must fend for themselves. We will try to travel together, but that may not be possible. Even so, all of us – all of the dispossessed – must leave simultaneously. Since the All Mother has been so devious in deluding us, it's likely she will try to stop our exodus now. Our strength will lie in our numbers and in the advantage of surprise.'

Just before they returned to the city Hora and Skjebne fired up the great engines of the Traveller. There was a grinding roar followed by plumes and billows of dark smoke which slowly cleared to leave a taint in the air. But then the engines pulsed busily and with a regular rhythm, and there were no further fumes. Hora reappeared grinning broadly. With Birca's help he folded up the heavy canvas sheeting and stowed it in a hatch in the vehicle's broad underbelly. Then Skjebne moved the Traveller slowly forwards along the meltstone road to within half a furrowlength of the big outer doors. Lights glared suddenly in a dazzling pattern across the Traveller's hull, most blazingly forward, burning two radiant overlapping circles on the dark metal portals. A moment later, as the noise and the brilliance ebbed, Kell felt a wave of excitement and pride at being part of this monumental adventure.

They went by a different way back towards Odal, making a brief detour so that Kano could point out a number of the other caverns where Travellers similar to their own stood waiting, primed and ready to go. Some had obviously been fully provisioned and tested, while others still lay draped in canvas with piles of boxes beside them. Kano made a sound of irritation and found it hard to keep the anger from his voice.

'Beorc's group have not worked hard enough. They won't have completed their preparations in time . . . And look here at Arrad's machine.' Kano indicated an oily pool beneath. 'I doubt if it will move half a pace, and yet he's said nothing about it to me!'

Feoh calmed him with a balm of thoughts and a hand gently placed on his forearm.

'They are not all like you, Kano. Not all bear such a hatred of the Goddess, or have your strength of trust in our enterprise. Balanced thinking tells you that some of the followers will change their minds. Others, through inaction, will have the choice taken from them. You have set the first spark; it is not your responsibility now to see that the fire burns well.'

Kano's temper subsided, though Feoh could still feel its heat deep within. She was his heartbonded and, as Shamra followed Kell, she had gone along with Kano's way; even when that way had led to a madness she could not at first understand. After his accident he had been a stranger, and only gradually and after much confusion did she come to see what he saw then through his eyes. The deceit, and the horror, of Perth – something so dreadful that she had sacrificed her beauty to be rid of it. Feoh had aided Kano in the surgery, and in fashioning the ceramic mask. At the time she believed that her sacrifice, for love of a man and for hatred of the Goddess, had been total. What an exquisite pain it had been when Kano had talked of the Outside and of going there and leaving Perth behind forever. The bleakness that swept over her almost destroyed her mind and the strong bond between them. Echoes of it still woke her some nights. So she could well understand that others, less forged to the cause, found ways and excuses to stay.

'As long as our hearts are firm.' Feoh added softly. 'The weakness of others is hardly our concern.'

Kano's immediate temper faded, but she knew he would not be pacified.

They made good time to Odal, walking briskly with no diversions this time and with little conversation. Skjehne estimated they would arrive just past the height of the day, and so it proved to be. They emerged some distance from the towers, having sloshed along in the kneedeep grimy water of a drainage tunnel; then up a rusted ladder; and through a grille that brought them out a few streets away from the shore of the Central Lake.

'Now we separate,' Kano said, 'as we have planned. Hora and Birca, go to the harbour taverns. Feoh and I will spread the word through the market-place. Skjebne, will you look after these youngsters awhile? We meet back here shortly before the ungathering – which will be our last; for at that time, with as many of us as we can assemble, we return to the caverns and make our escape.'

The others nodded briskly and were gone. Kano turned to Kell and Shamra, made the small bow that indicated respect, and then he too disappeared among the crowds with Feoh at his side. Soon Kell could see them no more, although Shamra felt the woman's influence like a gentle veil across her mind. Bitten by brief doubt, she wondered whether Feoh was right to trust her: was the All Mother hiding in her mind at this moment, seeing through her eyes, directing her actions . . .? Or was Feoh protecting her as she had promised? Time would finish the telling of that tale. But for now to leave Perth was to be her lot, constantly under the wing of Feoh, swept up in Kano's awful wonderful terrifying liberating dream.

The group had separated close to the market-place. Skjebne suggested they eat there, and buy some provisions for their journey back through the tunnels. Kell hadn't given it a thought before now, but suddenly he realised just how hungry he was.

'It will please me to pass on to you some of the things I have learned,' Skjebne said. They were walking through the crowded ways, with the Central Lake at their backs and the savoury – and sometimes unsavoury – smells of the market leading them on. 'You have an interest in the purposes of things. And I like the way you ask a big question, but also content yourself by enquiring over the smallest details. I think you will be an apt pupil – and you too Shamra, of course, in the learning of Feoh's powerful psience.'

Kell smiled at Skjebne's pleasure. It would be interesting to have him as a mentor, instead of the dull and dessicated tutors he was used to . . . Though he would miss Gifu's rough but sure and solid instruction. Indeed, Kell realised now that he would miss many things, even the small satisfactions of seeing soil fold aside under the plough, and the gleam of seed as it was scattered among the furrows. He would miss sitting alone at the end of the day to watch the sun disappear; and he felt sad to have lost the innocence of the sky gleams' simple beauty as they hung and drifted and swooped above the broad plains of Perth . . .

They came to a food stall and Skjebne bought some meatsticks and hunks of breadroot, and a small pouch of wineberries for himself. He handed over his coinage and then popped two of the purple globes into his mouth, closing his eyes and tilting his head back to let the rich, warm, flavoursome liquor trickle down into his throat.

'That's what *he'll* miss,' Shamra chuckled. Skjebne gave a shrug and sighed and put the rest of the berries into his belt pouch.

'Maybe they grow wild, and as big as your head, in some hidden woodland beyond the gates – Oop!'

Skjebne, lost in his vision and hardly looking, bumped into a fisherman stacking boxes of catch. The topmost box slid off and overturned, spilling yellow ingotfish at their feet.

'I apologise friend. Here, let me pay you for the ruined fish.' Skjebne knew the man would simply wash the fish and repack it, but he looked angry and the money perhaps would help to placate him. He fumbled at his belt for the coins. Shamra noticed the wineberries had been squashed, and their juice was now spreading like blood through the pouch's grey fabric . . . .

Something flashed in her head. It felt like nothing she had ever experienced before: a pain of light, a startling dismay echoing down from things yet to be.

She tugged on Kell's sleeve.

'This is not good. Kell, something terrible is going to happen.'

Skjebne had some tokens in his hand. The big fisherman looked on them with a towering disdain. He was like one of the boulders up at the place of the stones; huge and hard and unmoving. Even Hora would find it difficult to overcome him.

'Kell—' Shamra's voice sounded urgent and frightened..

'It's all right. Wait just a moment . . .'

Skjebne added more coins and jingled them temptingly. The fisherman sniffed, though his eyes had shifted a moment before, indicating the change in his attitude. He scooped up the tokens with his big calloused paw and grinned massively showing square yellow bac-stained teeth and a mouth startlingly black from years of using the chewing-leaf.

'There.' Kell began to relax. 'There was nothing to worry about after all—'

A hand appeared. Kell saw it out of the corner of his eye. The hand held a knife. The knife flashed forward and Skjebne's eyes went wide with surprise, and then shock. And then pain.

Kell watched blood speckling across the fisherman's waxed apron. The square, lumpen face seemed uncomprehending, before a slow understanding dawned.

Shamra moved quickly and caught Skjebne as he staggered. He looked at the girl's hands covered in blood and still didn't realise.

The attacker was a young man, dark haired, and may have been one of the Initiates at the Tutorium. Kell was haunted by a vague sense of recognition. His face was twisted and set with a purpose, and his eyes – *or the membranes covering his eyes* – swam like dark and troubled waters.

He glanced at the wound he'd inflicted and drew back his arm. Kell acted without thought. He swept the knife aside and the hand that held it and pushed the young man hard in the chest with the flat of his palm. The attacker stumbled backwards and trod on slick ingotfish: his feet slid from under him and he went down on his back, the knife tinkling away.

'Come on!'

Kell urged Skjebne and Shamra through pressing circles of curious onlookers, between narrow alleys of stalls in a deliberately tortuous route.

'He – he stabbed me.' Skjebne looked at the wet stain above his hip. He still could hardly believe it had happened.

'The All Mother stabbed you,' Kell corrected bitterly. 'She knows what Kano's plan is about. Maybe she knows everything.'

'Feoh has seen this,' Shamra told them. 'She has seen it through my eyes and is explaining things to Kano . . . He – says – Let us meet where Feoh first found us, Kell – In the alley by the moxen byre.'

Kell obeyed without question, for his thoughts were still back at the market and he was living through the stabbing again . . . again . . . again. The youth would have killed Skjebne there in sight of others. And then perhaps he would have turned his knife upon him and on Shamra . . . Kell had heard about such things, and occasionally Gifu in mellow mood would spin yarns about deliberate killings; farmers' tales intended to scare young ploughlads. But never in his life had Kell dreamed that he would see this thing for himself, this incredible act that history called murder.

He looked at Skjebne's face – it was pale and strained, screwed with pain. Then at the wound. Skjebne had one hand clamped to his hip, and blood oozed slowly through the fingers. That was a good sign, Shamra told him directly into his mind. No artery had been hit, Skjebne was not in danger for his life. Kell nodded his thanks and smiled weakly at the girl, not doubting her. He dared not, for there was already so much to distrust.

They came to a place where streets crossed and Skjebne asked to rest.

'It hurts.' He eased his hand away and shook his head at the mess of blood. 'He was so intent.' The boy's face haunted him, the hideous youthful face he would never forget.

'Be calm Skjebne,' Shamra said. 'We'll soon be at our meeting place and then others will help you – Hora and Feoh.' She used what ability she had to ease Skjebne's suffering: Feoh could do it much better, but Shamra was only just beginning to learn the skills of direct healing mind-to-mind. Even so, Skjebne felt her presence and noticed a numbing, a blunting of the blade that still seemed embedded in his flesh.

'We should be on our way.' Kell pointed out the direction – and a warning went through him like a light. Behind it was an impression of Feoh's face, her voice, the texture of her clothes; a startling and vivid assertion of danger.

Shamra sensed it too, more powerfully still, and she jolted.

'Kell – it's happening elsewhere in the city. People are dying . . . Kano's dispossessed . . .'

The last words came out in a whisper, for the madness was everywhere, and watching. And even as the three of them began to realise the size of the horror, a thin scream reached them from a few streets away; then the sound of raised voices; shouts, chantings, another scream.

'The cityzens are killing Kano's followers. The All Mother is trying to stop us from leaving.' Skjebne pushed himself away from the wall. 'We mustn't be caught here in the open.'

'Feoh will guide us. She is not far now.' Shamra opened her mind and, as though she was a fallen leaf, the stream of Feoh's thinking took her and washed away her indecision and some of the extremity of fear. Insight bloomed and she indicated a narrow passageway between the dwellings.

'Here, we must go this way.'

They hurried across the street, Kell supporting Skjebne, Shamra leading decisively. Over to the left came a commotion and people appeared; five, six, ten, twenty . . .

Kell had barely noticed them when a roaring filled the sky, like a flame blown by a strong and steady wind. The light changed suddenly, swinging this way and that, fluttering shadows like flags in a gale. A surge of shadow moved hugely across.

They reached the opposite wall and turned to gauge the distance of their pursuers; looked up, and saw a diamond of light sweeping in from the lake. It was a sky gleam, there in the sky, in the day. And beyond it a veil of reds and golds was blowing past the face of the sun. The whole huge globe guttered and dimmed . . .

'It is the end of the world,' Skjebne said very calmly.

Guttered and dimmed, flickered like a candle's last moment of life.

And then was extinguished entirely.

6

Thunder and Darkenings

The panic was total.

The darkness, torn by screaming, smothered like a blanket and stifled the people's capacity to reason. Kell could sense their terror surge upon surge through his mind – conveyed to him by Shamra against her will, as she too trembled on the edge of a madness that threatened to sweep her away.

But immediately Feoh's calming influence made itself felt, solid as an anchor in their heads. 'I'm close, and we're together, and we are going to live and be free of this place very soon.' It was a wordless message, but that was the sense of it; and it went deep, deeper than any power Shamra had ever known.

Skjebne's hands rested lightly on the children's shoulders. His voice was very close and a secret spell in their ears.

'This is the All Mother's doing. Her retaliation for our defiance. Come on, let's be going. We can use the darkness to our advantage.'

He eased them back and they felt the roughness of the brick wall and the sharp corner, and heard Skjebne's ragged breathing above the awful noise of the city's confusion. High above, sky gleams were massing; bright beacons dipping and swinging through the air. Some of them were quite low, and Kell was able to see them as mechanical devices bristling with points and reflecting faces. They made a fluttering sound like birds as they flew, although the means of their flight itself was silent and unknown to him. One sky gleam shone a sudden dazzling beam of white light down into the street – Kell had a frozen impression of many people with upturned faces and open mouths – then utter blackness and a flurry of ghosts fading slowly on his eyes.

'They're searching for us,' Skjebne hazarded. 'The Goddess does not know we're here!'

'Then why the darkness?' Shamra couldn't understand. 'Why is she making all of the Community suffer?'

'To prove her authority. To terrify us into inaction, or into changing our minds. Or into losing our minds,' he added seriously. Kell thought about the cityzens caught up in this catastrophe, and the people beyond Odal in the outlying villages. Poor Munin and Enjeck, and Gifu alone in the fields, and all of the helpless creatures . . . The cruelty of it was beyond belief. But that cruelty fuelled Kell's anger, and it was the anger that made him stay sane.

'We are not far now . . .' Skjebne said.

Kell felt Feoh's guidance again: Shamra's mind was radiating it like heat. He had never known her display such an easy openness of thought. It was as though the crisis had shaken loose her self-control and she was simply passing on Feoh's reassurances without deliberation. Kell held Shamra's hand, and her fingers were cold and limp and unresponsive. She was relying completely on the power of the other woman's word.

They had been easing themselves carefully step by step, moving sideways along the line of the wall towards the junction that would take them to their rendezvous. Kell's memory of it was that the alley lay a few streets down from the sprawl of the market. And indeed now they could smell the complex odours of the abandoned stalls, and the bellowing of terrified moxen and the shrieks and chitterings of other creatures not very far away.

'We must cut through to reach the meeting place,' Skjebne

93

said. Kell had been expecting it and dreading it, for it would mean moving from the security of the wall. Apart from that, there were many people hurrying and stumbling nearby; and others who had fallen to the ground. Some of them, by their cries, had been injured. Others, undoubtedly, would be dead.

'Do you think we should arm ourselves with weapons?' Kell wondered. It was a new and strange idea to him, but one that seemed appropriate now.

'Trust and a cool head are all we need for the present.' Skjebne shifted his grip and took hold of their hands, and they allowed themselves to be led out into the ocean of the dark.

'Feel forwards, step cautiously ... That's it ... I think there's an obstacle here — a canopy ... It's a crockery stall ...' Skjebne's commentry, calm and continuous, sustained them. Whenever he squeezed their hands suddenly, they stopped. When they felt the pressure ease off, they allowed themselves to be led. In this way they moved between the chaos of scattered goods, resting briefly when they crossed an open space, making better headway as they came to the next row of stalls. Once, unexpectedly, Skjebne stepped on a man who had fallen. The stranger gave a low moan, and in his startlement Skjebne let go his grip. For a few alarming seconds all three of them flailed randomly in a panic of the newly blind. Then Shamra's hand caught Kell a blow on his forehead. He grabbed at her and they clung to each other until Skjebne, searching carefully and systematically, found Kell's shoulder and held on to it like a treasured gift.

Skjebne laughed softly. 'This is already more of an adventure than I bargained for!'

His face flared into being with a loud crackling sound as someone nearby lit a firebrand. All three of them startled and ducked and screwed up their faces under this sudden painful drenching of light. The man with the torch waved it in front

94

of himself, its brilliance as useless to him as the blackness had been. He was one of the dispossessed, recently freed; his eyes were reddened and sore, and his fear was such that he would not be soothed even by the salve of Feoh's mind. But other followers, on seeing him, acted more purposefully. A woman with short-cropped black hair ran forwards and thrust a torch into his flame. As soon as it caught she touched the brand to a nearby stall hung with clothes.

The garments burned up with a whoosh of fire and pushed back the dark a little more. Skjebne and the children were shocked at this action, but at least now they could take proper bearings. Kell was surprised that they had come less than thirty paces from where he thought they had started. The alleyway was still some distance away, a good five minutes' brisk walk. But if the dispossessed could see, so could the ordinary cityzens of Perth. And they, under the influence of the All Mother, were looking at the world through her eyes.

Almost instantly two – three – four cityzens turned on the woman with the torch, clawing at her and lashing out with their fists. Briefly she managed to keep them back by swinging the firebrand to and fro in a dangerous arc. One attacker jumped clear with a howl as the brand cracked across his arm and singed the sleeve of his tunic. He spent a few seconds in a ludicrous dance patting out the flames, but then with renewed anger he moved in with his friends: the torch was knocked from the woman's grasp and she went down under the onslaught of their blows . . .

In Shamra's mind a glass vase dropped and shattered and the fragments were trampled underfoot.

Skjebne turned the children's faces away from the death. He felt guilty not to have acted to stop it. But his injury pained him horribly, and Kano's previous orders had been precise and final: if the Goddess attempted to stop the exodus, then the duty of the individual was to the others in the cell.

Whatever else happened, the integrity of the group must be preserved. At the time it had seemed like a harsh but distant pronouncement, and Skjebne had never imagined he would be forced to stand and watch in a torment of inaction as another human life was ended. Now he realised this might happen many times before the great portals rolled back to release him.

All across the wide square where the market of Odal had been held for longer than anyone could remember, fires were kindling and spreading; the darkness being traded for the light. By and large the scene was chaotic: many people still didn't realise what was happening. But some were hurrying with purpose to find other members of their team, and all the while little groups and clusters of cityzens were banding together to stop them.

'Let's go now,' Skjebne said. 'There's nothing we can do to change any of this.' By the dreadful light of a hundred fires they wove between the stalls towards the alley. Once a young girl, perhaps only two seasons older than Shamra and Kell, came stumbling towards them with a broken spar of wood held out as a threat. The girl's face was twisted in a senseless anger. She attacked blindly with a catlike scream. Kell parried the spar and pushed her forcefully away with the flat of his hand—

She came on again, jabbing and swinging the pike. Shamra released a blizzard of confused images defensively and instinctively. The girl stopped in her tracks. Shamra walked up to her and took the weapon away from her unresisting hands. She was a fisherman's daughter and her name was Tyr. Shamra gleaned this in the instant of their meeting. Then Skjebne was pulling her back and the little girl Tyr was a world away, then lost amongst the uproar of the night.

In the distance came a mighty shout, accompanied by a more controlled and meaningful message from Feoh. Kell saw Hora as he bellowed again. The huge figure held two blazing torches aloft to be more easily seen, and moment by moment he was touching them to the drapes and canopies of the stalls. Cloth and wood and careful wickerwork leaped into flame, creating a corridor of fire that closed in behind Hora and the others, helping to protect them from attack.

Skjebne brought the children to the alley and they waited to be joined there by the rest.

'The entire city is like this.' Kano's face was bleak. 'The Goddess is determined to put a stop to us and reassert her authority in the enclave—'

'It is not so bad in the villages,' Feoh said, catching a glimmer of Kell's concern.

'The main routes to the outer portals start here in Odal – the cleft you found is a freak flaw. The land must have shifted over the centuries . . .'

'We've had a difficult journey,' Skjebne began.

'I know that.' Feoh bent to him and eased aside the cloth of his tunic to look at the extent of his wound. She visualised the flesh whole again, and at the same time gave Skjebne's mind the gift of forgetting as far as the pain was concerned. That would help for a time, but she knew then – and Skjebne would know it later – that he was likely to be hobbled for life.

There was no time for the swapping of tales. Without warning there came a tremendous rushing sound through the sky, followed by a vast muffled thunder. High overhead a blue spark flashed intermittently, illuminating tangled swirlings of black cloud. Again and again the spark cracked and flared, until finally the sun returned as a huge red amorphous shadow of itself; an enormous spherical hull which cast a dull and melancholy glow.

'She tells us what we already know, that this is a dark day of blood,' Hora said. He passed one torch to Birca and the other to Skjebne, preferring his hands free now if it came to a fight. They were after all his most dangerous weapons.

'Look there.' Birca pointed upwards and they saw swarms of tiny black dots streaming in from the farthest horizons; clusters of sky gleams dropping fast towards the city.

Kano shook his head. 'The All Mother wants to make an end of it (*Things will get worse now*, Shamra snatched from his mind). Let's be on our way.'

Kell's last glimpse of the plaza was of a mass of burning piles, with figures running between them, and a dirty coppery pall of smoke rising lazily towards the scarlet sky.

Then they were in the alley and moving quickly towards the hatch that would take them to the tunnels. Here between the buildings the gloom was deeper and the dim red overcast made things difficult to see. The high walls kept out most of the sound, but occasional screams and cries came clearly through the hazy air and grated on the nerves.

They reached the place where the metal hatch was stamped into the roadway. Hora dropped to his knees, drew an iron spike from his belt and began to lever it up. Without telling them, Feoh and Skjebne moved protectively to shield the children, while Kano and Birca held the torches high to keep a lookout for danger; though when it came, it happened quickly and without any warning.

'I have it!' Hora heaved and gave a grunt and the heavy steel hatchway lifted free. He dropped it with a clang to the side and motioned Feoh to enter. She, being the first, could scan for hazards below ground.

'I sense nothing . . .' Feoh climbed quickly down the ladder and vanished into blackness. 'It's clear here—'

'Not here!' Kano's warning snapped like a whip. He had seen a jumble of running figures at the end of the alley: but more menacingly, above them, a flight of shapes that bounced and bobbed like floats on a turbulent stream.

One of the sky gleams disintegrated suddenly. It came apart in an explosion of black crystal. Kano threw himself down across Skjebne, who cried out with the agony of his wound, and the two of them tumbled into Hora, who only just managed to keep his balance. Birca, slower and more startled, did not have time to drop clear.

There was a swish and a hard pattering of little projectiles on the wall and fencing nearby. Kano glanced up to warn Birca, but the man was already dead, pierced a hundred times through. The fleens had cut so cleanly that he stood upright for another second or two, before the dumb weight of his body toppled forward and he fell on his face in the road.

'Oh – no – no . . .' Shamra's shocked, spinning mind had caught Birca's death-thought; a merest glimpse and memory of boyhood, casting flat stones on the shore of the Central Lake. And he'd counted the times each had skipped the surface: one – two – three—

Then a blackness empty of pain.

Hora lifted the girl with ease and bundled her down through the hole. Then Kell, unresisting, was delivered into Feoh's trembling hands.

'Now you Kano – now!'

Hora was in no mood for argument. He wrenched Kano down and pushed him through.

'Skjebne—'

Hampered by the stiffness of his hip, Skjebne took a few seconds to clamber clear.

Another sky gleam exploded. Hora snatched up the hatch cover and held it like a shield. Fragments sang and tinkled on the metal. A few pierced his leg. And one, painfully, sliced clean through his left hand in a splash of bright blood.

With a roar of outrage Hora hurled the steel disc towards the mass of cityzens who were now perhaps only thirty paces away. It banged and rattled on the roadway a little short of the crowd. A few stones were thrown weakly in retaliation. Hora disdained them. His big square face had been carved by what he'd seen into a mask of determination, and the heat of life burned in him now more resolutely than ever before. He did not bother with the ladder, but dropped cleanly three man-heights to the floor of the labyrinth and lumbered at a slow running pace to catch up with his dearest friends.

The network of stone and metal corridors channelled the noises of the fighting in strange and frightening ways. Fires burning above made a low and continuous roaring like a steady wind or a distant fall of water. There came clangs and bumpings, scrapes, shrieks, cries and other sounds that the children's imagination failed to grasp. Occasionally the group heard distant shouting from elsewhere in the tunnels: more of the dispossessed escaping below ground, making their way to the waiting travel machines.

After a first hurrying to be away from the open hatch, Kano called a halt and insisted on checking Hora's injuries.

'They are nothing,' he muttered gruffly, embarrassed as Feoh wiped away the blood.

'Even nothings can become infected . . .' Hora knew better than to argue with her and waited patiently as she bandaged the wounds and touched Hora's mind with her thoughts to stimulate his healing.

'Besides, we need you well to carry us when we grow tired!' Skjebne's smile was strained and his humour weak. The shadow of Birca's death would stay with them for many days to come, and their spirits would flicker low from the horror of it.

They moved on and a natural pattern formed – Kano leading the way with Feoh and Shamra just behind; then Kell walking at the side of Skjebne, and Hora like a prowling rock-bear bringing up the rear. Their conversation was brief and infrequent, though all of them felt the balm of Feoh's thoughts and were glad of it: and she, working hard, was also sensitive to Shamra's every change and emphasis of mood, and kept some of her attention cast like a gentle net all around for any signs of danger.

In this way they walked for several hours, making good progress by taking turns to help Skjebne along. The troubling sounds of the city in its turmoil dropped away behind them, and for a long while there was silence but for their footsteps and breathing and the sputtering of the firebrands.

Then, gradually, shortly before the tunnels sloped up towards the mountains, there came a distant cacophony, as of huge millstones grinding together. Kano stopped and looked automatically to Skjebne for advice.

'Who can know for sure?' Skjebne's sharp bright eyes, frightened though they were, still held curiosity's passionate light. 'The All Mother works the world with a marvellous machinery. We have discovered that. And do you notice how it has grown colder? I suspect she is making changes all across Perth – inflicting her punishments perhaps on those who are left . . .'

'All of the poor people!' Shamra's thoughts went out to them, and Feoh turned them aside and brought them home to save the waste of a purposeless grief.

'The Goddess will not destroy her worshippers. She is sustained by them as much as they are by her. Her lesson will be sharp and swift, and then over and done with.'

'We must look out for ourselves,' Kano said. 'Should we move on, Skjebne?'

'Where we have no choice, our action must be the right one.'

And this time he smiled naturally, and the other adults joined him.

As they moved on, coming at last to the upslope, the

grindings grew louder and the drop in temperature more noticeable. A weak yet steady breeze blew in their faces. Somewhere to their left metal scraped against metal. There was a dull *boom*, a silence, then a frantic scurrying of footsteps.

'Three people,' Feoh surmised. 'Terrified—'

Something shattered violently. A tinkling of metal. There was a scream.

'The sky gleams.' Hora came up level with the others. 'They have entered the tunnels.'

'They're searching us out.' Kano took stock of their position. 'We aren't far from the cache of weapons—'

'And then we come back,' Feoh said firmly, 'to help these others in trouble.'

'There isn't anything . . .' he began, and then saw the look on Feoh's face and knew that argument would be pointless.

She said gently, 'We want to make a human world, Kano. Let's start now.'

He nodded, and they moved. Skjebne with his injury found it hard to keep pace, so Kano decided that he would go for the weapons alone.

'I can stay in touch through Feoh, and by myself I can be back in minutes.'

'If you're caught you are vulnerable,' Hora pointed out.

'No more than we all are, my friend. Stay out of sight. I won't be long.'

They watched him dwindle along the length of the tunnel, until all that was left was a flame, then a memory of a flame; and then only Feoh's quietly spoken word that he was safe.

'And what do you glean of the others?' wondered Skjebne presently.

She looked beyond him and upwards. 'One of them is badly hurt . . .'

'I feel it,' Shamra confirmed. 'And his friend . . . Little mice . . . Little mice in the corner . . .'

Feoh comforted her with a hug. 'The sky gleams radiate nothing I can read. There could be many of them. Through all these years they have watched us! How could we have known?'

'Never mind it now,' Skjebne said. 'At least there are three of our friends still alive, and Kano will be with us directly.'

'He's returning now—'

A thought. A flame. The running figure of a man.

Kano came up to them panting and hefted the fire-rod across to Hora. He gave a similar though smaller weapon to Feoh and to Skjebne.

'And you'll just have to curse,' he told Shamra and Kell.

They left their path and took a side tunnel towards the commotion. Skjebne reasoned that the first sounds must have been of the sky gleams entering the labyrinth, happening upon the other group probably by chance.

'Let's hope it was,' Feoh said. Her black mask, turned towards him, reflected the torch flames like liquid. 'For if they are systematically hunting us, we stand little chance . . .'

It was not a thought to dwell on, and Kell tried to keep his mind focused on the task in hand . . . But again and again the vision of the beautiful little sky gleams he'd watched so often pushed to the front of his mind, and there transformed into the monstrosities that had killed Birca and how many others? Such was the measure of the All Mother's goodness, her true face a spray of cutting blades.

They hurried on as best they could through the tunnels, Feoh sensing ahead and filling their minds with what she saw. And so it was they anticipated the death of the other group well before they came into the cavernous space where the killing had happened.

Huge conduits soared upwards into the towering dark, disappearing into a high vaulted roof that their torchflames could never illuminate; equally below, where the pipes dropped into sheer pits many furrowlengths deep. Skjebne, experimenting, picked up a chunk of rubble and let it fall. Ten heartbeats later came the distant sound of its shattering.

'One of them fell down there,' Feoh told Kano alone. 'The other two have been mutilated. I think they are somewhere nearby. The children should not see it.'

'We are too late,' Kano said. 'The gleams have done their work efficiently.'

Hora gave a soft groan of horror; and Skjebne, a startled gasp as something glittered deep in the shaft.

'Kano—'

They held their brands over the pit and Skjebne deliberately let go of his and watched it fluttering wildly, and by its light caught a momentary glimpse of a shape as it came soaring upwards.

'Back!' Kano thrust his torch into Skjebne's hand, grabbed the children and ran with them, half dragging them, to the greater safety beyond the cavern.

Skjebne and Feoh retreated, taking cover behind the clusters of vertical tubes. Hora's withdrawal was slower and more considered. He back-walked as he unslung his fire-rod and swung it into position with a grunt; coming to a halt some paces from cover, steadying his aim on the rim of the shaft.

The gleam appeared seconds later, came buzzing like a meadowfly in a flurry of twinkling antennae. Hora discharged the fire-rod and the cavern boomed like a drum with deafening echoes. The machine exploded and fell in fragments of flame back into the pit.

'It was a scout—' Skjebne called, voicing his instinct.' Not a fighter—'

He had no time for more. Two other devices swept up into view, leaden jewels more solidly built. Feoh and Skjebne aimed and shot, and the higher machine burst apart into scraps that whined and ricocheted among the complex of pipes.

The other gleam showered scalding rays in all directions, then seemed to focus on where Skjebne was hiding. It launched a glowing projectile which struck the ground just short of his position. There was a *thud* of dull sound and brief flame; smoke and stone erupted outwards leaving a ragged crater in their place. Skjebne fired again and sent the gleam spinning. Hora took advantage of its confusion and loosed a further shot. It struck dead centre and the machine came apart in a shower of debris.

'There may be more,' Feoh warned. 'I cannot read them – they do not think like human minds.'

'There is nothing else for us to do here.' Kano beckoned his friends to leave. 'We aren't far from the Traveller now, though we should hurry.'

They kept together in a tight group, Hora back-walking with the fire-rod held high and ready. Only his huge strength made this possible: earlier Kell had taken hold of the weapon and had barely been able to lift it.

So it was they came to the place where the travel machine was housed, patiently waiting like a well-trained mox beneath its canvas cover. Kano ran ahead and began to unhitch the securing ropes while Feoh, Shamra and Kell started hauling the caul aside. Skjebne worked a pattern of studs at the rear of the Traveller: the back hatch folded downwards and he disappeared inside. Hora unhooked a clip on the fire rod and clicked a small metal stand into place. He positioned the weapon propped thus on the ground, and laid a huge heavy hand on Kell's shoulder.

'Now I need to open the outer portals. Take your position like this—' He demonstrated by lying out on his stomach, legs splayed, the stock of the rod tucked tightly into his shoulder. 'Use your favoured eye.' Hora showed Kell how to hold the weapon and look along its sights. 'You see, it's weightless mounted like this on its pivot. Let yourself relax . . . Grow easy in yourself Kell, that's it. Just be lazily alert in case more of the sky gleams appear.'

'And if they should?'

'Just assert your authority.' Hora gave his big, open, uncomplicated grin and padded away to do his other work, leaving Kell alone.

Meanwhile Skjebne was spinning his magic. Lights blazed across the Traveller's hull and the hunched beast shuddered as the great engines woke up from sleep. It growled with a first burst of power, then its voice settled to a quieter muttering. Feoh and Shamra went aboard. Kano ran across to assist Hora in turning the wheels that would force the portals to open.

Kell, only half aware of this activity, arced the fire-rod to and fro, to and fro in a daydream of things yet to come. So it was that he almost missed the appearance of the sky gleam, and yelled and fired wildly as the attacker hurtled forward into the chamber.

The rod's powerful missile hit the wall close to the gleam, the impact sending it tumbling. Kell fired again, losing all sense of Hora's instruction. The shot went wide.

But now, with the others alerted, Kano came to help. He did not humiliate the boy by taking charge of the fire-rod himself. Instead, he checked his own weapon and began shooting with a cool regularity as the gleam tried to reorient and focus in on its enemies.

Behind them, Hora cried out with the effort of freeing the portal-wheels, and then again in triumph as he succeeded. Deep inside the mighty doors some mechanism engaged: the lights in the chamber dimmed briefly and a cold cutting wind began to blow.

Smiling ferociously, Kano took pleasure in watching the

gleam lose its fight. A glancing shot took off one side of its many-faceted shell; while Kell struck lucky and destroyed the mechanism that kept the gleam aloft. It fell like a stone to the dust.

'You've done enough.' Kano tapped Kell's arm smartly. 'Get aboard with the others. Go now!'

Kell obeyed at once. He ran to the Traveller, letting out a whoop both of excitement and pain as the frigid wind from the outer world tugged and nipped and buffeted his body with a ruffian's hands.

Then he was in a small warm room of cramped spaces and skittering lights and chattering machinery, cosy darkness and the unusual tantalising smell of plastics. Shamra nearby was tucked into a bucket seat, strapped in place by a diagonal belt. Feoh likewise. Not five steps farther on Skjebne hunched over the Traveller's controls and played them like an intent and frenzied musician.

As Kell took the seat next to Shamra, he looked beyond Skjebne and saw a widening light, a pearly light filled with spinning flakes; and his heart seemed to loosen and dissolve with the wonder and the fear of it all.

Hora came aboard, having completed his tasks. He hung back near the rear hatch and watched as Kano performed a necessary ritual—

Feeling his body as tight as a tensioned cable, Kano drew one of the securing spikes out of the ground. He walked over to where the sky gleam was clicking furiously, rocking itself randomly this way and that with the aid of strange grappling appendages. Its shell had been ripped loose in several places, and inside the tangling of wires and mysterious jewellery blue sparks popped and fizzed and disappeared into smoke.

'This is how the future will be, All Mother.' Kano dropped to his knees. Now he felt strangely tranquil and passionless. The magnitude of his freedom had washed away his hate.

'This is how it will be.'

He raised the spike high and drove it down through the machine, staking it to the earth. Something crackled at its core and its clicking and trembling stopped . . .

But for a short while afterwards its systems stayed alive, and it watched with a baleful eye as its destroyer entered the Traveller. The back hatch closed. Then with a howl of engines the vehicle moved forward, through the outermost gates of Perth, into a confusion of rose pink blizzard-filled light.

7

The World Beyond the World

There was something a little different about the day. Gifu sat very still against the soft backrest of a cushiontree and listened to the peacefulness. Way out over the broad plains of Perth, and hung beneath the vague blue dome of the sky, the sudden amber sun quivered in a brief agitation. Then it shone more strongly and the morning had truly begun.

The night . . . Gifu struggled to remember the night. He somehow felt bruised by it, and a part of him had no wish to recollect. There had been much activity in the huge darkness; a gleam – yes, a gleam – of memory told him that the countryside had been alive and busy with great prowling hulks and flying things. They had swept and scoured the land on the business of the All Mother that was no business of men. Gifu's thoughts touched upon fragmentary scenes; a vast lumbering brute of smooth metal thundering by. It had had no mind, at least nothing resembling the slow contentedness he found inside moxen's heads. Its purpose was obscure, and his sighting of it had been fleeting . . .

Then there was the sky itself, alive with lights that had swarmed in greater numbers than Gifu had ever known. Earlier some of them had come in very close and looked at him with insects' eyes, and his simple soul had quailed and turned away at their scrutiny.

And across far distances, he realised now, had come screams and howlings. . ... And there had been fire in the city and rumours of chaos and death—

Something clicked in Gifu's brain and a warmth suddenly soothed him. His muscles eased and the memories faded away, so that his mind and imagination shrank back again to the immediate moment. Sitting quietly, doing nothing, summer was here and the grass grew by itself . . .

The grass. The beauty of the slopes. A sparkling dew on the fronds of the feathergrass. It was another perfect day.

Presently the old fieldsman stirred himself and struggled stiffly to his feet, as though he had sat there for an age. He clumped along the pale earth track, and once, and twice, made the high ululating whistle that drew his mox from its byre and brought it down to the place where the ploughing was needed.

Oddly, this morning, two beasts shuffled into view, their vast breath steaming in the dawn-chilly air. Gifu was puzzled. Though on reflection, it was not uncommon for the minds of these brutes to become somehow entangled and their purposes linked. He shrugged at this minor complication and went over to examine the other beast while his own came to a halt with a sharp hiss of pneumatics and scratched its flank against the trunk of a nearby lantern-apple tree.

This new one was a mystery; strange and without origin, and yet clearly it had been well worked and competently cared for over the seasons. Gifu's adept fingers found the nodules in its neck and read the brief simple story of its past . . .

But even as the information came to him, it was drawn back somehow and taken beyond his grasp. He saw a fair-haired, clear-faced young boy and for the briefest instant knew his name. Then the vision was gone and the mox's brain was empty of images. It gazed down stupidly at Gifu, who decided there and then to take it as his own and work it in tandem with his regular animal.

But the time for training was later. Gifu used the pattern of bony studs behind the mox's skull to tether it in place. Then he retrieved his own beast and led it over to the share, shackled it up and continued cutting the furrow from where he had left off the evening before.

They were driving blind, and the thought of it locked Kell into his seat. Despite Feoh's soothing mental reassurance, he could not help but conjure up scenarios of disaster and death—

The Traveller suddenly tilts and topples off a brink. There is a long and terrifying fall, a spinning weightlessness, then the universe smashes into a million tiny fragments . . . Behind them the rock opens and a monstrous thing looms out, twenty times larger than their machine. Its huge head seems to split apart, vast jaws gape, and the Traveller is scooped up and cracked open like a lake oyster . . . The engines fail. There comes a sliding sound over the top of the hull. The lights go out and suddenly the rear hatch is rent apart as many clawed fingers reach inside for their screaming wriggling prey—

'Kell!' Kano was in front of him, his face thunderous yet also concerned. 'If you keep this up I'm going to take you back to the All Mother!'

The idea was so ludicrous that after a moment's stark shock Kell started to laugh and the tension was broken – though not completely removed. They had come out beyond the portals and the snow and hurricane winds had engulfed them entirely. Even with the Traveller's solidity and weight, it had rocked and been buffeted by the punishing storm. Skjebne worked quickly. The machine's forward windows had become slitted to thin vertical chinks; the note of its engines deepened; and once, as the gusts reached a peak, grappling chains shot out from the sides to anchor the vehicle in place until the worst of the fury had passed.

From then on, over the course of an hour, the machine had made slow but steady headway through an endless curtain of flakes.

Presently Kano took Kell and Shamra to study the Traveller's controls. Kell instinctively lifted his eyes to look out.

'There's nothing to see.' Kano put his hand at the back of Kell's head and made him gaze down. 'It's all here.'

There was another window filled with glowing light, and within the light, a map. Kell quickly recognised the patterns of lines and shadows as the shapes of mountains and valleys envisaged in this unusual way. A red point, Kano explained, marked the Traveller's present position; the blue line, its route. Further illuminated windows gave other details of their place and progress through the wilderness.

'Much of this knowledge was already here, laid down in the mind of the machine – the Goddess knows when! Skjebne found a way to draw it out, and we can add our own observations too, and the discoveries we made on our earlier brief journeys beyond the gates.'

Shamra touched the smooth cool screens and the dull black surface around them, and found it all lifeless.

'The Traveller is not a living thing,' Kano said. 'And maybe it has no soul. But its mind is there, sure enough, and contains intelligence.'

'The vehicle was created to survive.' Skjebne worked the drive wheels as he spoke. 'Instincts are built into its metals. We can direct it, but only within limits. It would not allow us to steer over a ledge . . .' He smiled wickedly.

Shamra's mouth dropped open. 'You've tried it!'

'We had to be sure.' Skjebne favoured the children with a sparkling glance. 'And we found it to be very resourceful. It knows the lie of the land around Perth, at least in a general way. And it has senses beyond ours that can read obstacles and slopes.'

'It was designed to keep its occupants alive.' Kano tapped the roof with a knuckle. 'Though it has won Skjebne's faith more than it has won mine. What I don't entirely know, I cannot entirely trust. Feoh has worked hard to understand it more surely—'

'Much of its mind is shielded from us.' Feoh spoke up from the back of the craft. 'It has ideas and purposes deeper than I can reach, and that neither I nor anyone can modify. But it is a benign creation.' She smiled. 'It has none of the destructive urge we saw in the sky gleams.'

'How do you know the Goddess doesn't possess it?' Kell wondered. 'She could be leading us to our deaths right now . . .' Another thought struck him. 'Maybe she has created all of this inside our heads – It could be a nightmare, another way to torture us!'

'We are beyond the reach of the All Mother, at least for now.' Feoh's single clear eye looked at Kell and through him. 'Unless she is hidden in our hearts like a worm at the core of an apple. In which case, we will never outrun her.'

Kano looked at Feoh critically. 'I can understand the boy's doubts. I'll be much happier when we have come down into the valley.'

'And what will we find there?' Shamra frowned at the lack of instant response from Feoh's mind. The two were growing closer, and even over the past few days had developed an ease of anticipation that would soon do away with the necessity of speech.

'We have seen it only distantly.' Kano pointed to the outermost limits of the map. 'There, see . . . We are following a trail that cleaves down between these two peaks. I think Perth must exist inside one of them. At the base of the mountains, a jumble of hills, and past the hills lies the valley.'

'And here?' Kell touched the thick glass of the map window. He felt strengthened by Feoh's confidence and lack of fear. And as his own unease decreased, the thrill and sheer wonder of what was happening to him expanded.

'Ice plains,' Skjebne said. 'For all we can tell. The Traveller doesn't have that knowledge.' He chuckled. 'Although we named it, we don't think it has travelled very much in the past.'

'But somebody imagined it would . . .'

Kano nodded. 'Long ago. Yes, someone did. What we don't understand is how that somebody knew what the land would be like now: whoever could anticipate what changes the Ice might have made?'

'A mystery among a new world of mysteries.' Skjebne waved airily at the snow streaming past the window slits. 'For this we came!' Kell stood beside him and also watched the flakes whirling by. And deep inside, at that moment, he had never been happier.

They ploughed on, trusting to the machine's cold and alien judgement. The little dot that marked their position on the map of glowing lines continued to follow the contours of the ground. Occasionally the Traveller would stop, as if diverse and subtle senses were questing ahead into the gloom. And once there came the bump and rattling of the anchor chains, and warning sirens yodelled briefly in the cabin. Everyone took to their seats and buckled in.

A moment later the whole vehicle lurched and something sped away—

'What's That!' Shamra's voice was almost a shriek.

Skjebne followed the projectile's arrow-straight flight on the main screen. It struck an unseen obstacle. They heard the muffled *boom* of its destruction even through the hull of the craft, and pieces showered down with a wild and random clatter on the roof.

'I'm impressed,' Hora said. 'What it can't go around it smashes out of the way.'

'Your two personalities must be similar.' Feoh's face was serious, but the twinkle in her eye belied her mood.

Soon the Traveller retracted the grapples, its engines powered up and it moved on. For a short while it eased itself downslope, before regaining level ground. And shortly after that it halted and shut down entirely.

Inside there was a brief but panicky confusion.

'It's all right! It's all right . . .' Skjebne's hands came up to calm the others. 'Nothing is out of the ordinary. There are no warnings showing here . . .' They all listened nervously, and although the main engines were silent other systems hummed and clicked throughout the machine.

'I think it has simply stopped for the night, knowing we need our sleep.'

'What if we wanted to carry on?' Kano sounded critical.

'I suspect there is some way of overriding the Traveller's inbuilt instructions. I just haven't found it yet.' Skjebne grinned at them. 'But look, we're warm enough here. And safe enough.'

He touched a button on the angled fascia in front of him. The window slits expanded to show the gathering night. The snow's intensity had lessened, so that now only thin flurries brushed like moths against the glass. Beyond that, dim suggestions of rocks and to the right a vague angle of shadow that might have been a cliff face; all this glimpsed by the Traveller's array of subdued external lights.

'Not much to see just now. You'll have a better view tomorrow.'

They busied themselves in preparing food, while beyond their influence the Traveller hunkered down closer to the ground. It drew metal cauls around itself for protection, knowing by its ancient instructions that the temperature would plummet. Within the tiny enclave of itself its occupants could sleep – although one, the young girl the others called Shamra, lay awake for some time; her mind as still as an unmoving pond as she listened to Perth's fading memories of pain, before the All Mother drew her warm and brooding wings around her children once more.

The cold pooled quickly near the floor of the cabin and rose like a suave heavy liquid along Kell's legs and body. It brushed his fingertips with a delicate touch, crept along his arms, and at last reached his face. He felt it then and for a moment thought he was drowning. His eyelids flickered open and he saw the steam of his outbreath of surprise.

Hora loomed by and the cold air stirred and flowed in his slipstream. Kell turned his head and saw the big man walk out through the dropped rear hatchway into a blinding ocean of light.

'Day – It's day!'

'Good morning.' Foeh smiled at the boy's rising excitement. 'Why don't you go and look at the view?' She handed him a mox pelt overjacket and insisted he put it on before leaving the craft. 'The cold will freeze the grin on your face as it is. The others are already out there. You can help Skjebne make observations . . .'

This last point was lost on him: Kell was already scrambling along the gangway, then out into a glory of brightness and ice and air as clean as a draught of the purest water.

He stopped and his mouth gaped open at the sheer scale of his surroundings. And to *be* here, a part of it! Nothing had prepared him for this.

Skjebne was just ten paces away, standing beside his farscope making notes on a paper pad. Kano and Shamra had wandered farther off – Kell caught the glitter of her own mood – and were examining a clump of rockweed they had found. Hora sat close to the Traveller, perched on a flat-topped boulder, the fire-rod held across his chest. His eyes scanned the horizons, while his other senses swept the nearer ground for any danger.

'We can live here after all . . . After all my worrying,' was Kell's first comment to Skjebne. And he wanted to laugh, for Skjebne was wearing a blue conical woollen hat to keep the chill off his balding head. But Kell knew he wasn't just being disrespectful; the joy was bubbling up in him over everything he saw.

'I mean, we can survive in this land . . .'

'Hmm . . .' Skjebne's concentration was elsewhere. 'Take your hand out of your pocket and hold it up.'

'What?'

'Do it, Kell.'

Kell obeyed, and within the space of a few breaths his bare fingers were numb and aching to the bone, the fingernails turning blue.

'If you kept it there long enough the flesh would freeze. Lesson one – respect the Ice. Besides that, the sun has been up for some time: at night the cold is far more intense. On the other hand, I don't doubt that we can live here.'

Kell stuffed his throbbing hand back into his pocket, noticing that Skjebne wore woollen gloves the same colour as his hat.

'And beneath those are undergloves of a special membrane we found among stores near the Traveller. There'll be a pair for you, don't fret.'

Skjebne pretended to be absorbed in his notes, but secretly he enjoyed the youngling's company: the boy's mind was a fire to be lighted, and Skjebne felt pleased that their friendship was striking some sparks.

Kell let his gaze drift in an arc that traced the far horizons. Behind him was the broad stony upland flats they had followed from Perth; a high plain that wound its way among mounds of rock-slippage back to the towering mountains, which reached to the top of the sky. Huge beyond Kell's imagination, the broken peaks each streamed a plume of white cloud, while their bases were shrouded in shadows. Inside them was everything he had ever known, with no one and nothing in all of the great wide World the wiser for it.

Kell tracked the jagged line of the pinnacles downwards in the direction of the sun – a sun that at first could be mistaken for the one that brought daylight to Perth; except, again, here was a sense of scale and of range that caused Kell to realise this was something different entirely. It was a hard white splintering of glass an incredible distance away; frozen into place; seemingly changeless, unlike the moody globe of the enclave.

Ahead, the land opened out and sloped downwards. As Kano had told him, after the mountains came a confusion of hills, lifeless and grey, streaked with hard blue ice and brushings of windblown snow. It was indeed a wilderness, beyond which lay a sea of soft white froth, broken by rounded summits that reached an enormous distance away.

'Not water, but cloud,' Skjebne said on noticing his gaze. 'This is something we must accept – that the weather here is varied, and it happens quickly. And it will not be placated by prayer.'

Kell nodded and didn't understand. Clouds existed in Perth, of course, but there they were fleecy decorations gathering only to deliver rain after suitable prayers and rituals had been made. Gifu had once said that her Community's devotion sometimes caused the Goddess to cry, and that because of her weeping life could continue. Kell's little boy's heart had been moved by the story. He didn't believe it now, but did that mean there was nothing out here to control the snow and the wind? Was this truly a land without heart, where supplications were as meaningless as the stones?

'This morning the vapour is low,' Skjebne said. 'Yesterday the storm rose around us, and the moving sky was a mass of snow-bearing cloud. Maybe there is a pattern behind it, but I have not discerned anything yet.'

He pointed out that their way led into the mass. 'Where it will most probably be snowing again, and our journey made that much more difficult.'

Within a short time Shamra and Kano returned and the time had come to move on. Up on his rock, Hora stood and stretched mightily, and jumped down with surprising agility given his size and the fire-rod's burden.

'I thought I saw something.' He swung the rod towards a far edge. 'Maybe just rocks falling by themselves . . .'

Even so, Kano insisted on using the farscope to scan the distant bluff.

'I see nothing,' he said after long moments of quiet. 'Let us be on our way . . .'

Hora guarded their position while the others went aboard. And that gave Kell his next useful lesson: for while the prospect of life tantalised and thrilled him, it would be life born of the wilderness, regarding all others as prey.

Twice more during the day Kano stopped the Traveller. Once it was to check something they'd noticed inside; that the vehicle itself was adding to the maps it displayed through the glass. Somehow, in a way they could neither see nor understand, the mind of the craft was gathering details of the land and marking them down in maps of light.

'Very useful,' Kano said, his expression such that no one knew if he was joking. 'It means we can always find our way back.'

And again they halted when both Skjebne and Kell saw something moving on a cliff slope ahead – far away, a pale and gangling shape clinging to ledges, swinging easily across the all-but-vertical face.

Kano and Skjebne bundled out, but it took a minute to assemble the farscope, by which time the animal had gone. If it had been an animal. And if they had really seen anything in the first place. It was late afternoon now and the sun's strange movement had taken it down close to the opposite peaks: the air was filled with an orange light and shadows were as blue and hard and clear as the sky. It might have been that what they'd seen was a tiny thing, its size and movement exaggerated by the conditions. No doubt Skjebne would write it up in his notes, and no doubt he and Hora would disagree on the matter for some days to come. Even as they stood there, their imaginations tantalising them with possibilities, they felt the temperature dropping and were glad to climb back inside.

It was Kano's intention to descend below the cloud layer before dark. Skjebne's feeling was that soon after they would find the cover of the forest. 'I think the cold will not be so cruel there,' he said. And apart from that, and something none of them voiced, was the fact that at last they would be out of sight of the mountains and away from the All Mother's gaze.

So, as they had been forced to do already, again they put their faith in the Traveller's power and sat and watched the rugged countryside roll by. Skjebne drew back the window shields to their full extent, and ahead of them the downslope of the ground led towards the unbroken lake of the cloud-tops; now golden, now amber, now a fiery red pooling swiftly with blue shadows. The scene was breathtakingly beautiful, but Kano felt compelled to warn of the danger.

'So far we have been able to see our own way. Once beneath the cloud, things could be different. If Skjebne is right and the forest begins, the Traveller will not be able to move so quickly. Nor, indeed, might there be any way forward at all. And what lives in the trees will be able to approach us unseen—'

'There can be no turning back,' Feoh reminded him, referring to his earlier comments.

'Another route maybe?' was Kell's suggestion.

Skjebne shook his head. 'The Traveller's charts are limited to the area around the Perth mountains.' He worked some controls and the map-of-light shifted, and they all saw for themselves that the weavework of lines and points ended with a sharp edge. 'However we come down off the high ground our problem will still be the same.'

'This is where it is hard.' Kano watched the sun touch a high brink of rock and disappear from sight, and a few bright stars were suddenly visible. 'This is where we live with our decisions . . .'

Soon afterwards the Traveller entered the clouds and, as Skjebne predicted, the snow began to fall. Guide lights came on automatically, though these were of limited help. The map windows shone with new illustrations as the vehicle's unseen senses scanned the landscape around.

'What is all this?' Shamra, as keen as the others to see, pointed to a glowing mass ahead of them.

Circumstances answered for her. Suddenly, the chaos of the snow ahead was different, a steady and nearly vertical fall. Thick black pillars loomed into the light. Then the Traveller shuddered and came to a halt.

'Trees!' Skjebne's voice held an eager ferocity. 'Kano, we've reached the forest!'

'But why does the machine stop?'

'I think . . .' He touched a button here, a switch there. 'It guides itself with the maps it makes. Yes, that must be it. But now – look, don't you see? Now there is too much fine detail. Its mind cannot work quickly enough to assess the land and create a way forward as it moves.'

'So do we wait while it wonders what to do?' Hora said grumpily from the rear.

'The engines are still running.' Kano looked at the array of displays and controls. 'The craft has not shut down, as it did on the first night. So maybe . . .'

'Maybe we can drive it for ourselves.' Skjebne eased himself into the forward seat. Directly in front of him and at chest height a further screen bloomed into life. He reached out and gripped a small control wheel. A red light appeared on the screen. Within arm's reach were two sticks. Skjebne took hold of them, and two gold lights replaced the single red.

'It's teaching me!' he said with a boyish glee. The golden points became lines moving forward. Skjebne eased the drive-sticks forward and the Traveller crawled ahead. He drew the sticks back, and the vehicle slowed.

And so it went through the dark hours, the machine and the man each learning the other's ways. Skjebne grew in confidence, but was warned when he outdistanced his skill. One time, though the downslope was gentle, the craft began to gather speed and slither sideways out of control. Skjebne's impulse was to heave back on the sticks: but of their own accord one stick swung back and the other went forward, so correcting the slide. Simultaneously a great whoosh of air surged from forward vents; and out of the corner of his eye Skjebne saw two grapplechains sail away sideways and anchor themselves in the trees. The machine followed its action with an array of sparkles across the 'teaching screen', as Skjebne had come to call it, and a melody of cascading musical notes which meant nothing to him at the time.

'It's like being back at the Tutorium,' he mumbled ruefully, the Traveller allowing him to return the controls to a neutral point before they proceeded again. Later Kano came and sat beside Skjebne for company while the other passengers slept and judged it was best just then to keep his praise and compliments to himself.

Until then only Skjebne had had the experience of driving the Traveller. He had spoken with Kano and they decided that each of the others in turn would be guided by Skjebne into knowing the moods of the machine. Thus, if needs be, very soon they would be able to travel continuously, working in shifts until they reached easier ground.

'And then?' Skjebne asked. They were moving through a monotony of trees and softly falling snow along what must have been an animal track or perhaps a natural break in the forest. Nothing had changed for many hours, and the flickering of endless flakes in the Traveller's beams was hypnotic and exhausting. Kano peered into the whirling dance with weary eyes and sighed.

'Who can know? Maybe there is no place where we can settle. Maybe this is the best the World can offer.'

'The power of the Traveller's engines will not last indefinitely.'

'Nor will our provisions. I know that. But once, before the Ice and before Perth and before machines like this one, people who were flesh and blood and bone like us were born of this land and lived in it and made it their own. They must have endured the snow and the cold—'

'But not forever, as the world might be now.'

Kano felt his temper rising, but then understood his friend's ploy. By fighting argument with argument, Skjebne was forcing Kano to think ahead. And that, Kano now realised with a new strength, was what must have allowed the native peoples of this wilderness to survive here in the first place.

But it was easy in the warm quiet comfort of the Traveller

to view all problems as distant ones. The gentle swaying of the craft lulled Kano into a half sleep. And Skjebne allowed the enchantment of the snow to enfold him—

Until a sudden shrill beeping startled him awake. He remembered his teaching and kept a firm grip on the guide sticks and slowed the machine in a controlled and careful way.

A shape loomed out of the darkness and glowed in the machine's forward lamps; a hulking thing, hunched over, head hidden, with a low curved back like a dead mox.

'What is that beast?'

The others had wakened to the commotion by now. Feoh put out her thoughts and found no life nearby . . . Other presences, almost too distant to detect, were unreadable.

'Let's go round it,' Skjebne said. He wasn't thinking. The bulking form was blocking the way, and the trees all about were clustered too thickly to allow easy passage.

'We could use the projectiles, I suppose,' was Hora's assessment, not realising Skjebne had not yet learned how to release them.

'No.' Kano faced the others. 'I think we should discover what it really is. If it's a dead animal, we can drag it clear with chains—'

'If it's rock—'

'If it's a rock, Hora, the Traveller would surely have destroyed it already. Skjebne, you stay here with the young ones. Hora, Feoh – come with me now.'

So it was that Kell was forced to watch while the three adults scrambled quickly into their overjackets. There came a brief blast of chilly air as they went out through the hatchway, reappearing a moment later in the brilliant glare of the lights.

They trudged across to the motionless shape, Hora first holding the fire-rod out in front of him.

'I hope it's not just asleep—' Shamra started to say. But Skjebne was glaring ahead, his face almost touching the glass of the forward window.

'It is . . . surely . . . the same size, the same shape . . . as . . .'

And his suspicions were confirmed as Kano swept a mittened hand across the back of the object, clearing away the snow to reveal bare grey metal beneath.

'It's another Traveller.' Shamra picked up the synchrony of her friends' minds, and looked past them and found nothing beyond. 'There's no one inside.'

'No one *alive* inside,' Skjebne added carelessly.

Hora kept the fire-rod aimed while Kano and Feoh pushed aside the accumulated snow from the back of the vehicle. Soon a row of white rear lights shone blearily through a frozen coating of ice. Kano grappled briefly with the hatch release, then the door folded down and they clumped inside, leaving a mess of snowy prints. A few interior lights came on, and the others could see that the air inside the craft hung like a frosty vapour.

'Gone some time,' Skjebne muttered. *I wonder who they had been . . .*

Feoh returned to the hatch and beckoned, though her thoughts were more precise – 'Shamra – Kell, come over to help offload the provisions.'

'Don't worry. If anything tries to get you, I'll run it over.' Skjebne tried to sound confident but looked nervous, and that combination did nothing to reassure the two as they bundled on their outside clothes and hurried down into the snow.

The snow. Kell had seen it in his imagination a thousand times and felt its bite in the All Mother's nightmarish punishments. But this was the first time ever that he had actually stood in it and tilted his face to its fall, and examined a single flake on his fingertip to marvel at its crystal filigree beauty.

'It's lighter than air!' Shamra called through a plume of white breath; though she revised her judgement later when the need came to shovel some aside. But for now there was just the silent wonder of the forest and there at the heart of it, a mystery.

'This is Lagu's machine,' Kano told them as they entered the abandoned Traveller. He held up a belt with a distinctive leather sheath. The knife was still secure inside. 'Something made them leave without taking sensible precautions . . .'

'Then we should learn a wise lesson and be away from here.' Hora was facing the hatch, squinting to see beyond the glare of their own Traveller's lamps; no less alert than Feoh whose look of utter concentration gave Kano some cause for concern.

'What danger?' he wondered, even as he passed Kell and then Shamra a cluster of small boxes and indicated the way back to their machine.

'It's confusing.' Feoh, whose skill was such that she was rarely confused, felt a little tingle of alarm across her neck. 'Something's out there . . . I want to say it's dangerous . . . But I detect only gentleness and silence . . . Like the snow. But not snow.'

Hora walked to the threshold and looked out. 'Confusing is right then. If we can't blast this vehicle out of the way, then I say we must batten ourselves down tight in our own craft and solve the problem in the morning.'

Feoh's intense and serious expression held a moment longer. Then the thread broke and she nodded at the men.

'We should go.'

Far away the particular pattern of the mountains and the line and angle of the valley focused the night wind down through the forest with a gathering intensity as the temperature fell. The effects of it were lessened here deep among the pines, but even so the wind came round with a sudden swirl; it lifted the skirts of the trees' lower branches and the air was instantly filled with a fine frosty powder.

Kell, blinded, gasped as the icy crystals swept into his face. Instinctively he dropped his armful of packages, stumbled forward, fell and cracked his elbow on what must have been the Traveller's hull—

—While Shamra felt herself pushed by the wind three-four-five staggering steps sideways among the huge groaning trunks.

Then the gust was over and the snow itself had thinned to a fine sprinkling of glittering stars. Way above the trees' topmost canopy the night gale roared with a sound that was as meaningless to Shamra as the ocean. There was only that and the faint swish of lower branches – and a song so heart-wrenchingly beautiful it brought the tears instantly to her eyes.

A child was lost and lonely in the wilderness! A little freezing waif had wandered away from all he knew and loved. Shamra's mind was flooded with his fear and despair. Perhaps, she thought, he had strayed from the Traveller when the adults had left. Lagu, or whoever, must have instructed him to stay; but his terror was so great it had overwhelmed his sense and he had gone in search of his parents . . .

The story unfolded with ease inside Shamra's head, while the strain of loss and misery called from the depths of the night.

She was able to regain her bearings. There to the left was the blaze of the Traveller's beams, cutting diagonally away from her. The poor child's siren song came from the opposite direction, but she could easily keep the craft in sight; and if she reached out and touched Feoh's mind with her immediate intention . . .

Something distracted her, a grey and ghostly shape slipping swiftly among the trunks. There, and gone. There, and gone. It was a flickering shade that moved too quickly to make any sense. And all the while Shamra knew that the little boy needed her, and that he too was in terrible danger from these marauding forest spirits.

So it was that indecision trapped her as effectively as a snare.

The apparition assessed the distance swiftly between the youngling and itself. Its muscles gathered their power and then it leaped out from among the trees and came for her, still accelerating in a dead straight run, its mind already enjoying the glory of warm meat and blood and bone.

In that almost-final second Shamra saw its true face: eyes as hot as melted crystal, a long black muzzle and lips drawn back from wet red gums and gleaming fangs.

She had seen nothing like it in Perth, though her ancestry well understood its power and its single terrifying intent.

The creature sprang and Shamra flung up her arms in a useless gesture of protection.

So it was that she missed something even more rapid that hissed through the air and caught the animal at the top of its arc and transfixed it through the middle of its neck.

8

The Shore People

The creature's front paw caught Shamra on the shoulder and batted her easily aside, then dropped down with a thud in the snow nearby raising a small blizzard of flakes. For a few moments it twitched in a death-dance; its life heat faded and the body was still, and two thin trickles of blood ran from its nose.

Shamra's breathing was out of control. She gulped in great draughts of the numbing air and felt her head starting to spin. More of the animals moved with an elegant co-ordination among the trees: so graceful and calculating, they were playing with the darkness and the light.

But the pretence of their illusion was over. The lie of the lost child had given way to a deadlier dream – To terrify their victim all the more, they pushed into her mind anticipations of her own slaughter beneath their crushing, ravaging jaws. Shamra screamed at the pain-that-was-to-come. And her scream saved her, for it gave Hora a bearing on which to aim. A shell exploded from the fire-rod and struck a tree to Shamra's right, taking a great chunk away in a spray of spinning splinters. The impact caused the whole trunk to shudder, dislodging a shower of snowflakes and heavier masses that came pattering down.

Another of the animals appeared. Despite this greater danger to the pack, they were reluctant to relinquish their meal. This next beast came in slinking low to the ground, not to pounce but to bite at Shamra's exposed limbs and right side.

The fire-rod roared again and sent booms echoing away into the forest deeps. But the creature wasn't deterred: it was intelligent enough to realise Hora's tactics, knowing it couldn't be hit without injuring or killing the youngling. Its thin black lips stretched away from its fangs, just as though it was smiling in triumph.

Now the rest of the human pack was assembling ... Clever, as she was, yet slow-moving and weak. The one who carried the fire posed the greatest threat, but the gristle of his neck was unprotected and one bite would be enough to take out the whole throat. Besides that, his eyes were not adapted to the dark: neither he nor his companions knew of the other kin circling round to attack from the direction of the bright-lights.

Shamra calmed her breathing with the greatest of efforts: on the brink of a panic, she had no hope. The long lean doglike creature was watching her from ten paces away. She realised it knew that it had the advantage; folded in shadow, concealed by trees. Hora had little chance of killing it before it reached her – whenever it chose that moment to be. And there was no doubt that the animal was biding its time, revelling in the thought of its victory perhaps ... *Or waiting for more of its kind to gather!*

The intuition was sharp and deep and true, and it was out of her before she could stop it. Feoh picked up on it at once.

'Kano. There are more of them.'

He had also felt the raw edge of Shamra's alarm. Somehow he knew the impulse radiated from her, though he could not have explained how.

While Hora had moved ahead towards Shamra's supposed position, he and Feoh had snatched up smaller firearms from the Traveller and hurried back outside. They were standing in the glare of the forward lamps. Now Kano stepped aside and waited for his eyes to readjust, and in the second of their settling caught sight of the streaking grey shape as it curved round in a wide silent arc, then came hurtling towards him.

Feoh helped quiet his mind as Kano lifted the weapon and fired – and fired for a second time – and at the third attempt hit the creature squarely in the head. On dying it spasmed in the air, lost its momentum and went tumbling by in a spray of crystals.

Two more animals rushed in. Kano concentrated on one and stopped it with his second shot. The other, gathering for the leap, was slammed sideways and pinned to a tree by a long barbed spear that came out of nowhere. The beast writhed and whimpered in its pain. Feoh could not bear it. She sent out the thought-of-ending and the impaled animal relaxed, its eyes closing in a final peace.

Now the balance of the pack had been shattered. The younger neophytes were already losing their nerve and went scattering back into the fathomless trees. The older and more cunning of the kin assessed their chances, and one by one swung their lithe bodies around and loped away in defeat.

Shamra, however, dared not move just yet. The one close to her waited on for a further few seconds; and it startled her to realise that the creature was gleaning her mind, was harvesting her weaknesses and strengths.

Hora, moving cautiously, was coming up slowly behind her, each careful footfall causing the snow crust to creak. The beast looked up from the youngling's tender face into the eyes of the giant fire-carrier and acquiesced on this occasion, accepting downfall in the battle. But the greater war would continue, with neither side sure of victory.

Hora tensed as the animal lifted itself up effortlessly, turned with a fine disdain and trotted haughtily back into the forest. Hora knew he could have discharged the weapon then, could have smashed the predator's ribs or flanks. But while it was savage in hunting, it was not barbaric by nature and killed only to eat.

So he lowered the fire-rod, deciding he would be no less noble than these prowlers of the wilderness.

Kell came running and skidding through the snow, gathered Shamra up and sobbed and shook with her while their fear calmed. There was a sense of safety in the air now; the pack in leaving had taken away the tension.

Hora moved around to the other side of the Traveller, where Kano and Feoh and Skjebne were examining the carcass speared to the tree.

'The weapon has been well crafted,' Hora observed. Kano ran his fingers along the blade's barbs.

'Well made and well hurled.' He turned to face the forest and the hurler.

'It's there,' Feoh said. *It-he-she-them*, the impression would not stay still!

Kano laid down his weapon and held up his open hands. There was movement among the trees and a figure stepped out; then a second, third and fourth. Feoh frowned, because her instincts continued to register just one being, its mind as fine-tuned and clear as a single held note of perfect pitch.

These people were graceful and slim under their heavy pelts, and possessed of a deep understanding. Their mindskills seemed very different from Feoh's own; powerful in other ways. Something about them was unutterably strange, but like branches of the one tree, they and these renegades of Perth shared the same roots.

'We thank you! I am Kano. I and my friends are travellers through your land! . . . I think they understand us.' Kano kept his voice low and confidential, and Feoh laughed.

'No doubt of it. This is the leader of the Shore People. His name is Faras.'

She indicated the foremost of the strangers, and touched her own forehead to tell him that she too could speak without voice and see without eyes. He nodded and came forward ahead of his party.

'There is some confusion,' said Faras. 'We heard cries – mind cries that your friend Feoh will comprehend. And we set out to help. But we find you here, and you are not the ones who called . . .'

The man's accent gave the words a certain roundness. He spoke swiftly and ran the sounds together so that their meanings were all but lost. They were, though, accompanied by a powerful mental imagery that helped to clarify his purpose.

'Then we are too late, Kano.' Skjebne pointed back towards the empty Traveller. 'Lagu and the rest must have been tempted out, as Shamra was almost enchanted and then spirited away.'

'That seems to be the truth of it. The ways of the Wulfen are quick and clean and very effective.'

Faras went on to explain that these pack animals worked with cunning. Like most of the forest creatures their unseen and subtle senses were developed to a very high degree. 'In the dark and the snowgloom, the fear of a victim shines like a beacon fire. The Wulfen have minds that can pick it out half a day's journey away. They are our oldest enemies. They have grown and changed with us, and as much as we have done, at least until our recent generations. But this story is longer than your ability to outlast the cold! We can offer you shelter, and by using your travel machines we will reach it quickly.'

Kano accepted gladly and, not knowing the etiquette of these people, removed his glove and held out his hand for Faras to shake. The Shoreman did likewise, causing Kano to jolt as he saw by the light of the Traveller's lamps the pale membrane webbed between the other's splayed fingers.

Skjebne decided on his first Golden Rule for survival beyond the enclave. Use Everything. So, while their initial plan had been to strip Lagu's Traveller of its provisions, the wiser course was to take the second machine along with their own. A brief examination confirmed the craft were identical and, since Kano had experience of working the vehicle, he was voted unanimously to be its driver.

So Kano, Feoh and their hosts used one Traveller; while Skjebne, Hora, Kell and Shamra followed in the other. It did not take long for Faras to discover – much to Skjebne's embarrassment – that the means existed for them to talk between the two Travellers by speaking into a silver wand positioned near the mapping screen. Shamra gave out a thin squeal when Kano's voice came out of the very air, close beside her ears.

'My feeling is,' said Skjebne by way of defence, 'that a treasure hoard of unknown devices must exist within these machines. Only time and curiosity will uncover them for us—'

'And a little good fortune,' Kano replied. 'Faras tells me that his people have seen vehicles something like this before. They came from a place he calls West. They carried traders and their goods – Do you realise, Skjebne, that we are not the first! Others, many others, must have escaped from their enclaves. And they have survived . . .'

'Often with a struggle,' added Faras. 'And sometimes by sheer good fortune, as in our case, as you will see.'

They travelled on through the night, and beyond it into a fog-laden iron–grey dawn. At the outset, the incline of the path (a traders' route, Faras explained) was clear; but gradually the ground levelled and they made better progress on the flat, especially so given the sleek curvatures of the travel machines that clove through the drifts, and the powerful side vents that all but completed the clearing.

An infinite distance away to the left, the freezing haze took light and shone like pearl. The fog stirred in the morning's first warmth; a meagre beginning, but one that would see the mist burnt off by midday and a glorious blue afternoon.

Just as ripples from a dropped stone circle out through the water, without sound, without effort, so Faras sent his thoughts to the enclave-dwellers who had emerged like blind and innocent children from the egg. He edited his histories carefully, for too much knowledge all at once – like too much liquor – is not good for the heart. He offered them a perspective on the region; of the mountain range a day's good journey from the sea; and of the sea itself, almost entirely encircled by land, with a narrow outlet to the greater ocean. He conveyed what he could of the Wulfen and their eternal impulse, and the imperative of all creatures – to live . . .

At this point Skjebne interrupted with words, since the speed and subtlety of Faras's inner communication was dizzying.

'So is it the case that all higher animals have the mindskills we've seen in Feoh and Shamra and yourselves—'

'I don't know quite what you mean by "higher" animals, since even the bees can tell where the pollen is found, and the salmon return without fail to the same river to spawn. And in these creatures, who you might not think are intelligent, there is an essence; and this essence threads them like beads on a necklace, or more truly like raindrops on a spiderweb.'

Skjebne was not sure his question had been answered. Faras continued with patience.

'Beyond that, all the spiderwebs of all the different kinds of creatures are connected. Some do not realise it. Most realise they do not need to let it trouble them. Does that make sense? All things, in the struggle to become, express what they are in ways beyond words. In Feoh's case, and in Shamra's, the controlling influence of the enclave has engineered their skills. Here in the outer world more natural forces have forged us – although our suspicion is that the people who lived before the Ice took a hand in crafting their own descendants. But once we, the Shore People, started to move along this route, so the Wulfen somehow were drawn in our direction. As our minds became more obviously joined, so did those of the forest packs.'

'You talk about your minds,' Feoh said, 'but I can read only one, which is yours. How is that possible?'

'The joining is completed, and "I" do not exist. Faras is the name my body takes. "I" have no individual identity.'

And Feoh understood why. Underlying all of Faras's explanations was the ambient imagery of the sea. The Wulfen, down a thousand generations, had hounded the Shore People out of their original territory in the hills. Eventually, trapped on the thin coastal strip, they had faced a collective decision. And they had made their choice. Within a very short time – the anticipation of it burned like the sun in Faras's mind – his children's children would take to the sea as a single school and leave the land behind forever.

'Though in thwarting the Wulfen we will take on a range of new and interesting problems, no doubt,' he concluded, smiling. And his guests appreciated his humour, and knew it would be a help to him during all of the challenges to come.

Kell's mind was still struggling with big puzzles.

'We have noticed your changes – your adaptations to the life you have chosen. How has that happened so quickly?'

'I will show you later,' Faras replied, and would say no more on the matter.

'They have a guide,' Shamra whispered in Kell's ear, as

Faras turned his attention away. She looked distracted for a moment; listening. Kell realised that she was communicating with Feoh, and that the two of them shared this powerful secret gift that might always exclude him.

'What kind of guide?'

'Faras's impressions are being carefully hidden . . .' She gazed at her hand and frowned, flexed her fingers and shook her head in disbelief. 'We don't understand . . . Feoh also thinks we should wait for Faras to explain.' Shamra's expression cleared and she leaned close to Kell and slipped her arm around his own. 'This is all so strange – but so wonderful and exciting—'

'And dangerous,' Kell replied seriously. 'That Wulf could have killed you.'

'But it didn't. Maybe we have a guide also,' she suggested frivolously.

Kell felt angry towards her, because he was envious of the way she and Feoh linked mind-to-mind. The trait had always been stronger on the female side in Perth, but this bond had formed very quickly, out of necessity, ignoring the usual rituals of preparation – and Kell felt excluded.

'Blind chance,' he said sullenly. 'That's all survival can ever be. Blind chance.'

He watched her bright face darken and took a mean pleasure from it, then turned to stare out of the window; though in fact he stared at his own reflection, not liking what he saw.

After a lengthy journey they broke from the trees and left the last of the ice-mist behind. Over the shoulder of the Travellers a bright sun was breaking and all the world began to glitter. They reached a broad stretch of scrubby ground still white with frost, and pocked with thorny bushes that sported metallic looking armoured fruit. Faras conveyed an impression of Shore children scattering the spiky fruits around the village as protection against Wulfen beasts slinking in under cover of the night. When stepped on, the husks shattered like razor sharp glass, and released a noxious gas that clung to the Wulfen beasts' fur for days and made their lives unbearable.

'These bushes are the great survivors!' Faras joked as they trundled between the dunes and came out into a nestling of rounded low dwellings made of a shell-like substance and covered over with turf. Even from a short distance away the little village cluster would be all but invisible.

Skjebne brought the Traveller to a halt a few furrow-lengths from the settlement and shut down the big engines. Lights continued to blink and flicker on the panels in front of him since the mind of the machine, like that of a man, functioned even while the body was asleep. Kano parked the second craft beside the first, and a few minutes were spent hauling the canvases over.

A number of the Shore community came out from their homes to stare at the strangers – though Feoh more clearly than anyone understood how strictly unnecessary this was: Faras had communicated a vast swathe of impressions to his people on the journey through the forest, such that everything he knew about the travellers, so did the rest of his tribe.

One dwelling was bigger than the others, a communal hall within which a small central fire was burning. A table had been laid out and decorated with coloured pebbles and shells, and set with plates of delicacies; all unfamiliar, and a few of which were moving.

Kell's idea of food had been put into his head by dear Munin – well-cooked vegetables and meat, fruit and nuts and occasionally a pastry pudding to follow. He had rarely eaten fish or other waterfood from Central Lake, and was highly suspicious now of all that was strange.

It is polite to sample from several dishes, Feoh advised him, since Kell's intention had been to say he was wasn't hungry. But first came greetings from Faras's colleagues, open-mind-messages of welcome conveying more warmth than words ever could. And, as it must be with children from all times and all places, so the youngsters of this village pushed and jostled into the hall for a closer look at the strangers.

'You may stay as long as you wish,' Faras invited, though his tone was careful. He understood what these enclave people were feeling – that here was a refuge beyond the power of the one they called the Goddess; a place of simple peace where, perhaps, the beginnings of a new life might be found.

Feoh took Faras's cold hand between her warm fingers before Kano could answer.

'A few suns' rest, and then we will be on our way. We thank you for the chance to refresh ourselves, and to learn a little of your customs. The more we learn, the better our chances will be.'

'Well, there's knowing,' Faras said with a smile, 'and there's understanding.' And quite deliberately, he offered Kell a bowl of the most strikingly coloured food.

Kell startled and was about to draw back, but Feoh's wisdom soaked through him, so that he made a little bow of respect and put his fingers into the raw fish flesh and selected a few of the morsels.

They tasted surprisingly good, in a cold and fishy kind of way; juices and savours cascading through Kell's mouth as he chewed. The others took their lead from the boy, and piled titbits into scallop-shell saucers and ate – Hora doing so with especial relish, until one little ball of pink meat unravelled into a wriggling mass of tentacles and two black button-bead eyes looked up pleadingly into his own.

After the meal all the Shore younglings were sent from the

139

hall and Faras and a few of the other adults sat at the fire with their guests. There was drink; a bitter and, as it turned out, a very potent beverage made from the pulp of the armour-fruit. And there was smoke-leaf which the Shore people puffed with great gusto and which Shamra and Kell avoided entirely.

Then the storying began, and words were used extensively out of respect for Kano and the other male travellers who were not as adept as the females at the craft of inner tuition.

Kano's account of life in Perth, coloured and textured by contributions from his friends, amounted to a straightforward description of how life had been, and the way of their escape.

'It's not much of a tale,' he admitted when it was done. 'And we can talk only of our part in it. My hope is that many groups found freedom. Some, like Lagu's party, were unlucky. But ill-fortune has no favourites, and so I'm confident that others will travel this way.'

'Spores from a burst pod.' Faras nodded agreement. 'I'm sure it will be so.'

For his part, Faras joined with the minds of his people and presented tales of fabulous proportions. The Shore tribe had grown against the backdrop of the Ice. Their ancestors, reaching as far back as the global cold itself, had always been hunters and gatherers, living on the fringes of the great ice rivers, the glaciers that had come down through the mountain ranges year by year and decade on decade.

'Even then inexplicable forces worked on the glacier creatures. We have racial memories of beasts appearing suddenly, without progenitors. We wondered how that could be, and it was for a long time a very great mystery to us. Only recently have we come to some kind of understanding.

'Of these new species; sometimes we found ourselves in conflict with their ways, and at other times we could live harmoniously together. Gradually we moved to the margins of the land, as we have explained. At last, as the ice made its slow retreat, so the forests proliferated and out of them, like a bad seed, came the Wulfen.

'But everything has its purpose,' Faras went on. 'And through the Wulfen and their ruthless predations we came to choose our future.' He held up his webbed hand and Kell gazed fascinated at the network of veins and capillaries as the firelight glowed through the membrane.

'That is an important point. We *chose*, as you did. And because of that we will always be linked.'

Kell's heart was touched with a strange sadness to think that some time quite soon, the Shore People would be gone, their shell houses lying empty on this forgotten beach . . . For the sea seemed such a vast and cold and distant place away from the quickening pulse of the land.

Listen to what Faras is saying, came Feoh's soft thought in his head. *Distance and physical separation are not the same things, and never have been . . .*

Kell knew her intervention was meant to comfort him, and normally it would have done. But something else was gathering in his mind – in all of their minds – some huge anticipation that had no form or explanation. Skjebne and Hora were quite clearly startled by it, and Kano, instantly alert, felt threatened. His hand moved automatically towards the knife in his belt, until Feoh reached out and gripped his fingers, restraining him.

Shamra leaned close in to Kell, and her breath was coming quickly with astonished expectation.

'It's out at sea,' she whispered as the immense, profound, benign visitor filled their hearts and the entire hall and every house in the little village with its presence.

'What is it?' Feoh wondered at last, and truly didn't know

– though she realised more clearly than her companions that it represented the Shore People's salvation.

Faras smiled broadly, delighted at the reaction of his guests.

'I promised Kell earlier that I would explain the process of our changes. The time has come! Put on your coats and let us go to meet the tide.'

Faras led the party out of the hall and along the beach, away from the village. A number of his kinfellows accompanied them; tall, slim, quiet people whose bodies already predicted the streamlining their sons and daughters would need for the ocean. Feoh especially was pleased to be in their company, which was in itself an education. If the mind of Kano or Skjebne or Kell was a flame burning with its own individual light, the all-as-one soul of the Shorefolk glowed around them and through them, with no distinctions to be made.

Farther along, towards the cliffs of black rock which sheltered the beach and formed the curve and cusp of the bay, a thin rickety structure had been built: it was a path of wooden slats supported by stilts lashed together and strengthened with cross-pieces. It stretched out for many paces into the water, and Kell had assumed it was used as a platform for fishing.

'We're going *there* to see – it?' He couldn't keep the nervousness out of his voice.

'The ocean walker will not harm you,' Faras said. They arrived at the landing and, as a gentle test of Kell's trust, Faras invited the boy to go first.

It was late afternoon and the sun hung low in the sky to their left. Even in the few minutes walk from the village, it had visibly reddened and dropped closer to the horizon. Kell reminded himself to ask Faras more about why that was so. But for now his immediate circumstances took up all of his attention . . .

The pier was reached by means of a twelve-step ladder made of stout sticks. Kell hauled himself up and was only mildly disconcerted as the rungs creaked beneath his feet, and the structure moved as Faras and then the others began to climb.

At the top, Kell walked a few paces out along the path. A thin breeze blew here, keen as a glass edge, and the smell of the sea was salt and sharp.

Faras joined him and walked with him out beyond the shoreline as the water beneath changed from greygreen to aquamarine to a deep and translucent blue.

Much farther out, something broke surface and rose up clear of the water, and flopped back with a splash in a ragged coronet of white foam.

'What is that!'

'They are the herd seals, the outriders – But look, look beyond!'

So Kell looked and for a few moments could only see the sleek black shapes of seals streaking beneath the surface, zigzagging this way and that. The animals were bigger than moxen ... Then behind them, miraculous and impossible, something a hundred times larger was cruising in from the far ocean depths.

9

The Last Great Whale

Skjebne, the man of science, exclaimed aloud at this thing which challenged all of his precious beliefs. Hora, the Shield, took a step back and then stood his ground, determined to die unflinching. Kell's impulse was to climb quickly down from the landing and to run and run until he was sure this vast monster could not get at him. The women, moist-eyed from the wind and what they had already understood, imparted their trust to the men and so saved them face as Faras lifted his arms and shouted a greeting across the dark water.

An island, low and glossy and black, heaved up from the sea and sank back again, sending a slow swell rolling in across the beach.

The platform will be washed away!

Kell's panic-thought escaped like a flash.

'Very easily,' Faras confirmed. 'And that was our intention. By standing on this fragile pier we show our faith in the Seetus. By allowing it to remain intact, the Seetus shows his faith in us.'

Kell thought the sense of it was sound, but that still couldn't stop him clinging nervously to Skjebne as the colossus rose again, showing a great curved back and, many paces behind that, a graceful fork-fluked tail that whacked back down on the water with a loud slap; and then the beast's huge head, as big as Hora's fishing skiff, that lifted level with the platform so that the landfolk and the giant of the sea could regard each other eye to eye.

'They have come from a place in the mountains,' Faras explained – pointlessly, Feoh felt, for the Seetus had already swept up all of their thoughts with the inexpressible power of its mind. Its own inner voice, which filled their heads now, deep and sombre and profound, boomed out massively and for some reason seemed to be directed at Kell.

You are bigger than your size, landling, and as fragile as a shell.
Do not be fooled by others.
If you meet the Goddess on the road – kill her.
If you meet your sister – kill her.
Don't hesitate. Kill them all!
It's the only way.

Kell was awash with confusion. He glanced at Faras for guidance, then at Kano, Feoh, Skjebne – and met the same blankness, so that finally he was forced again to look into the tiny glittering eye of the Seetus and admit his own ignorance.

'I don't understand you. I'm sorry.'

You cannot read the path until you have become that path yourself.
From the beginning, nothing has been kept from you.
It is only you that has closed your eyes to the fact.

'How do I open my eyes then?'

How do I hold on to the water?

'That's not an answer!'

I have no answers to teach you, and if I tried you might well make fun of me.

Kell clenched his teeth in frustration, but Faras was smiling as though this was all a fine joke.

'He does not mean to infuriate you. His teachings are elusive only because you try to learn – and then, thinking you now understand, try not to try.'

'So how then *do* I learn?'

Faras immediately dug in his pocket and pulled out a small white globe which he pressed into Kell's hand and told him to eat. Kell did so, and at once spat the ball out, finding it unbearably salty. He began to splutter an apology, but Faras was laughing and the mind of the Seetus was still.

'So, Kell, how would you teach your friend Shamra about salt?'

And Kell held out his hand for a globe.

Even so, as an hour went by and the sun swung slowly towards the sea, they asked the creature many questions and the Seetus, not in such a mischievous mood, answered them simply and plainly. Because of the cold, they had need to move about constantly and to rub the circulation into their fingers and hands. But the Seetus seemed oblivious of it all, as though in body as much as in mind he did not entirely exist in this world.

He explained that in past ages there had been more of his kind, although before the ice the great whales had dwindled in number until they were almost extinguished.

But the engineers realised that what cannot survive on the land might flourish in the seas. And so they created my ancestors. While the ice engulfed the continents, men played with the threads of life and embroidered many new breeds.

'They made you?' Skjebne wondered, amazed.

They made what became me, and what I am to become. Because they didn't understand, the world is as it is. Because I understand, the world is as it is . . .

Kell opened his mouth to query, but closed it again as he remembered the pellet of salt.

What is the difference between a dead fish and a live one? The fishermen on the surface of the ocean have never known. But the Shore Folk know, and there are others in many places across the world who are trying to find out.

'Will they succeed, do you think?'

Do I think? All I can say is that the wish to be makes you wise. But the wish to have makes you foolish.

Then a change came in the evening around them as the last thin arc of the sun's red disc sank below the horizon. The air was very calm, but there was a deepening frost that must soon drive the party back indoors to the warmth of their fires.

The whale sensed their need and began to draw away from the pier: water sucked back and sloshed and gurgled about its supports.

Kell thought then that the creature would disappear from view and that would be the last he'd see of it. But there was something more, a final gift that was to stay with each of them for all the days of their life.

The big swift outrider seals were leaping and splashing about the enormous body of the Seetus. And yet its mind seemed tiny now like a minute seed you could hold in your hand . . . Kell gazed at his hand and the seed opened and bloomed. The hand was a wing, then a flipper, then a stranger's hand while all of the cells spiralled and danced as the seals had just done. Everything seemed possible in time, and time was only a dream and awakening was imminent.

Faras again lifted his arms, called thanks, and made the mantra of parting as the Seetus sank below the waves.

'He was born alone, and he will die alone. But he carries the whole world with him now.'

And without having to think about it, and without being able to explain it, Kell knew what Faras meant and realised it was absolutely true.

They walked briskly back then towards the village, and as they approached the low grassy humps of the Shore People's houses, Kell noticed that a shadow was moving ahead of him – his own; a crisp blue shadow cast on the beach's flat sand.

He stopped and turned and was startled at the round white light that must have just lifted clear of the dunes.

'It's only the moon.' Faras told them, delighted at their amazement. 'Tonight it is a Whole Moon. Soon, in a week, it will be a broken moon and rising much later into the night . . .'

Kell's imagination conjured a much smaller disc for the 'broken moon', but Faras perceived the mistake and corrected it.

'But what *is it*?' Shamra wanted to know.

'We think it's another place, a long long way from here. Since it is up in the sky, you cannot walk to it—'

'Then how?'

'We asked the Seetus if he had swum the ocean of the night. And he said "Why would I wish to go there when I am here?" So, we are none the wiser for that!'

Faras indulged his guests as they stood and gazed at the whole and perfect moon with a simple wonder. After many minutes Feoh put her arms around Shamra's shoulders.

'She's shivering. Let's go in.' Her voice like the sea was calm and flat and gave nothing away.

They returned to the hall to eat a final small meal, before going to the dwellings they had been offered for the duration of their stay. Very soon, and warm once more, they chattered and joked and went over their meeting with the whale again and again, and what his words might have meant.

'He seemed to be saying that all of us can change, like Faras and his people are changing.' Shamra had thought about this very deeply. She was sitting beside Kell and they had nuzzled against each other with an ease and an innocence that they had rarely enjoyed in Perth.

'And we can create those changes for ourselves,' Shamra added. She tilted her head to look at Kell's face. 'So chance is not blind. It has eyes, and a mind, and a sense of direction . . .'

He chuckled lazily, being too warm and comfortable and filled up with food to argue.

'That is very subversive. The tutors would say that only the All Mother, and only in Perth, can our fate be guided.'

'The Seetus would disagree, and Faras would ask you to chew salt.' Shamra smiled mischievously and felt closer to Kell in this moment than she had ever done before.

'And those changes happen in the flesh, because . . . Because flesh and thoughts and the world are all one thing—'

She sat up and glanced sharply at Feoh, but the woman was lost in conversation with the other adults and hadn't influenced Shamra's ideas at all.

'Well . . .' Kell stretched and yawned. 'Everything you say is probably completely correct, and I wouldn't dream of arguing. What will happen will happen, one way or another.'

'But we can still choose,' Shamra said softly. 'Whatever does happen, we can still choose.'

And the boy, dazed in his langour, failed to pay much attention, or see the tears in her eyes.

By and by Skjebne came and prodded the half-asleep youngsters and encouraged them to join in the circle. The men indulged in too much smoke-leaf, and even the sensible Feoh drank one cupful too many of the delicious armour-fruit wine. Kell and Shamra were sometimes helpless with laughter as Hora told his fisherman's tales . . . And sometimes they wept quietly as Kano relived with them the horrors of Perth and the death of their good friend Birca.

So the night wore on; the moon gazed down; and a white star sailed silently over the village, and then disappeared swiftly inland.

The dark was deeper than the cold. Kell woke, troubled by

the nothingness. Within the enclave – until the last terrible day – he had always felt safe. Inside the Traveller's robust and powerful shell, he had always likewise felt safe. But now with the whole wide unknown world about him, and the others asleep and half stupefied from their revelry, Kell was touched by apprehension. He became very still and let himself sink back into the silence and belong to it. And out of that silence came the merest clink of metal, the tiniest crush of dust under a careful footfall . . .

He had drifted to sleep by the greenish light of a luminous seashell, but gradually the glow had faded with Kell's consciousness and now was entirely gone. Faras had explained how chambers within the shell contained a radiant liquid, which could to some small extent be revived by shaking.

With the utmost caution, and feeling his heart beginning to race quite against his will, Kell reached out to where he knew the shell would be. He felt the cold curved edge of the little table at his bedside, then the delicate spirals and minarets of the seashell itself. He lifted it, remembering its weight, and tilted it this way and that—

A faint green shine came back to life.

In the doorway stood an insect shape as tall as a man; it had steel surfaces and probing antennae and a wicked black eye as glossy as a chestnut.

Kell cried out and hurled the shell. It shattered against the intruder and splashed it over with moonlight. The insect made a high chittering noise and swiftly withdrew.

Its action was surprising, since Kell had been fully convinced the invader would attack. Now with a surging confidence-in-triumph to balance his fear, Kell jumped up from the bed and set up a great commotion of shouting and crashing about in the room as he made his way to the door. He caught a fractional glimpse of the tall spindly figure darting into the night. It took three swift balletic steps towards safety, before something whipped sideways and wrapped around its thin neck and tangled up about its head.

The insect staggered and made feeble attempts to free itself. Then Hora's big bulk came running into view. Without hesitation he smashed into the thing and used his weight to drive it down to the ground.

A probe swished out and split the skin under Hora's left eye. Faras appeared with four – five – of his kind. He dashed forward and drove a spike through the insect's grey carapace. The hole spat fire and sparks. The trespasser thrashed, but its fight was finished. Its body trembled briefly and then all its limbs relaxed with a tinkling of metals.

'What is it?'

Faras's answer arrived in Kell's head before he had voiced the question.

I have not seen anything like it – There are others!

The warning came from another of the Shore Folk on the far side of the village. Kell had time to appreciate how effective the tribe's onemindedness was, before he was running with Hora and Faras through the freezing dark among a puzzle of shadows cast by figures carrying more of the glow-shells. Kano appeared, weary-eyed but furious at this slip in his defences. Feoh, somewhere nearby but unseen, was radiating a powerful concern.

'It's Shamra! They have come for Shamra!' The final word ended in a sob of grief and loss, and because the cold air was cutting Kell's throat. His lungs were filled with it, like a weight of dead iron.

There were more insect figures, lean swift scurrying shapes among the turfed-over houses. Kell felt Faras's clear thought cleave through the minds of his kin: they separated, each intent upon the one task. And as the Shore People moved in their beautifully co-ordinated way, Kell was reminded of the

Wulfen and how they too had worked together, locked into the dance of their single bright purpose.

'Stay with me, boy. Stay close!' was Hora's gruff command. Kell was too numbed and too painfully cold to think otherwise. He had not had time to put on his overjacket and was now shivering violently. They reached the middle of the village. Two of the Shore People came hurrying over with Hora's fire-rod, which they had brought from his dwelling. Skjebne followed carrying other weapons. This time he pushed one of the smaller wands into the boy's hands, and a spark of pride lit in Kell's chest.

'They don't seem to be attacking people,' Skjebne said, 'but rather just causing some – confusion—'

Far away, somehow cobwebby but clear and loud at one and the same time, Feoh's mind-voice rose above the general turmoil and brought a crystal understanding. The insect servants were no more than a distraction, a magician's sly trick to hide the truth.

'This way,' Faras said, running with a few of his kind between the houses. The luminous shells bobbed and dwindled in the dark, leaving a pale wash of moonlight behind.

Kell's eyes were streaming and he whimpered softly with his burden of hurt. But the pictures in his head were bright and sharp through Feoh's powerful gift . . .

Among the dunes, in the soft sandy hollows below the killing wind, stood a cadre of armoured men. A number of the insect forms scuttled and busied, attending a strange machine. One of the men barked words in an unknown tongue. The others began to climb aboard in their slow lumbering way.

Shamra was already inside!

The intuition came as a staggering blow, and Kell did not doubt it. Feoh was there crouched down amidst the wiregrass, overseeing the scene. She had followed Shamra's calls of distress to this place, but dared not go further for the enemy seemed cunning and well-organised and strong.

The insect devices began to disappear inside the craft like ants seeking the nest: a few slotted on to the ship's outer hull and locked themselves smartly in place. Many were not returning, it seemed, caught by the Shore Folk's rapid retaliation. Some small fighting was still going on in the village, and the insects would be crushed, their loss part of the intruders' greater winning.

'Can't we do something? Can't we stop them?' Kell's words came out flat and hopeless: anaesthetised by the cold and stunned by the sheer smooth efficiency of the invaders' attack, Kell felt wooden and pathetic, with his unprimed weapon useless in his hands. Not even his anger and grief could rouse him to faster action now. He moved his puppet body over the crest of the dune and trudged down into dry sand that slid away beneath and left him floundering.

A shadowy bulk and a slipstream of freezing air swept by. Hora pounded past and in a fury that Kano would later call foolish, hurled himself at the rearguard and smashed the armoured man off his feet. Around the metallic shell of the ship the insects stirred and bristled. A few gazed down at the scene below through their bejewelled eyes, but were detached from it. They already sensed the vehicle in final preparation to depart.

Get away from there now!

Feoh's warning cracked like a whiplash and stopped Hora dead in his tracks. He jerked upright and blinked away a storm of dazzling lights before his eyes. For a moment he swayed, faint and disoriented, then made sense of the signal and started to stagger away—

The hand of a giant caught him midstride and flung him like a broken doll ten paces upwards and twenty paces out.

The world tumbled about and went spinning over, and Hora seemed to fall upwards into a hard flat ceiling of sand that slammed the breath and the fight and the last sparks of consciousness out of him.

From their vantage point on the dune-top, Kell and the others watched the thin air ripple like liquid. A beautiful indentation, smooth as an egg, appeared in the sand around the vehicle. There came a deep resonance and a rising whining note: the machine lifted hesitantly like a weight precariously balanced – then soared and curved away swiftly and became a star among a night filled with stars, and was gone.

There was a moment of silence and stillness and shock, like a vacuum.

Feoh broke cover and ran towards where Hora was lying, reading ahead of herself his dimmed and disjointed thoughts. Kell, Kano, Faras and other Shore Folk walked more slowly down into the depression and stood around the smoothly sculpted crater the craft had left behind; and the crushed and splintered body of the guard.

'What is it?' Faras wanted to know – he, and the rest of his curious kin. Kano prodded the wreckage with his boot. Something had changed the structure of the armour so that now the steel crumbled like dried leaves, caved in to show hollows and ribs and blackened stuff, the remains of what had once been a man.

Kell was sickened by it, but more profoundly upset by the fact that Shamra had been taken. *Why?* was all he wanted to know, but on this matter the adults in whom he had placed his trust stayed silent.

'I only know is that she is alive.' Feoh spoke up from where she knelt over Hora's unconscious body. 'Frightened and confused, but alive.' The impression came to her of great height and great purpose; of circumstances meshing like immense gears. She seemed to be moving through oceans of stars, all hung in a wonderful weave of filigree light. It was too complex and too exquisite to dwell upon – Feoh's imagination failed her and all she had then was a memory-image of Perth; a garden and some toys and sunlight flickering down between the plumage of vast warm wings. It was Shamra's safe haven, the place where her mind had gone to be far away from the terror.

Hora groaned and flopped over on to his side. His eyes opened and he frowned, because all he had in his mind were mysteries.

'He landed on his head. He'll be all right.' Feoh smiled thinly, stood up and walked away from her friends, making light of the moment because anything else would betray her own fear.

'At least we can safely guess they would not capture her just to kill her.' Faras spoke confidentially close to Kano's ear. His common sense was a very small consolation. 'And however we can help you, so we will.'

Kano accepted the reassurance respectfully. But his thoughts were bleak; for if he had learned anything at all in his small and bitter life it was that worse things existed than death.

There was no more sleep that night. A group of the Shore Folk buried the body of the invader guard where it had fallen. No words were spoken and no ceremony followed. It was just an act of necessity. Then the whole population, bar the children who were told to stay indoors, scoured the ground around the village for any further clues. Kell was mildly surprised to be included among the searchers, and guessed it was significant that Kano had not asked for his weapon to be returned. Perhaps he was accepting Kell into his adult world. Or maybe in the aftermath of the crisis it was merely an oversight.

They searched at first by the light of the luminous shells, and then in the gathering glow of the dawn. A pinkness strengthened in the calm layered cloud beyond the hills inland, and by the time the first rays broke through, Kell was sure that their journey lay in that direction.

'Nothing.' Skjebne scuffed at a pebble in the sand and turned it over with his boot. Nothing to tell them who the invaders had been or why they had chosen Shamra – for a choice it had certainly been, carried out with stealth and cunning and impressive precision.

'Who knew of us to find us here?' Hora wondered. 'The Wulfen?'

'No,' Faras said. 'The forest packs keep to themselves and have no trade with men. At least that has been our experience. People have nothing to give them that they would want, or could not hunt out for themselves—'

He glanced pointedly at Kano. 'And we have already pledged you our friendship and help. How can you cruelly suspect us now?'

'Because I am tired and frightened and I have no answers to any of this . . . I apologise for my thought. It is not meant.'

Faras came over and clasped Kano's hand in his own, and the token was accepted and the pact between them strengthened.

The party trudged back towards the settlement, pausing on the outskirts to look over the pile of insect machines that had been collected and dumped there earlier.

'We will throw them into the sea today,' Faras declared. 'Where the water will rust them and the salt will corrode them away.'

Skjebne nodded his approval. He picked over the wreckage, checking that all of the devices were inert, and at one point bent down to recover something that caught his eye.

The others gathered round to look, though only the travellers understood what the glass lens might mean.

'No. The All Mother can't be out here . . .' Feoh's voice was a whisper. She touched the smooth black surface of her mask. 'She is . . .'

'We don't know that. The glass might be a coincidence, or perhaps these machines were built before the Ice.'

Kano was about to snatch the lens away and dash it to the ground, but Skjebne closed his fist around it and smiled in a devious way.

'All we have done so far is destroy things,' he pointed out. 'That has brought us here but has not allowed us to understand very much. There may be meanings inside the glass. Wouldn't it be better to find them out? Don't you think that answers would make better weapons than questions?'

Kano weighed the dilemma up in his mind but couldn't reach a decision.

Hora said, 'We have two Travellers now, which means that not all of us would come under the thrall of the lens if that was its danger. And Feoh would know – she would sense at once if the thoughts of the Goddess emerged from the glass.'

Skjebne could not help but smile at the big man with his bruised face and his simple solid reasoning. 'He has a point, Kano. His way we get the best of both curiosity and caution.'

'Then keep the thing,' Kano said brusquely before he was caught up in more doubt. 'But if there is the faintest suspicion of danger from it, I will destroy it myself immediately!'

As the morning brightened Kell felt an increasing urgency to leave. The sky ship had travelled at great speed and could be a vast distance away by now, and growing farther. He checked with Feoh a number of times that she still kept a sense of Shamra's presence. And the woman answered him tolerantly each time that yes, the link was there – but becoming more tenuous as one hour and then two hours went by.

'And do you know,' Feoh confided with a kind of amazement, 'I think that the Seetus has a role in all of this. He keeps secrets that he cannot tell, but that people throughout all the lands are looking for. The idea comes to me that whatever we do, and however we make our way, it is part of a pattern that is still being built . . . Do I make sense?'

Feoh chuckled: she was asking it of herself. 'Of course I don't! Because the pattern is not yet complete. Perhaps it never will be, or maybe even if it were we would fail to recognise it.'

'Now you are *talking* like the Seetus,' Kell said. He was reminded of what Shamra said to him the evening before and felt marginally better. 'So I know your insight is sound.'

Shortly afterwards, as his friends packed up their few belongings and Hora and Skjebne rekindled the engines of the Travellers, Kell walked down to the edge of the sea and stared out over the flatcalm water. There was nothing to be seen – no gigantic seals or the vastly greater bulk of the Seetus; only the clean line between ocean and sky that marked the limits of the world.

Or did it? If Kell had learned anything at all it was that limits are illusions and that the unseen exists as surely as anything visible.

It was a comforting thought, and one that would need to sustain him in the days and weeks to come.

The Shore Folk had suffered some injuries but no fatalities in the attack. Kano paid the courtesy of visiting every one who had fought on Shamra's behalf. He thanked them simply, since that was the only gift he could offer, but the best.

'I hope we meet again,' he said to one. And Faras, behind him, put a hand on his shoulder.

'If you come by in the future you will not find us here. The changes in the flesh of our children are gathering pace. The sea is calling, and we cannot resist its song for much longer. But the links between us will never be broken, Kano. Our brief time together is woven into what we are to become. Let us take that with us on our own separate ways.'

Seriously, but not solemnly, each of the travellers shook the hand of Faras, and in so doing said farewell to all of his kin.

Then they walked together a little beyond the village to where the vehicles were waiting. Kell climbed aboard one with Skjebne and Feoh. Kano and Hora took the other.

There was a small window set in the rear hatch. Kell gazed through it intently, wiping the breath-mist away again and again, as Faras and his people dwindled, and their homes dropped out of sight behind the dunes, and the swathes of armour-fruit bushes beyond gave the land a scrubby and abandoned look.

Soon the place of the Shore Folk could not be seen at all. Presently the Travellers entered the trees. And shortly afterwards the snow once more began to fall.

10

Trade Ways

Several suns and moons went by, and Faras's observations proved correct: the Whole Moon soon wore down on one edge, like a ball of chalk rubbed on a stone, rising later and later into the night.

'There are complex geometries involved in all this,' Skjebne said during one early hour. They had travelled long and hard that day and for once found themselves too weary to sleep. Kano and Skjebne had backed the Travellers together into a V and Hora kindled a fire on the triangle of ground between them. There they sat round and ate from their provisions and, tentatively, from the roasted carcass of a small animal that Feoh had hunted that day.

Skjebne pointed up at the moon through the veil of woodsmoke that hung above their encampment.

'It is clearly spherical, given the shape of its shadow. And just as obviously it moves against the background of the stars – which are either frozen on to the sky, or are places in their own right, though immensely farther away . . .'

Kell thought cynically that Skjebne was talking to impress rather than to inform. Nothing in the mind of either Traveller had been able to answer their questions – although there was some obscure guidance about using the stars to steer by. Nor had the Shore Folk been sure. But once, long, long ago, someone surely *had* known. Was it all lost knowledge, Kell pondered, or would it be rediscovered again one day? But for now tiredness mixed with the wonder, and he was content to let life be a journey to enjoy, rather than a puzzle to be solved.

'It's this place I'm concerned about,' Hora said gruffly, only half trying to deflate his friend's sense of self-importance. 'We have neither seen nor heard anything of the Wulfen, for a start—'

'They suffered a defeat at our hands. No doubt they are looking for easier meat.' Kano was puffing at the last of his stock of smoke-leaf. It had been a parting gift from Faras; and now the sweetish yet pungent smell of it brought back bright memories of the brief time they had spent with their friends.

'They are intelligent animals. News of our presence will have travelled ahead of us.'

'How far ahead of us, Feoh? And to whom?'

'Time will tell.' Feoh smiled levelly at her man. 'And that same news might speak of the other dispossessed out of Perth – for it's unlikely we are the only ones to have come through.'

'Can you find out?' Kano tossed his dune-reed pipe into the fire, the last of the smoke-leaf gone. 'Can you read the will of the pack?'

'And can you still reach Shamra?' Kell added in a small and plaintive voice.

'All . . . All of it eventually . . .'

Feoh's eye seemed to gaze far away, at other distances none of the others could see. She pretended to concentrate in the alert-yet-lazy way that brought the insights to her; pretended, because she needed to decide how much to say. Just lately her dreams had been vivid and complex, welling up from the deeps of her mind. As such, they were highly symbolic and she had not yet fully clarified either their meaning or their final import. She knew with certainty though that significant days lay ahead, and that many forces were precariously balanced.

'The Wulfen bands are far from us at present. As the season of the deep cold makes its changes, other creatures are spreading into the forest. And you are right Kano, they will avoid us if they can.'

Her expression cleared. 'And Shamra is resting peacefully right now, Kell. As I think we should all do. Don't you?'

Morning brought a short flurrying of snow which quickly cleared as the clouds thinned and blue sky showed through. Gentle chimes within the Travellers had woken their occupants at first light. The controls at the front of the craft had brightened, the map windows had come to life and the engines were powered up even before Skjebne had taken his seat and the others were properly awake.

Today Kano's was the lead machine. With a deep growl of power and a gush from the snow-clearing vents, the Traveller swung back on to the track and Kano set course for the place called East, the direction in which the invaders' ship had disappeared.

All through the morning they made their way undisturbed, and for long quiet periods Kell watched the gentle sway of the forested land around them, and compared his limited view through the trees with the maps of light the machine was endlessly creating within itself – extensive downslopes back the way they had come towards the sea; mountains ahead and to the left, cleft by steep-sided valleys. There also seemed to be a region of lakes before them; deep trapped pockets of water scattered over rubble-fields crossed by high passes.

'How does the Traveller know what the terrain far away is like?' Kell asked idly. 'It doesn't have eyes to see for itself. It doesn't have friends who've been there before . . .'

'We don't know that,' Skjebne pointed out with just a hint of sternness. 'Perhaps its eyes are not visible to us. And who can say that it has no "friends" – other machines who whisper the knowledge of the land into its mind? It would not be wise to assume that the world is set as we see it.'

Kell felt suitably chided, and recalled his own insights as he'd stood and looked out over the sea.

'Nor would it be wise to assume the same is true of the Traveller . . .'

Feoh had moved up quietly behind them, startling them both. It was a lesson in itself.

'There are people nearby. Many of them. Two groups . . . One along the way, the other more scattered on the high slopes . . . There is no smell of the Wulfen here . . . And the situation feels different . . . I sense wealth . . . Dark wreaths of fear . . . That is a motive – to end the fear . . . And there is greed . . .'

Feoh's voice became a quiet monotone as she let her words pace the impressions that arrived in her mind: she spoke as she saw, and had long regarded that to be the purest and most accurate way of reaping the information.

'These other . . . the ones high up . . . They do not know of us yet . . . Soon we will be spotted . . . It is an ambush . . .'

'We don't have to be involved,' Skejebne said – and Kano's voice replied out of the air as he spoke from the other Traveller.

'We have escaped from Perth and come into this world. We have to be involved.'

And so the order was given.

They halted the machines and shut down the main drives, gathered their weapons and stepped out into the crisp clear air of the bright afternoon.

'These others – this marauding band – they are nothing like the Wulfen.' Feoh smiled as she said it, gathering up understandings of ragged disorganised bandits whose only strength was aggression and whose main strategy amounted to nothing more than blunt opportunism. They had happened upon a passing caravan of traders and decided to attack. The river was rich, and sluggishly flowing . . .

'Probably just warning the peddlers will be enough,' was Kano's opinion once Feoh had told of her gleanings.

'Yes . . . Perhaps . . .' For another few seconds Feoh was absorbed by her inner seeing: there seemed to be a complexity present which she found unexpected and surprising, but then again she may have misread the welter of subtle signs, or placed her own interpretation on images which meant nothing in themselves.

Kano was securing the Travellers' hatches and Hora was checking the mechanism of the fire-rod. Kell and Skjebne hung back waiting for instructions.

The moment passed and Feoh's eyes were once again focused on the simple outer world.

'Let's go carefully. Keep to the trees.'

Kano broke into an easy run, trotting towards the heavy shadows to the right of the track. He ducked into the trees and the others followed, Hora last of all as a safe solid anchor.

They were surrounded by the forest immediately; green thoughts in a green shade; puzzles of moving colour through the dim speckling sunlight. Kell found the pine smell almost intoxicating, and the soft swift whisper of their feet through beds of dead needles somehow strangely sinister.

Keep at least one of us in sight. Feoh's advice was sharp with apprehension. *We should stay together—*

Kano slowed and turned, crouching low. The others came up around him.

'No, we ought to separate. Hora and Skjebne, go ahead to the caravan and announce yourselves. Warn them of the danger—'

'That is a danger in itself,' Feoh insisted. 'They may well be suspicious, frightened . . .'

Skjebne shrugged. 'Then let us simply ambush the ambushers.'

'That's wise,' Hora said, and with the weight of opinion against him Kano was forced to acquiesce.

'Though we could do with the spears and arrows of the Shore Folk.' He hefted his weapon and primed it. A code of green lights flickered to red. 'As soon as the first shot is fired the bandits will be alerted.'

'But the advantage will be ours,' Feoh replied, 'if we act now.'

They hurried on, strung like beads on the thread of Feoh's mental direction. Ahead of them and to the left lay the trade way, and perhaps five furrowlengths along it a slowly moving train of big wagons, some hauled by moxen, others self-powered. There came sprinklings of laughter as a joke was made; whistlings and shouts as the jest passed from one rig on to the next. A man, an outrider, stood up in the saddle as though to mimic the object of their fun—

And something rose up beside Kano and swept him off his feet.

Kell cried out. Among the trees the pine needles were seething as though the dead were climbing from their graves. Five men, then ten, then too many to follow appeared out of the ground; wild haired, scruffily dressed, their dusty faces outrageously painted to shock. One drew back his arm to hurl a throwing-knife – and Hora flailed with an elbow and drove it against his skull with a dull clunk of bone. But other knives were sprouting like claws in a dozen fists and there could be no avoiding them all.

Skjebne lifted his weapon to the sky and discharged round after round, setting up a cacophonous din. Dust and bark scraps and splintered branches came spiralling down. The brigands ducked in unison, momentarily startled. Then one man, taller than the others and more imposing for all his tattered clothes, grinned a slow sly grin of victory and pointed his blade at Skjebne, at Kano, at Kell . . .

Feoh gathered her force and projected a pulse of confusion. One or two men grunted and staggered; others shook their heads stunned. The leader's smile was wiped from his face in a sudden bewilderment.

Feoh's tactic by itself would not have been enough to save them. But with her energy spent, circumstance took over.

Somewhere out in the sunlight there came a thunderous clatter and a towering wave of destruction. Chunks of wood, bitten from the trees, flashed past and splinters spat through the air. Clouds of smoke and a haze of particles and fragments whirled by. Even the ground itself was being chewed up into clods and clumps of wet soil and little hurricanes of needles showering down.

Kell dived behind one of the larger trunks nearby and pressed himself flat to the earth. There was movement everywhere; people running and plunging for cover; and the terrible noise of the timberland being shredded . . .

Then a momentary pause and echoes boomed out over the valley.

It's not over!

Feoh's warning was swamped by a loud *whoosh* of something skittering at head height swiftly through the trees. Fifty paces deeper into the forest it erupted as a ball of flame rapidly expanding ignited the nearer pines and singed those farther out with its heat blast. A second later Kell felt the dreadful breath of the fire and there was a crackling above him and many tiny popping sounds of vegetation crisping.

This retaliation was more than enough for the brigands. Their leader gave a shrill call and set off into the undergrowth, closely followed by his men. They left in chaos — but behind that disarray Feoh discerned a more calculating mind, a strong and forceful presence.

She hurried over to Kell and dragged him to his feet.

Come with me. You should see this—

'But Kano and the others!'

The traders have the measure of the situation. They are not wanton killers. Now keep up!

They ran together; Kell in a helplessness of ignorance with Feoh determinedly leading the way. There were no tracks in the forest, yet Feoh's path was sure and her expression grim and set. The ground tilted upwards, the trees thinned and Kell felt the warm sun on his back. It was harder keeping pace with the woman; he staggered in an ecstasy of struggling.

Just up ahead a pale slow animal moved, dragging something behind it. In amazement Kell sensed the heady whirl of Feoh's satisfaction and wonder and foreboding.

She lunged forward, grabbed the creature by its hair and pulled it backwards into full view.

She was a vagabond girl of about Kell's age. She wore the tough hide clothing of her nomad kind, equally ragged but without the showy colours of the men. Indeed, her leggings and tunic and torn overcloak had been dyed in subdued browns and greens as though for deliberate camouflage – and even as Kell noticed the chain on her leg and its burden of heavy scrap iron, she seemed to melt like glass and swirl away towards liquid invisibility.

Oh no sly sorceress – You will show your face, if not your true face!

Feoh's reprimand cracked out commandingly and Kell felt it deep in his flesh. The girl squirmed and writhed as a cat might wrestle to be free, but Feoh's leash of thought was tight and sure, and her captive had no choice but to reveal herself to their eyes . . .

She was grubby and scratched, wretched in every way save for the impression of power she gave off like a heat. And yet it was a limited force, confined to illusions and tricks of unseeing, *of blending out of people's sight* – or so Feoh surmised and passed her reasoning automatically to Kell.

You do it to survive. And you have both the reason and the right . . .

'And your name is Sebalrai, and mine is Feoh.'

The older woman knelt down beside Sebalrai and examined her encumbrance of chains. Kell stood a little back, not wishing to intrude on the flow of their understandings. And besides, he felt unaccountably hollow and his heart was beating fast in noticing the spark in the nomad girl's eyes and the pitch of her cheekbones, and the tousled scruffiness of her cropped yellow hair.

She ignored him of course, and that served only to intensify his symptoms.

'There's not much I can do here. We should get you to our Travelling machines, where we have tools—'

'The traders will kill me!' Sebalrai's fear was immediate and genuine. 'I have abetted Chertan and his raiders – Alderamin will spike my head on a pole!'

This was accompanied by a reflex image which hit Kell's mind before Feoh could snatch it back.

'We won't let him do that,' Kell said. 'We warned the caravan of the attack. We may have saved Alderamin's life!' He tried to sound reassuring, but had no defence against Sebalrai's cold and cynical smile.

'So what's your intention?' Feoh wanted to know. 'To crawl back into the forest and die slowly like a snared rabbit? Because it's likely Chertan and his wayfarer thieves will be far away from here by now, and you'll be out of their protection . . .'

Feoh sensed the shift in Sebalrai's heart, away from suspicion and doubt almost to an acceptance and the first small seeds of trust . . . And then to a dawning horror of the danger she could suddenly see.

Kell spun round and Feoh started to turn her head—

A looming figure in black armoured leather pointed a silvery wand.

And the sky and the daylight and awareness itself was engulfed in a wave of oblivion.

Kell opened his mouth before he opened his eyes and heaved up a thin dribble of spew. Close beside him Feoh groaned and glared at the world through her one bleary eye. Sebalrai remained unconscious, curled like a sleeping child around her dark pearl of forgetfulness. Her leg was bruised and the skin torn where she had roughly been dragged by her chains.

'Do you suppose we would have fired our weapons for any reason other than to warn you!'

That was Skjebne's voice, high-pitched with outrage. Kell jerked and spat out the bitterness on his tongue and, filled with unfamiliar pains, he slowly sat up. A dull headache drummed at the back of his skull and his whole body felt sensitive, as though it might discover new agonies at any time.

He had been thrown like a blanket against the base of a tree: the ridged roots under him added to his discomfort. The forest around glowed with a redder, later light – he had been unconscious for some considerable time. Lodged among the trees stood the wagons of Alderamin's caravan train, drawn round roughly in a circle as a shield against the keener evening wind. Hearty fires lent the encampment a certain cheer, and on its fringes moxen-like pack beasts cropped the pines lower branches, occasionally lifting their heads to let out a sonorous call. Beyond the canopy, a purple sky lit with shreds of crimson cloud warned of another night of penetrating cold.

Kell's drowsy mind took in the greater picture before he focused on one particular group among the many; Skjebne and Kano and Hora lashed like trapped animals to rings pegged in the earth. Hora, particularly, looked murderous, and even while he listened to the flow of conversation, his muscles flexed and strained to test the limits of his bonds.

Feoh woke fully, her mind rising like a sun in Kell's mental sky. She checked on him and diminished the throbbing in his head, and tended briefly to Sebalrai before returning.

She has been frightened and exhausted for a very long time. I think she will sleep through till morning . . . Don't worry – she added, clear as a crystal bell *– these peddlers don't have the facility to think outside their heads. That is why they still fail to trust us.*

How can we convince them?

Skjebne is artful in his words . . . And I suspect that this man Alderamin is just playing clever games.

They both looked towards him as he sat solid as a cask on a stout oaken chair. He was a big man, grizzled, iron-haired and bearded; corpulent rather than muscular, his broad shoulders draped with grey Wulfen furs overlying plates of light, finely wrought metal brightened by jewels and inlaid gold. Standing a little behind and at either side of him were huge guards clad in black armour: they seemed to be carved out of coal. From each of their belts hung a sword and a silver oblivion-wand and other esoteric devices. Each carried a double-headed axe that looked as though it could split a man with one swing. Kell wondered briefly if they were truly alive and entire in their flesh, or strangely hybrid like the invader they had buried by the sea . . . And following that came a pang of misgiving and loss as he thought again of Shamra, and where she might be. And what she might be suffering.

'You could have shot wide at us, being clumsy in your attack.' Alderamin's flatly accented voice rumbled up from his chest and he showed a flash of bright teeth at the cleverness of his unfolding gambit. He was obviously enjoying the sport.

'You know I shot from deep in the trees. I had no clear line of sight. By aiming into the air I alerted you to the presence of the bandits, and I provoked your return fire, which dispersed the raiders, thereby saving ourselves.'

'And two of your party fled from us, as the foragers ran.'

'Foeh and Kell pursued the girl, knowing something of her special talent—'

'How did they know?'

'They saw her vanish. They discerned her ability – and it is a useful one, this craft of concealment; a gift she can share with those around her. That's why Chertan's band could hide from you so well. And that's why we, in our clumsiness, could not have been a part of it.'

Alderamin's fierce smile faded somewhat as he found himself caught in Skjebne's logic. Kano and the others sat quietly and did not interfere, though Hora still eased at his ropes and Kano's mind, Foeh saw, was filled with schemes of revenge.

'All of this may or may not be a lie. But in any case, what matter is it to me? I now have Sebalrai in my possession – as I have you and all that you own.'

'But you cannot get into our Travellers,' Skjebne countered confidently.

Alderamin leaned forward. 'How do you know?'

'Because we are still alive. We are the key.'

'Keys made of flesh can be made to open anything . . .'

'Unless they choose to die first.'

Feoh's clear voice cut across the men's pointless bickering. How similar were Skjebne and Alderamin in their will to out-talk one another! The deal was clear, shining like a torch in the trader's mind. He wanted the Travellers and the gift of

Sebalrai in return for his prisoners' lives. Sebalrai wanted only to be free. Poor lost Kell wanted to find Shamra, and then perhaps truly to find himself. Why wasn't this out in the open? Why hadn't the ultimatum been issued?

Feoh stood up and smiled within herself. Neither she nor Kell had been shackled: naively Alderamin saw no danger from females or children. She walked calmly towards him and felt the guards' defences stir like the red rage of dogs at the approach of a stranger.

'You are not a stupid man, Alderamin. You know that Skjebne tells you the truth. But neither, apparently, are you a just man, else you would thank us for saving your life.'

Feoh saw the fury rising in his face, and continued.

'On the other hand, this is the situation in which we find ourselves. We are your prisoners. Now we both know you get nothing for nothing. You cannot have both our travel machines and Sebalrai's power. If you try to force us, we will die—'

Effortlessly she projected the memory of the Wulf she had ended in the forest, and felt gratified to see Alderamin visibly startle as the idea took shape in his head.

'In all of us lies both the life-wish and the death-wish – though we deny this for our own peace of mind. You cannot squeeze our secrets from us before we have ended ourselves. Do you think we would dare not to do this?'

She let the question hang. And nearby the campfires crackled and far above the stars were absolutely still.

'I know you would do it,' Alderamin said at last, and with a dawning respect. 'So, once you have spoken with your men, they can come and bargain with me.'

'No. Untie them now and give us food and some drink and I will discuss our arrangement in a grown-up and civilised way.'

A number of the trader's compatriots gasped at the

172

woman's brash answer, and a few chuckled, anticipating Alderamin's temper. But instead he tipped back his head and let out a bellowing laugh as he realised the bartering had already begun.

It felt strange to Kano to let go his grip on the moment and allow Feoh to trade on behalf of them all. For so long he had demanded rigid control, because his had been the vision and his the only path that would lead to it. That strategy had brought them out of Perth. But these were new lands and different days, and it was time to put trust in his friends.

'So. You give me one of the ice-wains and show me how to use it . . .' (Alderamin's pride swelled at the thought of owning this new toy). 'In return, you keep the other. I reprovision it for you and allow you to go free.'

'That is also my understanding of the agreement,' Feoh said.

'And I keep the girl Sebalrai for her gift of concealment—'

Her face hardened. 'No. She must choose her own way.'

'The bargain isn't balanced. You ask for too much.'

'And you give too little . . . And I know why!'

Feoh's suspicion had started with the merest shift of light in Alderamin's eyes, and the way he had reacted whenever Sebalrai was mentioned. Even the idea of disguise had something to do with it . . . masks . . . hiding . . . cowering . . . chained to the past, locked in the fear . . .

And as though it was time for a release of the secret, an admission long overdue, the source of Alderamin's shame and impotence came clearly to the surface of his mind: his eyes brimmed and he wept openly in front of his men.

None of them dared respond except to hold back and wait to see what happened; and it embarrassed even the most hardened of the trader's followers that their leader should be brought to tears by this woman – or more accurately by what this woman had realised.

For long minutes Alderamin said nothing, his head hanging forward, his great body shaking with sobs. No one moved to comfort him, for consolation was not appropriate here. Only Feoh knew what to offer.

'You are a better healer than you are a trader,' Alderamin said presently, looking up and wiping his wet face on his Wulfen skin cloak.' And you are a better diplomat than you are a healer – you did not tell my servants the source of my pain.'

He held out his big rough hand through which fortunes had passed, and grasped Feoh's hand and wrapped it completely around with his fingers. And every finger was jewelled, and none of those jewels had ever brought him true joy.

'Sebalrai's resemblance to your daughter is minimal, Alderamin. Your eyes are as veiled as mine once were.' She touched her mask absently with a flash of bitter memory.

'And you know, it occurs to me that Shaula is only wintering the storm, not realising that storm has now passed.' Feoh smiled. 'So it was in the land where I came from, although some of us came back to the light.'

'Take your ice-wains. Take Sebalrai. Go with my gratitude. My men here think they see weakness, but you have given me strength.'

Alderamin almost pushed Feoh away from him, as if her power was suddenly too much, and he wanted to be alone with his ghosts.

But Feoh gripped his hand and clung on and would not be dismissed.

'No, you misunderstand me, trader. Our bargain stands, as your reputation for barter must stand. But I didn't just want you to acknowledge your child. Hers is an illness of the mind. I can go into that territory, and I can recover her . . .'

11

Edgetown

Perhaps it was a mark of man's raw recency in this land that the place where Alderamin made his home had no formally agreed name, though the people in their gossip called it Edgetown.

'Very apt, since it marks the outermost point so far on our travels,' Skjebne said one evening as they talked around the topic. And Kell's blood thrilled to wonder what lay beyond that edge.

As Feoh had discerned, and as Alderamin confirmed for his guests now, his trade was in jewellery, and in the metals and stones that went into their making. His present business had taken him far to the west, halfway to the coast, in search of a substance called amber. On the evening before their arrival at Edgetown, he brought a leather bag to where Kano and his party sat around the fire, and tipped its contents out on to the dust—

Feoh's breath caught at the beauty of the amber lumps as they absorbed the glow of the campfire flames; like chunks of solid honey, some mellow gold, others polished copper, a few so richly red they might have been distilled from the blood of fallen heroes.

'And look at this!' Skjebne snatched up a piece in his surprise and showed them the little burnished green beetle trapped inside. 'How is this possible?' His mind swept on for explanations and sparked with excitements.

'The men of wisdom who dig amber from the ground say

it is the ancient resin of trees,' Alderamin explained. 'Long ago, too long to imagine, this beetle landed on a pine trunk one dawn day; and the resin oozed from the wood and the insect was caught for eternity. Despite its defences, despite all its determination to live, it died in this most unexpected way. A lesson for us all, little shadowling . . .'

Alderamin's dark brown eyes turned their emphasis on Sebalrai as she sat nestled up against Feoh's side. A thin, silent, fearful child, her gift flickered nervously even now, so that to the onlookers she seemed to fade in and out of their sight. It was a reflex that troubled Feoh's mind, for no one should be so frightened of the world despite its dangers.

The trader then showed them an assortment of amber pieces containing all manner of small items; a leaf, a mosquito, an ant, a seed. 'And in my home I have a chunk the size of my fist that imprisons a lizard, perfect in its preservation though it died ten thousand lifetimes ago.'

'No wonder people are eager to purchase such treasures,' Kano said. Alderamin shrugged his broad shoulders: he was warmed by several generous draughts of wayberry wine and felt expansive.

'It's not just the rarity of these substances that gives them value. For many of the tribes in this part of the continent amber and jade, amethyst and pearl and certain precious metals have a symbolic quality they use in their worship. And there are others who—'

Suddenly self-aware, he broke into a bout of coughing and quaffed more wine from his goblet and then called for another barrel to be broken and shared out; and meat too, a piglet to be roasted from the stores. Let them celebrate their new relationship, the people of Edgetown and these brave wayfarers; let them celebrate the fact that they were not trapped in amber!

But Feoh had seen through the door that opened

momentarily to show Alderamin's innermost heart. There he hid his deepest desires, his darkest secrets, his profoundest fears. And there Feoh glimpsed a suspicion of horrors so evil that Alderamin kept them locked tight away, denying them even to himself.

Just a glimmer, just a gleam of possibility. But it showed Feoh the road to the future, and perhaps the reason for young Shamra's taking.

The depths of the night brought a light snow, a crystal dust that hardened on to things through the clear-sky cold of the predawn dark. Skjebne emerged from the 'ice-wain' and breathed in a lungful of blades. He spluttered and coughed and his breath rose around him in clouds.

'Wrap your mouth with cloth and inhale through your nose,' advised one of the armoured guards. The man had been standing out all night, sealed in his leather. It was like being spoken to by a black monolith. 'In this place no man can afford to breathe his warmth away.'

'Thank you – er, sir.' Skjebne was amused to realise that here was a man who would have taken off his head without pause just a few days ago. 'I apologise – I don't know your name.'

'Nor will you. Part of my pledge of duty is to give nothing away. A name is a word of power. Sharing it leaves you vulnerable.'

Skjebne nodded and did not quite understand. Even so, he thought the warrior's view a strange and sorry thing.

A short time later, after the morning ablutions, the caravan went on its way, led by the two ice-wains, one of which now belonged to Alderamin. It had been planned that he would parade his convoy proudly into Edgetown driving the lead machine; so this was his last chance to practise. He sat with Skjebne beside him, while just behind Feoh and Kell repressed their giggles, and even Sebalrai was moved to smile at the trader's impatience.

'It is a simple matter of a light hand on the control sticks and allowing the vehicle to use its own wisdom!' Skjebne sounded snappish, like an irritable Tutor. 'And you can speak with it too – the Traveller knows your voice now and can appreciate your commands—'

'Then why does the wain jerk so, slowing and speeding? Look how it frightens the beasts!'

One of the screens showed a rear view, and sure enough the big animals, normally placid, were stamping and rearing a little farther back along the train.

'Because you are unsure yourself, and that reflects in the vehicle's behaviour.' Skjebne tutted and was hard pressed not to take the controls himself.

'Do it like this, Alderamin,' Feoh intervened. She placed her hands on his shoulders and pressed them until they relaxed. Then she touched the man's temples with her fingertips and imparted to him what she had learned of Kano's and Skjebne's expertise, and of her own brief periods at the helm.

It pleased her when he reacted, quickly and easily; letting go, easing into the process. He let his blood learn; let his flesh and bones be guided by this woman's sure touch and knowledge. He felt his confidence grow and came to relish the wain's easy power and its sensitivity to his wishes. It was like training up a hound to know the meaning of your sound and smell and intention . . .

'Yes, that's just how it is,' Feoh said. He had not even noticed her taking her hands away. 'I hear and I forget. I see and I remember. I *do*, and I understand.'

'You make a good teacher . . . And would make a good wife.'

Then Sebalrai did chuckle out loud, and Kell grinned, and Feoh was surprised and complimented enough to blush.

They came upon Edgetown in the early afternoon. For most of the morning the long line of waggons followed the course of a river along the valley bottom. At either side slopes of rough scree piled up about the base of sheer cliffs that rose to a high plateau, beyond which lay a jumble of hills and more mountainous terrain to the East. Scrubby bushes and a fuzz of tough grass were beginning to secure the scree, while the forest was growing back into the valley; a mixture of pines and broad-leaved trees, the first that the travellers had seen outside Perth.

'Some time soon this will be a handsome land,' was Skjebne's opinion. 'A rich and settled land.'

And a land under threat.

Feoh felt the butterfly touch of Alderamin's doubt in her mind and then flitter away. She was not sure whether to curse or bless this ability of hers to look into the tiny chinks and crannies of thought and to see things the thinker did not wish to be known. But at least this confirmed her perception of the night before had been true – some dark shadow was cast over Alderamin's land; a knowledge he could not bear to face. And Feoh knew that she was already a part of it, engulfed in its amber forever.

The ground upsloped gently, and as the Traveller crested the rise Kell and the others got their first glimpse of Edgetown. The track became a wide road, and along the road stout log dwellings had been built, interspersed with corrals and stabling for moxen and spaces where wains could be parked. A scattering of houses had also begun to spread across the valley flats, and there was one bridge over the river sturdy enough to carry people and carts to settlements beyond.

The centrepiece of Edgetown was a spacious caravanserai

bordered on one side by the river, and on the other by workshops. So it was an easy and efficient matter to offload the trading waggons as they arrived, and for the craftsmen whom Alderamin had assembled to begin work at once.

It was Kell who first noticed that the road reached beyond Edgetown on its far side, meandering beside the river until it vanished into the distant hills. And innocently he asked where it went.

'To the Barbaric Lands,' the trader said gruffly. 'To a place you would not like to go . . . We must of necessity deal with the savages who dwell there. They mine silver and iron for us, and a number of exotic materials which are of use to us only to trade on for other supplies we require . . .'

'How can they be savages if their industry is so well developed?'

'He asks from curiosity rather than impertinence,' Feoh counselled, noticing Alderamin's expression.

'It is possible to be civilised in your trappings yet barbaric in your arts. Do you understand that?'

'No sir.'

'Well I am not of a mind to explain. Just take my word on it and be satisfied.'

Kell nodded and did not argue, and was silent for the remainder of the journey.

What must have been the entire population of Edgetown came out of their houses to greet the return of the merchants. The caravan had been gone for two months, Alderamin said. Kell was briefly baffled by the term, though caught the backwash of Feoh's understanding that it had something to do with the moon – he saw it as 'moonths' in his head. So, almost at once, there was food being served and wine and beer handed round in big metal juggons, and children dancing while minstrels played – all of it the warm and rough and ready welcoming of a well-bonded kin.

The leadsmen of the caravan positioned their vehicles as appropriate outside the workshops, where apprentice lads did the dogwork of unloading and stacking the stores. Alderamin's expedition had been a successful one, and he had traded all of his stock of well-wrought jewellery for large quantities of raw materials and other provisions his people had not the ability to produce for themselves.

'Once it must have been like this everywhere,' Alderamin commented as Skjebne quizzed him on this and other matters. 'Communities thriving through their wit and skill, trading what they have for what they need. It builds up the bones of a people, and puts heat into the blood!'

'Have you always lived here in Edgetown? What came before?'

'Your thirst for knowledge is greater than your thirst for ale!' Alderamin jested, though he saw that Skjebne was intent in his asking.

'Before this I was a skinny half-starved youth who came up out of the ground with a handful of others from my enclave. It was a dark and dismal cavern, a failed society that had been faltering for some generations. Deep underground we burned the dead trees to stay warm, and prayed to the empty dark for a salvation we knew would never arrive.'

'And what . . .' Skjebne hesitated to mention it. 'What of your eyes? What of the All Mother?'

'I know nothing of that particular deity – though tales were once told of a nurturing presence, a spirit in the nature of things; the hlaf-weard who was the provider of bread, and who deserted our land lifetimes ago . . . As for your mention of eyes, the forefathers all wore the weorthan–glass; at first to know how to live, and latterly in desperation, for its visions faded and have never returned.'

Skjebne was eager for more, but Alderamin held up his hand to dampen the other's enthusiasm.

'Friend Skjebne, I admire your quest to know everything. But now I am tired. So, I am going to spend some time with my wives, then I am going to get drunk . . . And then I have to oversee an important meeting between the glorious Feoh and my poor daughter Shaula. And if I am still of a mood, I will speak again with you after that.'

Feoh herself, from a short distance away, had followed the conversation with interest. Even as a small girl she had realised that a few spoken words were accompanied by a flood of linked thoughts; as though one told page revealed the whole unopened book. And so as Alderamin talked briefly with Skjebne, his mind released a glut of memories and dreams, anticipations and fears – far more than Feoh could notice and reflect on at the time, though they did serve to reinforce her impression of this noble man who was filled with energy and life and yet with a bleak foreboding.

Then he was walking away towards his own dwelling that was no grander or better appointed than any other in Edgetown. And for a few moments more Feoh thought of him and wondered about the future, and calmed herself for the trial that was shortly to follow . . .

In thinking of Shaula, she glanced at Sebalrai and her mood immediately lightened. The girl had begun the festivities as a shade; pale and quiet, nervous and silent. All her short life she had spent in hiding, or in helping others to hide on pain of some torment or other. She had been six summers old when Chertan had raided her village and snatched her away, leaving her family dead among their burning huts. Then had come her training, through whippings and blows and other worse cruelties, so that her power was bent to the brigand's will. Ultimately, while he kept Sebalrai near him, Chertan could feed on her energy and make himself vanish from sight. The cloaking worked perfectly with people, but less well with Wulfen and other forest creatures, whose keener senses still detected him and his cut-throat band even when there was nothing to be seen.

So it had been for eight summers and eight longer winters, the last four spent in chains after Sebalrai's one reckless bid to escape. Chertan recaptured her, of course, having laid traps around his encampment for brush-swine, but catching a fleeing prisoner instead. He had fractured her jaw as a punishment, and staked her out on the ground at night until the cold had almost killed her. After that she simply obeyed him and expected nothing, and was never disappointed.

Now the life was coming back into her face. She was growing more vivid by the hour, chuckling at the children's antics, delighting at the musicians' fine tunes, staring with a certain spark in her eye as young men went by and played the fool to keep her attention. She was allowing herself the possibility of tomorrow.

'You know,' said Feoh in the lull between tunes, 'you are fully free now to be yourself and to do what you want. But whether you travel onwards with us, or decide to stay here at Edgetown, you will find protection and companionship. I want you to realise that.'

'I do realise it,' Sebalrai said, her face glowing. 'You have given me that certainty. And all I can give you back is the hope that, whatever *you* do, you will never hide from life as I have done.'

It was well said, and sufficient. And the two sat on, listening to the music and choosing from the delicacies that were offered to them. The afternoon waned in celebration, and then Alderamin appeared at the doorway of his home, and Feoh knew that her moment had come.

Upon seeing Shaula, she apologised to the merchant for her earlier mistake.

'They look nothing like in the flesh. But your daughter is as well hidden as Sebalrai ever was . . .'

The chamber where they had gathered – Feoh, Alderamin, Shaula and her birth-mother Jadhma – was a place of solitude. Heavy drapes hung over the windows, and a shaded candle provided the only light.

'She can tolerate the dark,' Jadhma explained. 'The daylight seems to pain her . . .'

She's aware of neither. Feoh bent low over the girl and moved a hand slowly in front of her eyes, which failed to flinch.

'Tell me what happened to cause this,' Feoh said, looking directly at him as she did so, in a way that told him she demanded nothing short of the truth.

'We don't know—'

'Then pretend you do and tell me anyway!'

The man sighed heavily and eased his weight into a nearby chair. He rested his gaze on Shaula's face as he spoke. It was as calm and still as a frozen lake, and had been since the time of her tenth summer.

'We were a younger community then – no less vigorous or productive than we are now, but perhaps less alert. Less suspicious. Our original number had grown rapidly over the course of a generation; in part because of our reputation as artisans and honest traders, and the prosperity which accompanied that. And in part because we welcomed those with a skill to offer as members of our bonded kin. When I dug the first post hole in the virgin earth to build this place, my dream was for a community of freemen, where each by his abilities served the needs of all the others . . .'

Alderamin waved the memory away, as though it was a trivial thing.

'Our mistake was that in trusting one another, we trusted the world. We had escaped from our various hells and believed we had left them behind, never thinking that the past would follow us out into the light of the day.

'This river valley is extensive, as you have seen. And beyond it the land is vast, and the early communities who settled here were well scattered. We were establishing our trade, making links with other tribes and settlements and forging new routes. In those days men often travelled with their families, since expeditions could last for many weeks, and with minimal protection. Yes, there were the Wulfen, but their patterns are predictable and they hunt men only as a last resort, in the season of the hard long dark when forest food is scarce. Similarly the other wild creatures could be avoided or frightened away.'

'And robber bands like Chertan's?'

'Brigands hadn't yet arrived in this region.' Alderamin gave a brief and fierce smile. 'They are a new annoyance.'

'But there was another danger, a greater danger that you hadn't anticipated?' Feoh said. Alderamin's thoughts ran ahead of his words, unfolding the story even before he told it: and already Feoh was seeing his fearful impressions of what had happened to cause Shaula's insanity.

'Yes. A threat that even to this day we do not fully understand . . . Our way took us northeast, into the Dawn Mountains. I travelled with Shaula and Jadhma, one or two other of my wives and our children. Several of the merchants did likewise. We had received news the previous season of a mining community there, and we were interested in making contact for our mutual benefit. We took horses and a few mox-drawn sleds, for we guessed that the tracks would be crude and the terrain very difficult.

'So it proved to be. We journeyed for the best part of a month, and at the start of the second week came to the mountains and entered the high passes between. It was a bleak place, still raw from the gougings of the Ice. And even though this was the time of the longest light, the night cold was bitter and the wind streaming down off the peaks unrelenting.

'There were some pockets of wealdland tucked into sheltered corners, however, and these we sought out whenever we could. One day, quite late in the afternoon, we encamped in such a wood, pitching our tents a little apart from one another for privacy. We lit fires, and the men took their turn in guarding the boundaries. We had weapons such as yours, and better, which we believed would protect us from any intruder.

'The night came on and a thin and freezing haze rose up from the ground. Men became ghosts; campfires turned into glowing flowers of mist; the moxen were shifting shadows on the edge of our sight.

'My family was asleep, and that part of the camp was guarded by Lesath, an old dear friend of mine. I was alert on the opposite fringe. Looking back, I think we all noticed the strange tension in the air; the sense that something was prowling nearby. And yet the feeling confused us, because the moxen were untroubled, and our experience had always been that they are sensitive to danger.

'Our unease intensified, until at last all the guardsmen were up on their feet and convinced of imminent attack. But there was nothing. And then a woman screamed, and a child cried out. More screams, and a terrible alarm.

'We fired our weapons blindly at the mist, in a panic. I turned and ran back to where my wives and children were sleeping . . . And as I approached the tent I thought – I don't know – I thought there was something hideous over by the trees. But what was I seeing? An illusion of shadows and fog and my own imagination? I shot at it. I fired until my weapon was empty, and by then it no longer existed . . .

'The horror came and went away, its damage done. All of us were shocked. Another of my wives, Talitha, has never entirely recovered her mind since the experience. All of those who were asleep at the time still carry their nightmares of that experience. But Shaula was the worst affected; neither asleep nor awake, she lives in a limbo of unlife that I can end with a bullet, or that maybe you can end, Feoh, with your healing gift . . .'

Alderamin fell silent and looked at Shaula, and at the floor and at his own hands. But he would not look at Feoh.

'You have not told me all,' she prompted him gently. 'Nor do you need to. Lesath died that night, didn't he? Torn apart by the "phantom" your imagination conjured. And you lie to yourself that it was Wulfen, or perhaps some mountain cat.'

'It is natural enough.' Alderamin sounded a little defensive, but not shamed. 'At least I can understand the wish of the Wulfen to kill. They too have an imperative to survive. I will have no truck with superstition, Feoh!'

'Nor am I asking you to. But the frame that our minds put on the world is not the whole world. Things lie outside, not yet part of what we know or believe—'

'What Shaula knows has done this to her!'

'No one can teach her to un-know it: that is not healing, just self-deception. The secret is to allow her to understand her knowledge.'

'She is a frail child.' Jadhma spoke up for the first time. 'She cannot deal with your truths.'

'As you expect her to be, so will she be. Besides, they are *her* truths,' Feoh said sternly. 'And I think they are better for her than your lies—'

'We are not here to be insulted and blamed!' Alderamin thundered. 'We have cared for the girl as best we can – we have shielded her, we have nourished her!'

'And you have not cured her. Without that, she will be shielded and nourished into the grave.'

Jadhma lowered her head at this and and began very softly

to weep. Alderamin's anger blazed up, and for an instant his hand moved towards the knife at his belt.

Feoh regarded him openly, and unafraid.

'So, after all of this, what am I to do?'

'Go—' Alderamin said after just a moment's hesitation. 'Go and find her, and bring her back.'

It was a bleak place, still raw from the gougings of the Ice. And even though this was the time of the longest light, the night cold was bitter and the wind streaming down off the peaks unrelenting.

Alderamin's encampment was settled amongst high woodland tucked into a fold of the hills, out of the wind in a quiet nook that allowed the mist to rise. Men were ghosts, campfires were turned into glowing flowers and moxen were shifting shadows on the edge of sight.

Years ago something had come this way and done its damage. Yet here in Shaula's mind the terror had remained. Feoh allowed her imaginary self to shine, blazing out so that things could be clearly seen. She went towards the tent where Alderamin's family had slept, and was briefly startled and then revolted at the sight of Lesath's sundered corpse and the violence of his disembowelling.

'Who is it?' came Shaula's quivering voice from within.

'You know who it is,' Feoh said. 'I am in your land now. You know everything about me.'

'Go away!'

'Only if you come with me—'

'It's out there!' A shriek, followed by a moan of utter torment.

'No more so than it's in here. And in here, as you well know, you are alone.'

She opened the flap of the tent and went inside. Shaula sat huddled in a corner. And inside her head was another shelter just like this one, and another Shaula cowering alone.

'You aren't allowing anything to change,' Feoh told her. 'The thing you realised has imprinted itself on the clay of your mind. That

second of understanding has become a word you will not stop repeating. But stop now, and come with me and see how your sisters and brothers have grown!'

Then Shaula allowed herself a small warm smile.

'Ancha will be eleven by now.'

'Yes, and you haven't seen him since he was a baby.'

The smile disappeared. *'It's out there.'*

'We can deal with it out there. Let go of it in here. Come with me.'

Feoh held out her hand and Shaula reached in return, her fingers shaking as though with a terrible effort while the battle was fought.

'Out there . . . out . . . out . . .'

Feoh radiated strength and reassurance, but nothing that was hollow or untrue. Yes it was a dangerous world and there were enemies to fight – but nothing that could not be defeated by courage and determination and love.

'I don't deny you.' Shaula spoke to something unseen. *'You have killed Lesath, who was my father's friend. You have terrorised my family. And you may kill me yet. But you are nothing here if I make nothing of you. You have lorded over me for long enough. You are nothing here!'*

Their fingertips touched and Shaula came into the light. For several minutes it was all a kaleidoscope of moving colours until Shaula's vision cleared. Alderamin wept and laughed with joy, and Jadhma hugged her daughter so hard that the breath was squeezed from her body. It was a homecoming more important than the long-awaited arrival of an entire caravan.

Then, while Jadhma and Shaula began a conversation that would last long into the night, and while Mirach, a close friend, summoned the rest of the family for the sharing of the gladness, Alderamin took Feoh to one side and spoke to her very softly and earnestly.

'What you have done for us today is a miraculous thing.'

'I used my skill to create something, as you and your artisans do—'

But Alderamin would not allow Feoh to belittle her achievement. 'The creation of a completed individual far outshines the making of a bracelet or a ring. We do not understand the ways of the mind, and certainly have no means of entering that inner world, as you do. Therefore, as I said, what you have done is a miraculous thing. No payment is enough, but whatever I have is yours; and whatever in my power I can do for you, so I will do it . . .'

'Two favours,' Feoh replied without hesitation, for she had given the matter some previous thought.

'I have talked with Sebalrai and pointed out that she is free now, as free as you or me.'

'So she is.'

'I also promised her that if she chose to stay here in Edgetown, she could be sure of a home and a family . . .'

Alderamin threw up his hands in pleasure and surprise. 'That is hardly a reward to you for your help!'

'But you will do it?'

'Any of the kinfolk here would be delighted to welcome Sebalrai as a daughter and friend.'

'Good enough.' Feoh regarded him levelly. 'The other favour is not quite as easily given . . .'

And she explained about their time with the Shore Folk, and how Shamra had been spirited away by the armoured machine-warriors in their strange flying craft.

'We watched it disappear in this direction, Eastwards, which is what brought us this way. And I have also maintained a link with Shamra, the thinnest thread, almost a forgotten memory. But I am still with her and she knows that I am . . . She has been taken to a region in the Dawn Mountains, the place from which the terror came that locked your daughter's mind within itself. It is—' Feoh's eyes drifted upwards to the right. 'It is a city, a broken place in a corrupted and disordered land. The impressions are dim and confusing . . . There is – a sickness.'

She looked at Alderamin straight. 'Whatever visited your camp was spawned there. Those of us who go to rescue Shamra will face extreme danger.'

Alderamin seemed to give Foeh's words serious and weighty consideration. But then in a childlike change of mood he shrugged his shoulders lightly and his face broke into a broadening grin.

'You have just given me a second good reason to put my men and equipment at your disposal, and to accompany you myself. Foremostly I go out of gratitude to you for saving my Shaula. But now, in light of what you've told me, I have another motivation.'

'Which is?'

'One as old as men's blood,' Alderamin said. 'Revenge.'

Feoh and the others received the generous hospitality of Alderamin and his kin. He insisted on showing them all around Edgetown, taking particular pride in his workshops – where not only jewellery was made. Hora especially took a keen interest in the armoury, where a startling range of weaponry was both crafted and maintained. Skjebne's curiosity was whetted by the logical principles behind some of the devices that Alderamin put on display . . .

'It seems that a number of these weapons have an intelligence of their own, much like the mind of the ice-wains.' Skjebne weighed in his hands a side-arm that fired bolts and darts of various kinds. He was reminded of the Traveller's console by the pistol's sparkling lights and displays.

'Quite right,' Alderamin said. 'In that case, the weapon assesses the target and chooses the most appropriate missile –

although as controller you can always override its decision. Some of these machines are clever enough to adjust and maintain themselves, within limits. Others without that power lie useless when they malfunction, for we haven't the wit to repair them.' He picked out another object, a beautifully jewelled cylinder which he passed across to Hora.

'Minds as well as blades have need to be sharp. Concentrate, my friend – envision a sword.'

Hora did so, and within a moment a long slim cutting edge had appeared and clicked into place.

'Now a spear—'

As though magically the swordblade retracted and a shaft emerged, tipped with a razor-sharp point.

'I earlier explained to Feoh that I did not understand the subtler ways of the mind, much less the ability of thoughts to influence the outer world directly. You see it in the ice-wains and in some of these armaments. They were created by smiths in a settlement well to the south: their knowledge of applied energies and the storage of intentions in crystal remains unsurpassed – except, perhaps, by those who dwell in the city that is our destination . . .'

The tour continued, and Alderamin was pleased to present each of his guests with a weapon he felt was appropriate; the sidearm for Skjebne, the multiblade for Hora, a crystal eye for Kano which defied the attraction of the earth; an exquisitely balanced throwing knife for Kell, and a faceted blue stone for Feoh which was half the size of her fist: all of this, plus accoutrements of armour and other provision as they required, or he advised.

'Don't fret,' Alderamin joked as he saw Feoh fingering the stone. 'I won't have it made into a pendant for you. The gem contains a power like the sun, a blinding light of great destructiveness. Its little soul will come to know your mission, and will understand when the time is right to unleash its terrible force. It can be your guardian angel, Feoh, a protector – but yet a demon on the backs of your enemies. I know you will use it wisely . . .'

Later, when Alderamin felt satisfied he had adequately entertained and amused his guests and shown them the necessary courtesies, he left them to themselves in the large house he'd put at their disposal.

The lodge consisted of a central hearth-hall with private rooms leading off. A fire in the middle of the stone-flagged meeting room filled the building with cosiness and warmth. Close by stood a table laden with food and drink, the best the people of Edgetown had to offer.

Feoh bade her friends pull up cushions and chairs closer to the fireside, where she could tell them her news.

'. . . And so, when we are ready, Alderamin will provision an escort for us to go to the city where, I believe, Shamra is held. I think he has given us these weapons as an indication of what he feels we will face there – a strong and merciless foe who on first impulse would kill us, or else use us for their sinister and mystical ends.'

'And what are those?' Kano asked. 'Does Alderamin have any idea?'

'Some,' Feoh answered, nodding slowly. 'There is much that he denies even to himself, even now. But since Shaula's disturbance he has gathered up snippets of gossip, scraps of rumour and hearsay that might have been connected with his pain. And in his mind there already exists an image of the city I told him about. He knows of it, and in this land all the way back to the sea, people fear it and call it Thule.'

'Then that is the source of the unease you have detected in these folk,' Kano said. 'Why then haven't they banded together and destroyed the wickedness?'

'Partly because, by Alderamin's own admission, his people do not understand the ways of the mind – and there is something in Thule that goes to the deepest roots of men's thoughts. And partly,' Feoh continued, though more hesitantly, 'it is to do with what happened on the night that Shaula was changed . . .

'All of the travellers in the camp were disquieted. There was a tension. Those that slept were troubled by nightmares. Then the shadow appeared which tore poor Lesath to pieces, and which drove Shaula into herself for all this time.'

'But why her?' Kell wondered. 'Why not the others?'

'Simply because the shadow passed close to where Shaula was sleeping. She woke to Lesath's screams, and peered out, and was the only one to see the beast – *the very creature that lay at the heart of her terrifying dream.*'

12

The Broken Place

'I'm still not sure I understand it,' Kell said, this being the outcome of much mental struggle. He felt slightly ashamed to admit his ignorance so; but as Skjebne had frequently told him, that was just a ghost from his time at the Tutorium. A purposeless haunting.

'The whole history of humankind has been one of not knowing.' Skjebne studied his weapon minutely and made a fractional adjustment. 'And the entire future of humankind lies in us *wanting to find out.* Asking the question with many answers is our greatest capability, therefore never feel diminished because you don't know.'

'I see. So what exactly was Feoh talking about?'

'I don't know.' They both laughed. 'But do I feel guilty? No, only frustrated.'

It was two days on, and preparations to travel to the Dawn Mountains were well advanced. Alderamin's plan – one which Kano heartily endorsed – was to go under the guise of a trading mission. The entire region east of Edgetown was opening up to the traders from the south and west, part of an ever-expanding network that Alderamin said formed the new life-blood of the land. Despite the dark reputation Thule had acquired – and the threat it increasingly posed – it would not be unusual for strangers to go there under the banner of commerce.

'One or two modest wains' worth of goods to begin with . . .' Alderamin smiled slyly. 'Just a few select little treasures to prick their curiosity and interest. We will not be regarded as a threat—'

'But we'll have weapons, easily found,' was Hora's objection.

'As the people there would expect us to, in order to protect our belongings. Marauder bands such as Chertan's are more commonly seen these days. We have to take precautions. It's the only way. In any event, we could never approach the city unseen, much less mingle with the populace and find our way around.'

So it was set. And while the wains were loaded and the finer details of the scheme were discussed, Skjebne and Kell kicked their heels and got in some useful target practice.

Skjebne lifted his gun and looked along his arm as Alderamin had advised. The target was a tiny dark disc in the distance, with the drift of the river beyond. Skjebne concentrated – *Too tense! Too tense!* – and sighed with barely held patience, and allowed his muscles to relax.

Hit, or destroy?

'Just hit,' Skjebne said aloud, though he had no real need: the tiny sharp mind of the weapon could pick up his basic intention and adjust itself accordingly, and feed him back advice.

He touched the firing fingerpad and there was a little exclamation of air. A small dart whispered silently away and disappeared. Kell stepped over to the farscope and checked Skjebne's efforts.

'Dead centre – again!'

'It is almost too easy . . .' He holstered the weapon and ignored the brief and waspish complaint that touched the edge of his mind.

'It's reassuring to have a reliable weapon – but to be *nagged* by it . . .'

They walked closer to the target, where Kell could practise with his knife.

'Feoh dwells in a different world,' Skjebne said, picking up their earlier conversation. 'What we see around us is just a part of her reality, and no more solid than the territory of her mind. For us that target is far away – three furrowlengths of space, two minutes of time to walk to it. For Feoh it is a point on the map laid out in front of her: she can touch it with her thoughts in an instant, just as she communes constantly with Shamra's mind, despite their physical separation.'

'That comforts me, Skjebne. A little. But I think about her constantly, Skjebne. I can't help worrying in case they hurt her . . .'

' "They"?' The man rested his hand on the boy's shoulder. 'We know nothing of them. But we can surmise that their actions were not random. This thing runs deep: Shamra was picked for reasons that are completely unknown to us. She is of worth to someone, somewhere. It's not likely she would be kidnapped and then simply killed.'

'But I still don't see—'

'Let your mind rest from it now, Kell. We are doing what we can by going to Thule. That's where Feoh says Shamra was taken. Her thoughts will her so – and thoughts are things for Feoh. We have a nightmare and dismiss it upon waking. But for her it is not the same; like walking from one room into another – both rooms are equally real and always there. That's why you can trust her when she says Shamra is alive.'

They set off early next morning through a rose-pink mist, in the direction of the just-risen sun. It was a quiet farewell, for this was a journey of a different kind. The people of Edgetown came out of their houses and stood silently by while Alderamin and his companions walked grim-faced to the waggons. They waved solemnly at the crowd, Alderamin reserving his only smile for Shaula and Sebalrai standing together in the doorway of his lodge. It was perfectly right that the girl had chosen to stay here, in the first place of safety she had known for years.

'We go!' he called. The engines of the two ice-wains fired loudly into life and the lead-wain, driven by Kano, set off at a leisurely pace.

Within a few minutes the frost-mist had shrouded the buildings and the dark low line of the river, so that these things were no more solid than the territory of the travellers' minds.

'It will take us seven days to reach the Dawn Mountains,' Alderamin had explained the day before, 'and another seven to pass through them to the valley of Thule – and that given fair weather and a trouble-free journey.'

'What troubles are we likely to have?' Kano had wanted to know.

'Not Wulfen, for they prefer the lowland forests. Possibly bandits, though we are well armed and alert for them. I don't know – I am reminded of the armoured men who captured Shamra, and the sky-vehicle they used. We know of nothing like it, and it would certainly have the advantage over any ground-based Traveller.'

'If, as you say, traders journey to Thule quite regularly, why should the people there destroy such caravans on the way?'

'Most likely I'm worrying needlessly,' Alderamin said and moved off the subject. And, while his expression changed, Feoh knew without doubt that the worries remained.

As the days went by the Dawn Mountains gradually lifted above the horizon like a showing of fearsome teeth; great grey granite peaks topped eternally with snow and plumes of white cloud trailing forever downwind.

'There is a theory,' Alderamin said as they camped in the

foothills at the end of the sixth day, 'that as much land exists to the east of the mountains as to the west and the north.' His calculating eyes glittered at the prospect. 'It makes sense to suppose that caravans just like our own are plying the trade routes westward to do business in Thule . . . Such opportunity! Such bargains to be sealed!'

'Don't you think—' Kell began, then paused timidly at the thought of his transgression. 'Don't you think life amounts to more than just bargaining? I mean, all the things there are to learn!' He noticed Kano's disapproving glare, but Alderamin was in mellow mood after half a juggon of wayberry wine and of a mind to argue his case without losing his temper.

'When I was not much more than your age, Kell, I left my enclave and crawled up out of the ground into a new world. I had nothing but a stout knife and the sharper desire to survive. The small group of us that had escaped thus came to a small busy stream of fast clear water bedded with coloured pebbles. My companions were looking for fish, but I selected from the stones. Some were unusual – I found rough nuggets of a heavy yellow metal which later proved easy to work. And when the stones dried and became dull, I found ways to polish them up with silksand to make them shine again. In my youth I loved to draw, and so I drew my ideas on the pebbles' faces and called them story-stones.' Alderamin chuckled at the memory. 'I earned my first money walking the byways from village to village, having the people pull stones at random from the bag so that my tales were always different. It taught me to think on my feet.'

'I can see how you got pleasure from that—'

'And doubly so when folks invested symbolic meaning in the pebbles' designs, and believed they foretold their destiny, and wanted to *buy* my stones from me, to keep that destiny secure. I had no choice but to make more . . . And then to ask my friends to help me produce them in even greater quantities. That's how Edgetown had its beginnings; based on trade; based on one man's crazy ideas.'

He said it with a touch of pride, and Kell could not help but admire him more for his endeavours.

'And let me show you something else, if you are not already convinced . . .'

Alderamin heaved himself to his feet and went to rummage in his wain. He returned a minute later and plumped back down with a grunt.

'Here, look at this. It is immensely old — the man from whom I bought it thinks it might even predate the Ice . . .'

Alderamin unfolded a soft cloth and held out the object for all of them to see; a squarish thing of a size to sit comfortably in the hands: it was made of many thin leaves arranged within leather casings, and each leaf on both sides was covered with intricate printings.

'What is it?' Hora wanted to know in his usual blunt and ready way. But Feoh smiled delightedly anticipating Alderamin's reply.

'It is called a *book*, and once it seemed the world was filled with them.'

'What does it do?' Kell wondered.

'Each of these sequences of markings is an idea,' Alderamin pointed out. 'Think of that — with my story-stones I scratched one or two meanings on each pebble. But here there are thousands of expressions, all joined in subtle and complex ways. Why, you could tell the story of man's whole life in the space no bigger than this. You might mark out any dream or observation in this way . . . And if you had many copies of books, then everyone could share your ideas.'

'Books are not the only way of hoarding ideas, of course,' Skjebne said, determined not to be outdone. He went into the other wain and retrieved a number of the crystal discs they'd gathered in the lost storehouses of Perth, and showed

Alderamin glimpses of distant places and times. He watched patiently, and worked the discs for himself, but passed them immediately back to Skjebne once the demonstration was over.

'I have no wish to demean the merits of these things. All I will say, Skjebne, is that a great superstition and a great fear exists in this land as far as picture-glass is concerned. Is it not a short journey from these innocent crystals to the bewitchment that existed in your enclave?'

'They are surely not the same!' Skjebne blustered, but Alderamin was not to be swayed. He was clearly excited by his books, and went on to describe his plan to learn the secret of the strange tiny markings so that one day he might make them himself.

'And to do that I need wealth, for how else am I realise my ambition?'

So the evening passed, while notions and tales, jokes and schemes flowed amongst the group gathered about the fire. And later, when even Alderamin had quaffed enough wine to slur his voice and muddy his thoughts, Hora helped him to his bed; the campfires were doused and the wains huddled down among the rocks out of the grip of the deepening cold.

Kell dreamed in a troubled sleep; unsatisfying fragments that would leave him vaguely afraid the next day. He dreamed of people hurling rocks and breakings of glass: he dreamed of Shamra drowning, and of Wulfen shadows stalking him relentlessly: he dreamed he was lost and could not find his way, because a voice was distracting him, calling his name. *Kell, Kell* . . .

'Kell – Kell, wake up . . .'

He startled and found Feoh leaning over him. She touched his lips with her fingers and looked towards where the others were still sound asleep. For a second, the subdued light from the Traveller's forward controls reflected on the ceramic surface of her mask.

'What's the matter?'

'Your dreams are my dreams too. They woke me and I came to see if you were all right . . . But as I crossed from the other wain, I saw something you too ought to see. Put on your overjacket and come outside.'

Kell didn't relish the prospect, but hurriedly obeyed because of the concern in Feoh's voice. When he was dressed she silently slipped the handle of the vehicle's rear door and they stepped out into the dark.

The sky was afire with stars, so many and so varied that they looked like Alderamin's treasured jewels scattered in heaps across a vast black ground. By their light, Kell could see the tight slopes of the defile in which they'd camped, and the more distant line of the mountains far ahead, and the smooth hulls of the Travellers dusted over with starfrost. He felt breathless before this beauty.

'But why have—'

She directed him with her mind, leading his gaze over the sky to a point above the peaks, where the stars gathered even more thickly into a meandering river of frozen crystals – except for one, which drifted slowly across, and then back, like an ever-vigilant eye.

Kell's heart gave a single deep thump and he suddenly felt a coldness spreading from within.

'It's a sky gleam!'

'Yes.' Feoh nodded. 'Or something very like one. And I would wager it guards the road to Thule.'

'But has it come from Perth? And has the All Mother sent it to pursue us? And will it recognise the waggons, do you think?'

She smiled inwardly at his child's tumble of questions. 'The worst we might imagine is that the Goddess knows of our presence here and is setting a trap. But it is just as likely that other enclaves apart from Perth made use of the sky gleams, yet know nothing of the All Mother and her suffocating ways.'

'But how can we find out?'

'That's the point of it, Kell. We can't except by completing the journey to Thule. Unfortunately, although I feel my abilities are growing and strengthening, I cannot catch thoughts born of wires and metals and glass: the gleam is as much a mystery to me as it must be to you. So, we have to decide and take our chances.'

Kell looked up at Feoh's face, at the contrast of passionless mask and pale skin taut and drawn with tension.

'Why?' he asked in a bloom of breath, acutely feeling the burden of the moment. *Why am I the one to decide?*

These are strange days, Kell. Our course has become more involved than we imagined. I find it hard to explain, but the impressions gathering in my head lately seem to come not just from the minds of others . . . I feel I know of things yet-to-exist, although I have been tempted to dismiss all of this as my own pointless worrying. But it may not be such mundane foresight, in which case what you choose and what you do carry a great significance. You may be the point where many roads cross, and so I ask you about tomorrow first of all.

Kell glanced again at the slowly drifting speck of light in the heavens. It looked so tiny and harmless, like one shell cast upon a marvellous beach of a billion shells. It might be nothing at all, or it might lead them surely to their death.

It took some seconds, but at last the decision was made and the matter settled at the centre of Kell's heart, in absolute silence, there under the fathomless sky.

The final day began with a fitful fall of wet sleet before the morning brightened. Shortly before noon (what Kell still called high-sun-time), Kano's lead wain crested a ridge at the end of a pass, and suddenly the city was spread out before them. Alderamin drew his vehicle alongside and they all surveyed the scene in wonder . . .

Far away, nearly lost in the haze of distance, a mountain had once crumbled, and out of its shell had spilled the hordes of Thule. Unlike Kano and his band, this kin had evidently not sought to escape, but had settled in the region and expanded through all of its high valleys and even, often precariously, far up its slopes. The sheer variety of buildings spoke of many influences, a blending of numerous cultures.

'This place is far more ancient than Edgetown,' Alderamin commented. 'It looks industrious and rich.' And he grinned at his friends, for each of them knew exactly what he was thinking.

'I'm not interested in how it appears – but how it turns out to be. You said yourself, Alderamin, that Thule was barbaric in its arts. And we know from Feoh's instinct that Shamra has been brought here, and we have fought with the warriors who took her. This is a dangerous city, however much profit you might make from it!'

'I am well reminded, Kano.' Alderamin made a small bow of acquiescence and apology. 'Forgive me. Shamra's rescue must be uppermost in our thoughts. On the other hand, if our disguise is to succeed then we must behave like traders. I'll show you how.'

And the grin was back, and Kano knew he'd been properly answered.

Out of caution they hid one of the Travellers in a quiet place some distance off the main track. Alderamin loaded what goods he'd need (he called them 'temptations') into the remaining vehicle, which he then piloted with surprising skill and much care along the twisting way and down towards the city—

'Though I think we will not reach the centre of Thule today. My advice would be for us to lodge at one of the outlying hut-towns; get to know the gossip and something of the local people; plant the seeds of our trading mission, and then press on tomorrow.'

Kell wanted to speak out in disagreement, because the impulse was strong in him to go to the heart of the city, to find Shamra quickly and be away from the place . . . And as it was becoming his habit to do, so he looked to Feoh for her reaction.

He makes good sense, Kell. There is a nervousness amongst the people here, for all their bustle and commerce. A dark thread of suspicion runs in them . . . Something that links them with Shamra . . . with us . . . A shadow . . . A madness—

'It's settled then,' Kano said, and Feoh's concentration was broken. They forged on over ground that was empty of trees; bleak land covered with tough winter-bleached grass and brushwood and clusters of black rocks, following the winding way until a markstone loomed ahead of them. Alderamin slowed the wain and then stopped it beside the tall pillar of granite.

'We must all get out. I've come across this before. It is the boundary mark of the outermost town,' he went on to forestall the clamour of questions. 'We need permission to go farther. Bring your weapons, since we will have to declare them.'

They all did as they were told, save for Feoh who wove a wreath of lies around her sun crystal and pretended it was a harmless, though valuable, family treasure.

Alderamin left the wain's engines liquidly idling, secured the hatch, and joined his friends who stood in the lee of the pillar to wait for whatever might come.

They had no need to wait long. Somehow their presence was noticed, and after just a few minutes a horseman appeared on the moorline, accompanied by a quickly moving animal of some kind beside him and – Kell looked again to be sure – and by a flying ball of lead-grey metal that soared without effort or sound above them both.

'Just be polite,' Alderamin quipped uneasily, stepping out into plain sight and laying his sword on the ground with exaggerated care.

The rider reined in his horse. He was clearly of warrior stock, upright and broad-shouldered, well-weaponed; a throwing axe on one hip, a short stabbing sword on the other, and a wooden shield strengthened with metal studs and bosses lashed across his back. He wore a rough cotton shirt and leather breeches beneath a heavy cloak of black ursus furs, and there was a wide mesh of decorative ring-mail strapped across his chest. His hair and beard, long and wild and straggling, was dyed a bright blood red.

His companion was equally striking. It was a boar, massively powerful, slung low to the ground on strong stubby legs and mailed, as was its master, with interlinked steel and hardened leather plate. Its terrible upcurving tusks shone with a polished black lacquer, and its wicked little eyes and the top and back of the skull were protected by a steel helmet, intricately designed, and glittering with many tiny points of light.

The flying ball, scaled like a serpent but otherwise featureless, remained enigmatic and, as such, inspired in Kell the greatest fear.

Alderamin's companions followed his lead and placed their weapons down. The boar barged forward and sniffed each one with its sensitive wet snout. It cocked its head briefly to look at the rider and grunted out guttural syllables.

'Verres says your wargear is varied and intelligent and comes from far afield.'

'He is correct on each count.' Alderamin, with just the right degree of obsequiousness, smiled at the animal and then faced its master with legs astride and hands boldly on hips. 'My business is business. I buy, I sell. That's how I came by these armaments, and that's what has brought us to Thule.'

'What do you seek?'

'A profit,' Alderamin answered simply. 'Isn't that what all traders desire? But I forget my manners . . .' He introduced his friends and they learned that the rider was called Zauraq, their exchange of names being an expected and traditional thing.

'Verres says that the woman has insight. Does she belong to the Sustren?'

'We don't know anything about that. But yes, Feoh sees inwardly and has the capacity to heal.'

'Verres says that you are hiding something—'

Zauraq's posture remained unchanged, sure and arrogant and contemptuous of these strangers; but Feoh noticed a change in the tension and wondered which way Alderamin would play it.

'Sir . . .' He chuckled conspiratorially. 'I'm sure that everyone, in all honesty, can admit to keeping secrets. I have travelled long and far to accumulate the goods I bring to Thule. To get the best prices, I like to keep the element of surprise. If buyers know in advance what's being sold, they are more likely to harden their view and lower their offer. Besides,' Alderamin added airily, 'certain of my wares are illegal to sell in some parts of my region.'

As he spoke, Feoh crept softly inside the head of the boar. There she found a rage with its roots in ancient survival and conflict. The heart of the animal regarded all others as enemies or rivals: its passion was to rut and to tear out the bowels of its foes. Some time long ago however, this raw power had been moderated in the species by the sharp though limited intelligence she now observed in Verres. His ancestors had been wrought anew, recreated with the gift of speech to voice their suspicions and anger. Left alone they would have shouted and warred in the hills until the penultimate boar was gored by the last left alive. But latterly, after the breaking of the mountain and the emergence of the Thulians, the breed had been leashed-in by cunning wires piercing deep into the brain. The killer's trail was being directed by Zauraq's kind, and by others too vaguely imagined for Feoh to learn any more—

Verres growled irritably and shook himself, as though plagued by flies. Feoh withdrew and came back to herself and let the animal be.

Zauraq regarded the strangers suspiciously. Whether or not it was within his power to refuse them passage, Alderamin didn't know. But the horseman was playing his part to the full, and after lengthy feigned inner debate, agreed haughtily that they could go on. And, as etiquette demanded, Alderamin made a gracious bow and dug in his pocket for coin, which he handed up in a small leather bag.

'I wish you an interesting stay,' Zauraq said, tucking the fee in his tunic without giving it a glance. Then he whirled his horse around and set off back along the track. Verres followed a moment later, after glaring at the group as though he would rather eat them than let them go by.

The metal ball was the last to leave, striking vertically upward without warning or sound and vanishing into the threadbare canopy of cloud.

'So, welcome to Thule.' Kano sounded aggrieved, loathing the warrior's superior manner.

'I found out he belongs to a clan called the Wyrda Craeftum; it means "having skill given by Wierd", which I think refers to the pattern of all-that-exists. He is one of a strange kin . . . He is here on a mission that remains vague in my mind . . . a path of some sort. He earns his bread as a way-keeper here on the fringes. Zauraq is strong and sure, yet even he lives in fear.' Feoh's expression was knowing. 'Didn't you notice? *Can't you feel it now?*'

'You're doing a better job of scaring us off than Zauraq did.' Skjebne stooped to pick up his weapon. He was not smiling.

'You could have bested him, Hora,' Kell said confidently. The big man sniffed.

'Aye, while you held the boar down, eh boy?'

Kano looked at the sky and the mountaintops, assessing the weather. 'Let's be going. I smell more snow . . .'

They left one of the vehicles hidden and took the other wain on towards the city. The hut-towns on the borderlands were shabby affairs of bone-white wood and crudely shaped stones and some kind of compacted mudstone packed in the cracks to keep out the draughts. This was a mining area, and these outlying settlements, evidently housing the poorest workers, had sprung up among the bare heaps of tailings and the crisscross tracks where the slag-waggons ran. Here and there illicit subsidiary mines pocked the land where men had dug down in hopes of earning more from their own findings. Kell found it to be a dull and depressing place.

The sun went early, hidden by the overtowering mountains. Very soon the hollows were filled with blue shadows and a swift wing of darkness. Lights sprinkled into being through the valleys; thinly here on the outskirts, where simple luminous globes were strung on cables between the dwellings. They swung in the stiffening wind, making the ground seem to sway, their inadequate yellow light picking out the first light drizzling of flakes.

Inside the wain, Alderamin, Kano and Feoh bent around

the forward screens and watched the maps of light grow, and stared by turns into the sparse blackness outside the windows. The snow came on more heavily and the vehicle adjusted its speed to compensate. Even through the shielded hull came the sound of crunching gravels and the wet splash of slush in the ruts of the track.

'Maybe we should just call a halt and settle by the roadside until morning,' Kano suggested. The worsening weather worried him.

The wain jonked to the left and its engines roared; there was a shudder as the machine righted itself and laboured on. All of them staggered and grabbed for handholds, save for Feoh who stumbled back and half fell into Skjebne's arms.

'Feoh, are you all right?' Kell's voice sharpened as he noticed Skjebne's expression.

'She's pale . . . She's fainting. Quickly, quickly help me!'

Alderamin brought the wain to a juddering halt and came back through the push of people to see what the matter was.

Skjebne had lowered Feoh to the floor. She was trembling and beneath its flickering lid her eye was glassy and confused. Kell, who was becoming more sensitive to the woman's thoughtwords, picked up a panicky scatter of ideas and the impression of loss and defeat; wave after wave washing through him.

'Feoh—' Kano dropped to his knees and supported her lolling head. Her eye opened wide and she gasped, as though breaking surface after a long time submerged. She gripped his wrist and held on desperately.

'I can't see her now – I can't find her—'

'No Feoh . . . No . . .' Kell felt the blood drain from his face.

'It's Shamra – my mind-link with her has been broken . . .'

13

Shahini Tarazad

'Let her be – let her be!' Kell pushed at Hora and Skejebne and Alderamin as they crowded in, urging them to give her space. 'Let her think.'

Kano settled himself down cross-legged and gently cradled her head in his lap.

'What does she mean?' Alderamin looked stupid in the depths of his concern, and Kell wanted to yell at him and hit out and tell him what use were all of his gaudy baubles now.

'She has lost Shamra – But how can that be, unless . . .' Skjebne left the silence too late, and Kell knew precisely what he meant. Feoh too, for she shook her head groggily and struggled; her pupil contracting as the bluegreen iris lensed round.

'She is not dead—' Her hand snuck out and gripped Kell's reassuringly. 'It doesn't feel like death or violence or anything at all like that . . . And she has not gone farther away. Shamra is still within Thule.'

'What then?' Kell's frustration was intense, and contended with his fear so that he didn't know which caused the greater pain. 'What's happened to her?'

Feoh indicated that she wanted to sit up: Kano assisted her and Hora, like a big friendly frightened dog, came and sat down beside her and gave her a beaker of hot wine infused with invigorating spices: it was a drink he had learned about from Alderamin, who swore by it, smelt it now, and went to pour one for himself.

'What's happened to her?' Feoh sipped the mull and wiped a blood-drop of juice from her lip. 'It's so strange. So very strange. Have you ever started out on an errand, and gone part way, and then forgotten what you were doing?' She waited for their several nods of recollection. 'Then, you will appreciate, in that state it is easy to be drawn down another road and distracted. That's the closest I can come to it . . . Before she vanished Shamra *has simply forgotten* – or been made to forget. We are an absence to her now; our names vaguely glimpsed but not remembered; faces not seen any more in memory. She knows she is missing something, I feel. But even that too will fade.'

'Then we'll be strangers to her?' Kell tried to imagine it, and failed, and felt a fresh wave of despair.

'Unless we can find her – and *re-mind* her.'

'Can't you do it from a distance?'

Feoh shrugged heavily. 'Where are her thoughts? Where do I begin to look? It's like holding on to water.'

'Then we have to go into Thule now,' Kell said. 'And talk to people, and search, and ask questions.'

'But the risks—'

'I've done it before, Skjebne, to find you.' And Kell looked at them all, one by one, and in the softening of their faces they acknowledged the boy's bravery.

So it was decided without further argument. Kano took over the wain's guidance, since Alderamin had, it seemed, indulged himself overmuch with the spicy wine. The sleet outside had become steadily heavier, so that Kano was forced to steer solely from the machine's maps-of-light, while Kell and Skjebne gazed through the dreary and mesmeric storm of flakes for any useful landmark.

But not much later the mud track through which they'd sloshed gave way to a lane of compacted gravels, and then to smooth meltstone not unlike the roadways of Perth. The mineworkers' huts were replaced by larger and more substantial buildings; the swinging necklaces of bulbs by more useful and powerful lamps at the tops of tall sturdy poles. A few other vehicles went by; one fleet and silent, another chugging heavily atop a complex of churning pistons and great white belchings of steam: and there was a rider, a small cauled form clinging as though terrified to a tall grey lizardlike steed that ran on two legs like a man, and whose face looked vicious and intent.

'Ahead,' Skjebne said. 'An inn. Might be a good place to start.'

Kano noted the smudgings and cross-hatchings of light on his screen and briefly compared them with what he could see of the street. This was still the hinterland of Thule, though close enough in for the temperature to be fractionally raised: now the sky was full of rain that slashed across the road and made it shine.

The inn was a substantial wooden building several stories high with roadside space where vehicles could be left. It was constructed of stout beams sealed with pitch and a steeply-angled roof down which the rainwater ran in heavy cascades. Beneath the crude overhanging gable-ends, yellow light glowed from a few cramped attic rooms. Stronger lamps shone above the solid central door. There seemed to be no guards or obvious traps.

'Places like these are welcome way-stations.' Alderamin came forward and squinted through the glass. 'I've visited such hearth-halls before. Incomers make themselves known here, and if you are leaving the city, it's a provision-hoard for varied and fairly priced goods.'

'Then I say we spend some time inside!' Hora was thinking of his stomach, and Feoh, despite her weariness and the shock of Shamra's fading, barely muffled a smile.

They all went armed, concealing most weapons beneath

furs and overjackets and raincapes of noctus-bat skin. Alderamin led the way, bidding Skjebne to carry his satchel of temptations. 'Every respectable trader needs an assistant . . .' Then Kano, Feoh and Kell in a cluster, and Hora as rearguard with his multiblade conspicuously in view. So it might be reasoned that here was a wealthy merchant with some travelling companions; an aide, a man and his wife and their son perhaps, and a mercenary paid to protect. As he approached the entrance Alderamin assumed his bluff arrogant mask, pushed the big iron-bossed portals apart and strode imperiously inside.

Heat and noise pushed into their faces: the smoke from a number of hearthfires blurred figures moving murkily within the haze. Kell rubbed his stinging eyes. Feoh was instantly consumed with coughing: Alderamin drew a deep appreciative breath and gave a low chuckle.

'Home from home,' he told her with a wink.

The bones of the building were formed from rows of treetrunks of enormous girth – Kell doubted that even Hora could get his arms half round any one of them. Evidently similar boles, split, had been used for the round tables scattered between the pillars. There were also crudely but sturdily fashioned chairs of nogs banded with iron. Most of them were occupied, but one table away from the fires had some empty places, which Alderamin now claimed; enough for his party except for Hora, who in his guard's guise was expected to stand. Within a few moments of them settling, a menial appeared and asked what it would be their pleasure to drink. And there was a food table across the way – the servant pointed to trestled longboards sagging with fare.

'Cooked meats of every variety; moxen, Wulfen rib, gull, and a whole pit-roasted hemoth.'

'Hm . . . I think—' Alderamin glanced at Hora. 'I think all of them.'

They ate and drank, refreshing themselves; but more importantly absorbing the complex tensions and undercurrents among the scores of people in the room. Here and there groups of soldiers occupied their own spaces and conversed in low tones. They were all red-hairs, like Zauraq; paid guards who worked perhaps for anyone, but whose final allegiance was only to themselves. Under the massive tables sat their armoured boars rooting through slops, their little hoggish eyes glittering with hostility if anyone passed too closely by. Elsewhere, Kell caught sight of a crew of gaudily coloured men laughing and joking with the serving girls who were pouring out their wine. They were certainly raiders, possibly Chertan's crowd, though Chertan himself seemed not to be among them.

Nor would you want him to be, Kell, Feoh said mindside. *Alderamin might be here for vengeance, but ours is a different mission.*

Then we should get on with it. 'We've sat and eaten our fill and taken our leisure. Don't you think we should go and find Shamra now?'

Kano looked startled at the boy's impertinence, but Alderamin, a juggon halfway to his lips, paused and saw the pain in his eyes and slammed the tankard back down.

'If he were not right I'd thrash him,' he said good humouredly. 'Besides, he's saving me from my own bad habits.' He lifted the bag of temptations and pulled out some jewels and chains, rings and pendants and brooches.

'Nothing of enormous value, but enough to buy a few snippets of gossip and perhaps a secret or two. I suggest we split up; Kano, Hora and Skjebne; Kell, Feoh and I – each group then having its own particular wiles.'

'Agreed,' Kano said. 'And Feoh, you can be the link between us. We meet back up when we have useful news.'

Alderamin draped his fur cloak across his chair and told the others to do likewise, so marking their right to the spot.

'Until later, then.'

Alderamin and Kano shook hands and they separated, none of them guessing that they would never truly be together again.

'I have heard it said that every road leads to Thule; that it is the end of all striving.'

'What do you mean?' Kell was puzzled. 'You have never been here before . . .'

Alderamin had taken them away from the main fires and the bustle around the food tables, to a quieter corner of the huge room where there was little conversation, where people slumped in shadows, their faces hidden by masks. Some of the masks were brightly decorated with painted designs, or inlays of silver and jewels: others looked plain: others were fashioned into almost-human faces, their various expressions frozen.

'They are dreaming,' Alderamin said with a kind of wonder. He kept his voice low, though there seemed to be no need for the seated ones were totally preoccupied.

'More than that,' Feoh said. She was reaching for things beyond herself, but gathered only little glimpses and scraps. 'The disguises are clever – they keep the dreamer in and the enquiring mind without. These people are almost entirely sealed in the world behind the mask—'

'You are interested in the weorthan glass, then?'

A stooped old man had joined them from somewhere, quite without their noticing. 'The glass of what is and what may be,' he added, holding up a chipped, cracked many-faced nugget of the crystal, turning it before them in his cramped and sticklike fingers. Kell was both fascinated and repelled by the elder's deformity; his hunched back and skeletal hands, blue-veined and blotched with spots; and by his wrinkled and papery skin, which he could not help but scratch, on his palm, under his chin . . .

'We are interested in the *purveyors* of the glass.' Alderamin affected a bright and cheerful manner. 'And even the creators of it. I am Alderamin of the wide river valley to the west of the mountains. I buy and I sell—'

'Hmm, then our occupations are similar. And these, your friends?'

'Feoh and Kell of Perth – travellers this way, and friends of mine . . . The crystal you're holding, that is weorthan glass?'

The old man lifted it up and turned it in the flickering light. He hunched his shoulders apologetically. 'A rough and uncut example, I'm afraid. I use it just as a sample, for demonstration purposes only . . .'

'Then demonstrate. And if I'm impressed—' Alderamin jiggled the money-pouch at his hip, 'I'll buy.'

'Weorthan glass is never for sale, it is only the experience within the glass that carries a cost. But, if that is your desire . . .'

He passed the nugget to Alderamin, who tilted it this way and that, and brought it close to his eyes and held it away at arm's length, and finally tutted with irritation.

'It's a puzzle stone, meaningless.'

'It works better for some than for others,' the old man explained. 'It's temperamental. You look and look and find nothing. You look again – and suddenly all is revealed. Perhaps the lady will see quickly into its depths . . .'

Alderamin passed the glass on. 'I have heard this kind of talk at a hundred fairs and markets, Old Scratch. These people here, accomplices aiding your deception—'

'That is a very cynical view,' the old man said. 'And as you well know, cynics are those who doubt the goodness in the world.'

'Tell me more then, and ease my doubts!'

'Weorthan glass is not created, only ever found. All the minings in these mountains – yes, for silver and quartz and other useful minerals, but ultimately, so the legends run, ultimately for more veins of the glass. And within those mysterious deposits, the hope of the one perfect crystal.'

'This sounds like more storytelling.' Alderamin looked at Kell and grinned. 'He wants us to give good money for bad lies! How do you come by the glass – you don't have the muscles to mine.'

'Ah, I am only the keeper. All weorthan glass belongs to the dream pedlars, to the Shahini Tarazad who came out of the broken enclave many generations ago. It is their first and final treasure, and they would be a worthless and desperate people without it—'

'They seem a mercenary and godless lot all the same,' Alderamin suggested, testing the old man's limits. And the Keeper of the Wierd laughed and showed them yellow teeth and a black mouth.

'Accusations of "mercenary" from a merchant! Very good . . . But the Tarazad are not entirely godless, for it seems that the falling of the city did not so much send the god of Thule away as awry. She is here, as everywhere, behind the machinations of men.'

'And so is this god, then, the true owner of the weorthan glass?'

'Maybe not true, but undisputed. Some say that she and the glass are one and the same. Some say that she comes from the crystal at the heart of the enclave – but that this is one outgrowth of a more supreme structure that branches into every enclave throughout the world: and the root of the Incomparable Mirror lies within the very core of the earth. So—' The old man shrugged with a strange repulsive rippling of his body. 'That is the essence of the story. But is it truth, trader? What would you trade to be sure, knowing as you do that I always tell lies?'

Kell yawned and hid his boredom behind his hand. The men were playing with words and achieving nothing, it seemed. Besides, not knowing where Shamra had gone was a constant worry to him, and he was itching with eagerness to reunite with the others and for them to be on their way. Alderamin talked a good talk and would happily chat with this old trickster all night! And by and by he would order some wine or strong ale, and they would sit and debate the origins and motives of 'the god of Thule' (whoever that was) for hours. Meanwhile Kell – only a young ploughlad with a head full of cloudy notions – would stand impatiently and wait, while Feoh seemed content to be lost in the gemstone she cradled . . .

A glory. An endless effulgence.

For a short time she had wandered; the crystal's reflecting faces had disoriented her and sent her this way and that in search of a glimpsed possibility. At first the nugget had seemed like an intrusion – Feoh had held the glass, but gradually the glass had come to hold her, until now she had forgotten it and ran with a focused intent after a girl who seemed always ahead of her, tormentingly elusive, just out of reach behind the next tilting mirror, and the next.

I know you, Feoh thought with a leap of the heart. And a piercing joy replaced her earlier apprehension. Another reflecting face presented itself, and Feoh disdained it and pushed it aside and saw the running girlchild not more than a few steps ahead. Realisation gave her speed: for many years she had been running away; from the cold embrace of the All Mother, from the pain and sacrifice of knowing her own mind, and at last from the stifling confines of Perth itself and out into the free and open world. But now she was moving towards her goal rather than away from the fear—

Just ahead, just ahead—

The running girl turned briefly and for a fleeting second it was Shamra. Turned away, and Shamra was gone.

Feoh reached with a final great effort and grabbed the girl by the shoulders, dragging her round.

The shock of recogniton was intense, though not immediate. Feoh had almost forgotten that fair and completed face, those two bright innocent eyes and the spill of tumbled black hair. Seeing her brought a poignancy so sharp that Feoh felt a sob tear loose from her heart and clench in her throat.

'Little sister, oh little sister . . .'

She held the girl's arms tightly and gazed at herself with a terrible longing. All of her years of struggling had brought her back to this, her perfected form.

'I won't leave you,' the woman whispered to the child. 'I won't ever leave you again.'

And she drew Feoh towards herself and was content.

Kell took the glass from Feoh's hands and knew that something had changed. The Keeper was watching him closely and paying no attention to Alderamin who jabbered on and on and on. The Keeper had a guilty look, and as Kell realised that, he saw the old man's eyes shift slyly to one particular seated form nearby—

And he moved towards it and snatched away the mask.

Shamra's body heaved, bowed upwards, and she gasped in a great gulp of air. Her eyelids fluttered and a thin stream of blood began to dribble from her nose.

'What have you done to her!' Kell shrieked. The Keeper started to shake his head to and fro, to and fro, to and fro, took a step backwards, and then tried to run.

Kell flung the nugget after him and watched it shatter against his bent back. The Keeper shrivelled like a flower.

There was a soft *boom*, an expanding absence of sound; and

in the tiny fleeting vacuum Kell watched understanding dawn on Alderamin's face. The merchant shouted something in anger, all the sound in the words soaked up. He reached inside his fleece tunic and drew out a hand weapon such as he had given to Skjebne. His expression hardened into a warning. He jabbed a fat finger over Kell's shoulder into the foggy dimness beyond; lifted the gun and fired – fired – fired with three blazing flashes of flame.

Kell turned slowly and saw a number of big powerful shapes looming in the smoke; the Shahini Tarazad, the armoured warriors who had first taken Shamra away. They had come in by the hearth-hall's main doors and left them open. Wave after wave of chilling gusts and sparkling rain blew through the huge room, howled among the rafters, roared over the piled fires so that they blazed up with a rush and sent sparks showering everywhere in blizzards.

One giant Tarazad warrior hefted what looked like a squat grey pipe and pointed it squarely in Kell's direction—

Kell yelled a warning to Feoh, but had time only to drag Shamra to her feet and dive with her behind a nearby pillar.

The warrior fired his weapon, and something flew swiftly towards them with a gentle whickering sound: it clipped the pillar and ricocheted off into the depths of the building – exploding a moment later with a huge thunder and a rippling liquidlike waterfall of fire.

Kell went low to the ground, pulling Shamra down with him. The dragon's breath blew over and soaked the pillar in flame, so that it burned from floor to roof all in an instant.

'Come on!'

He pulled the dazed girl back to her feet and ran with her, stumbling, away from the blaze. There was suddenly no sign either of Alderamin or Feoh – certainly no glimpse of Skjebne or of Kano. But, in the midst of the rush and the screaming, Kell sighted Hora striding through the scattering crowds. One Tarazad soldier tried to stop him – Hora dealt him a mighty blow that felled him like a storm-snapped tree, and waded on towards the other with the fire weapon.

That warrior, sensing the threat, swung round and down and began to bring the weapon to bear. The jewelled cylinder in Hora's fist grew magically into a shining spear which Hora hurled, threading the smoke like a needle. It struck the Tarazad square in the chest and slipped clean through the breastplate, flung the man backwards and pinned him struggling to the rooftree behind.

Hora waved Kell clear and ducked back into the haze. There was no time for reflection, no opportunity to hesitate. Kell took Shamra's cold and trembling hand and hurried with her towards the great open doors—

And out into the wet and darkness of the street.

The entire hall was alight, the sky filled with falling rain and rising sparks. Low fleet clouds streamed across, their sagging grey underbellies aglow. A growing heat, and a strong wind that lashed the flames about like ragged flags, added to the risk and forced Kell away and along a side alley where he and Shamra were shielded by other buildings.

Only then did they pause to catch their breath and wipe the stinging smoke out of their eyes, and then stand panting in the rain.

'You found me Kell. I was lost in the glamour of the glass, but you found me.'

Water streamed down Shamra's face, mingling with her blood. She wiped a hand across her mouth and flicked the mess away, disgusted.

'I would have kept searching . . . There is so much to say . . .'

Kell smiled, and watched in fascination as a single snowflake amongst all the raindrops settled in the tangle of

Shamra's hair. Then a second flake, a third, fourth – each as perfect as a rose – touched her hair and did not melt.

The temperature dropped. They felt it fall. And the bluff and gusty wind became meaner and colder, cutting and nipping them now, worrying at them like a dog.

'What's happening?' Shamra asked.

Kell already knew, and in that knowing, shivered. He understood with Feoh's depth of instinct that all roads led to Thule, because here was the source of every soul's dread.

A blast of freezing wind channelled down the alley and a vast veil of snow lifted beyond the buildings.

Out of the veil, a thin keening cry.

The cry of the Ice Demon.

14

The Ice Demon

For a few moments only, Kell saw a monstrous machine moving up taller than the nearby buildings: ten, fifteen spans high, it resembled the two-legged running vehicle they had seen when entering the city—

Nearby people began to scream, and their eyes were filled with the sight of the fiend of the glaciers. And Kell's mind could not struggle against the crowd's weight of conviction.

The Ice Demon's very presence cast a slick of frost over roofs and walls and roadways, and the cold was so intense that it seemed the monster's knives were out and stabbing even before it came into view. Soaked as they were by the rain, Kell knew that he and Shamra would quickly die without the demon even touching them. And this was what he had been told to fear all his life; what all the people of Perth had feared, deep down, since the very earliest times. For the All Mother had been right about the killing cold; and Kell should have listened to her and her ministers at the Tutorium – the pompous Praeceptor, the ridiculous, malicious, self-important Aquizi and the lesser clerics; all of them knew what he had denied, so that now he would learn the final lesson by paying the greatest possible price. And Shamra must needs bear her share of the cost.

Out of the blizzard came the creature ... No, Kell corrected himself: the creature *was* the blizzard. The tearing winds and the whirling hurricane of snowflakes were its screamings and its breath. The huge head, iron-grey-blue and cracked and spiked with icicles, lifted up over the nearer roofs. Whatever its fingers touched became dusted over with white and froze rigid instantly, locked and creaking inside the ice. It was the Bringer of the Cold. It was the reason that all of humanity had lain cowering in the earth these thousands of years!

Kell felt these ancient fears sweeping through him. All he wanted to do was crouch down and hide like a child behind his hands – or else give himself up to the beast and meet his death swiftly and be done with it. The urge to surrender was almost overpowering . . . Until Shamra tugged at Kell's sleeve and broke the fatalistic spell.

'We could go through here. It might not see us . . .'

There was a gap between the buildings; less than an alley, a channel where water could run. It cut back to the main street, since Kell could see the reflection of flames on the wet meltstone where the inn was still burning furiously.

'Yes.' He ushered Shamra through first and followed immediately, though he found it a tight squeeze. The walls of the buildings pressed him chest and back, and he was only able to move at all because the wood was slimy with freezing rain.

They were perhaps halfway along when a gigantic foot smashed down into the alley they had just left, and the air was filled with wintry fog and tinkling splinters.

'Hurry up!' urged Kell – for now the whole of the alley that he could see was filled with the body of the beast; a great grey-white mass of primeval ice. Its head, above the rooftops, swung this way and that. It roared, and the streets shuddered and boomed.

They had squeezed to within a few armspans of the channel's far end, when the Ice Demon glimpsed their little wriggling movements in the dark. It dropped down and jammed its fingers between the stout houses, gouging out the walls, ripping wood and plaster away in ragged chunks. The intense cold of its touch seared the surfaces with frost, which spread like hoary cobweb and caught Kell unawares and stuck his jacket to the wall.

With a cry he ripped himself free, pushed Shamra out into the street and followed her a second later. They began running towards the blazing hearth-hall, which had now become a refuge.

There were many people about in the roadway, completely blocking the thoroughfare: mox-wains and horse-drawn carts and mechanical waggons had come to rest before the gathering, their drivers and passengers likewise pausing to watch the spectacle.

Kell began shouting and waving his arms, and Shamra joined him in the warning. But the great fire itself and the crumbling of the inn beneath it set up a thunder that was deafening. People laughed and cheered and prodded one another in their excitement, and made jokes about the ill fortune of the lodgekeeper and his ugly wife . . . And only gradually did a few faces change in the comical slide from humour to horror as they saw what was rising above the rooftops.

Then a panic flashed quickly through the crowds. Laughter turned into shrieks, friendly jostlings became a desperate effort to escape. A howling whirlwind surged down twisting from the sky, swept across the street and filled it with a blinding hurricane of snow.

Almost instantly the world shrank tight as the horizons closed in. A stumbling man staggered into Shamra and nearly knocked her to the ground. Kell shoved him out of the way and grabbed the girl's hand: he had some vague plan to move closer to the burning tavern – maybe the monster of cold would be fearful of the heat.

A huge shadow swished by at great speed and there was a

frightful crash: the Ice Demon's cloven foot had smashed into a mechanical wain and sent it tumbling up into the air. There came a further thunderous clatter moments later as the machine hurtled into the side of a building and shattered them both asunder.

These cacophonies, mixed with the screaming of the people, the endless wailing of the blizzard and the cracking-banging-roaring of the fire made speech impossible. Indeed, it was all Kell could do to keep hold of his grip on Shamra's fingers as the fierce chilling gusts threatened to rip them both apart.

But now Kell had a sense of where he was – he could see the dancing fire-glows ahead and feel the heat of the conflagration. As the wind changed, moment by moment, it brought the cold sweeping in at their backs; then that was whisked away and a scorching wave blew across to steal their breath; the snow became warm rain and the menace of the demon seemed reduced.

He noticed that large portions of the crowd had gathered near the fire, snatching at the same idea of safety. The ice monster, trapped between the urge to kill and the fear of its own destruction, lingered on the fringes, daring only every few seconds to swing its clawed hand into the sphere of the flames. Once they saw the awful talons hook a man up from the ground and spin him away into the dark. His fading cry was brief and abruptly stopped. Shamra turned away appalled, but Kell's gaze was locked on the creature, on its pattern of backing off and then lunging in for more prey . . .

Now it came forward again, enraged by the sting of the flames. As it did so, its head necessarily dropped below the roofline for its vast hand to scoop along the ground. People scattered like insects to be away from the terrible blades.

Kell looked up into the Ice Demon's eyes above the chasm of the jaws and the frigid cliff of the face, and saw stupidity there behind the ancient senseless fury: the pupils, cracked and glassy, had long forgotten their origins. The only thought, chained deep in the frozen cavern of its mind, was to drain the world's last atom of heat and then forever lord it over a dead and unchanging wilderness.

Well, no more! Kell was tired of being scared and intimidated. All his life everyone he had ever known, somewhere inside themselves, had been fearful of the beast. Many in Perth had denied it; some had admitted their terror but kept it safely wrapped within the security of the enclave. Only a few had dared to emerge and test the truth of the Mythologies, and in finding that truth attempt to change it.

Maybe it would make no difference at all – maybe it would spur the demon on to a crescendo of destruction and Kell's own death – but if he failed to make this gesture, only a token perhaps, then he could never cross the line from childhood to man.

There was no time to explain or reflect on his plan. All around was chaos. As the colossus loomed down again, Kell let go of Shamra and pulled the knife that had been Alderamin's gift from its sheath. The beautiful thing of silver and steel and inlaid gems balanced perfectly in his fist.

Kell remembered his practise time with Skjebne, recalling the little moment of calm just before he'd loosed the blade; that brief stillness when all doubt was absent and there was only himself and the target and no separation between . . .

He tossed the knife spinning, caught it blade first and, continuing the same movement, swung his arm down and then up like a pendulum and flicked the weapon swiftly into the air—

Good fortune or skill or both sent it surely on its way almost too fast to follow. Even before Kell had time to assess his aim the knife pierced the demon's eye to the hilt.

The wind's moaning lifted to an immense and terrifying

screech. The massive head jerked back and rushed upwards into the gloom above. The monster staggered, blinded, blundering back across the street in its agony, then forward again towards the flames. But some part outside the pain realised the greater danger of the fire. The giant turned its shoulders to the heat and bellowed, casting its one remaining eye across the crowd—

It saw Kell, and instinctively recognised its foe.

The time for all decisions was ended. All Kell knew how to do then was put one foot in front of the other, faster, faster, to increase the distance between Shamra and himself. If he was far enough away from her, the monster might be satisfied with his life alone.

He bolted into the cold and dark – diving aside as a wain rumbled past at top speed – the Traveller, the one they had brought out of Perth. For a fleeting instant he saw Kano bent grimly over the controls. And then it flashed by him and the force of its slipstream made him stumble. He overbalanced and fell to his knees, glancing up at the very moment the wain hit the ice giant and toppled it and sent it crashing into the inferno of the burning lodge.

An enormous gust of fire and sparks exploded outwards across the street in every direction, while a vast geyser of steam shot upwards and flattened against the clouds. Seconds later gouts of meltwater washed and rippled over the roadway from the crumbling colossus, who even now in its devastation thrashed and attempted to rise. But its strugglings grew feebler second by second until at last its piles of dirty slush and cage of ribs and scattered bones – all that was left of it – quivered and were still, succumbing to the residual heat of the pyre.

Kell saw this in snatches. He was shocked and in pain after the ordeal, and the throng was still frightened and confused. There was much bustling and shouting, and a number of people alone or in groups took advantage of the bedlam and began looting nearby houses and stores.

A shot was fired and the crowd surged away.

Kell was caught up in it and found himself carried helplessly along. He called out Shamra's name again and again: but not even the people closest to him paid him the slightest attention. The Ice Demon was dead, but their superstitious fear was alive and driving them on blindly like a stampeding heard of senseless moxen. On and on, until by chance Kell was jostled to the fringes and pushed past the edge and dragged himself free . . .

Stumbling and exhausted, he made for some nearby trees that seemed to form a little park away from the main thoroughfares. A narrow roadway ran through the park, and Kell followed this for a short distance until leaves and branches shielded him from the cut of the wind. Then he flopped down against one of the trunks and hugged his arms around his updrawn knees, closed his eyes and drowsed for a time . . .

The merest touch on his face woke him some time later. He sprang awake, briefly disoriented.

'Shamra?'

And so it was, for a second.

A young girl was kneeling beside him, looking as startled as he. She could have been no more than seven ploughings old and was dressed only in her sleeping gown, a long white garment of simply woven cottoncloth. Kell assumed she and her family had become separated in the turmoil of the night. She smiled at him tentatively, and Kell tried to smile back, wearily, painfully.

'Are you lost, little sister?'

'No more than you are. Yet you look as though you have also lost someone, while I am alone. And I can find my way back at last, but can you?'

'The burning lodge, that's where my friends are. Once the streets become quieter – once the crowds have died down . . .'

'Yes.' The small child nodded and her long dark hair fell forward. 'Maybe that would be best, just to rest here awhile until things are settled, and the daylight comes . . .'

'Yes.' Kell felt comforted and pleased that the girl seemed to understand him.

'We can rest now. Just the two of us here together. Until the time is right. Until the daylight comes.'

He took it as permission. Like his closest friend or a pet cat the child settled down beside him and leaned against his side. She had no weight at all, but great trust. She sighed contentedly and the sound reminded Kell of the wind streaming upwards over stones.

'Good night, Kell,' she said, and he went gently into it, sinking down past all thoughts of Shamra and Kano, Feoh and the others, and the dreams and impulses that defined him, until at last there was only the dark and a single sleeping boy and the night breeze.

It was a kind of peace.